Praise for the Melan~

THE ROSWL

Readers Favorite: If you're a fan of TV shows like *Stranger Things*, you're going to love *The Roswell Quest*. Author DJ Schneider masterfully incorporates real-life events to craft an engaging narrative that keeps you hooked from start to finish.

The UFO Detective: DJ Schneider captures some of the very REAL truths about Roswell and delivers them in an entertaining novel.

Night Owl: I loved this book, plain and simple. The plot revolves around aliens which I love, and had a great feel to it with the kids interacting in an honest, believable way.

Amazon reviewer: Ok. Wow!!! Such a fun read! I lost half of one day because I could NOT stop reading!

Amazon reviewer: I love this book! DJ Schneider has managed to make you feel as if you are a character in his story.

Amazon reviewer: I could not put it down and I had so much else to do.

Amazon reviewer: You will feel as if you were right there with the characters.

Amazon reviewer: The characters have great personalities that really shine throughout the whole read.

Amazon reviewer: Once I started this book, I couldn't set it down.

Amazon reviewer: You won't be disappointed with this summer read!

DJ SCHNEIDER

THE ROSWELL QUEST

Melanie Simpson's Adventure Begins

Prequel to the Melanie Simpson Mystery Series

This novel was originally published as *Hoaxes Roswell*

This novel is dedicated to my kids,
Nathan and Tyler,
who were the very first to hear this story,
and the motivation to publish it.

What I saw I couldn't believe…
it was not anything of this earth.
That I am quite sure of!

Statement by Major Jesse A. Marcel, base Intelligence Officer at Roswell Army Air Field in 1947, on his observations about the materials found at the crash site during a filmed interview with WFFT television, Fort Wayne, IN.

Chapters

THE
ROSWELL
QUEST

Prologue

July 4th, 1947

A man sits at a camp table examining Indian arrowheads spread over a weathered cotton cloth. He moves an arrowhead from a group in the middle to one of the corners of the cloth as he sorts it for size and type. He is young, but the light from the gas lantern makes him look older. He has two days of stubble on his face and his brown hair hangs down his forehead as he leans over the arrowheads. Desert dust is matted to the sweat stains of his shirt.

The late summer sun has just set and an intense orange glow filters up from the horizon to touch the bottoms of the dark clouds above in only the way a New Mexico sunset can.

The clouds are building and he knows a summer storm is not far off. Thunder has already sounded in the distance. The flash of a lightning bolt breaks his concentration, illuminating the Creosote brush and Beargrass of the desert.

He looks up to the ominous clouds above and counts softly, "One, two, three, four, five..." The thunderclap reaches him. "Getting closer."

He has been through the violence of summer storms before and knows he needs to prepare. He rolls up the arrowheads in the cloth and ties a string around them. He folds up the table and chair, carrying all to the jeep and placing them in the back. He secures the rest of the camp as the storm grows stronger and closer with each new rumble of thunder.

He looks up as a lightning bolt dashes across the sky above his head, a giant thunderclap chasing it. An eerie light forms in the cloud where the lightning has just vacated. It builds in intensity, casting a glow over the landscape. Then a meteor breaks from the spot trailing a flaming, blue-steel tail. It is angled straight toward him.

He throws himself to the ground as it dives just overhead, crashing to earth less than a mile away.

"That wasn't a meteor!"

He stands and brushes himself off while looking in the direction of the crash. All that remains is a red glow where it hit.

"What *was* that?"

He pinpoints the direction as another flash of lightning brightens the desert floor. A gust of wind shakes the flap of his tent. He looks up to see the storm is now on top of him. Giant drops of rain smatter his face. It will be a long night. He looks one more time in the direction of the crash, wondering what it was, and at the same time knowing it was nothing he recognized.

Another bolt of lightning dances across the sky. He heads into the tent to weather out the storm, knowing that in the morning he will find out.

It is early morning and still dark. A flashlight beam waves a path across the ground ahead of him. A thin sliver of first light shows on the horizon. He is following a ravine he had marked the night before. It looked like it would track in the general direction of the crash site. The going is slow. The ground is still wet and muddy from the storm and there are pooled areas of water.

He climbs to the top of the ravine once in a while to re-mark his direction and make corrections. He has to cut over to another ravine to keep his track, but his progress improves as the morning light grows stronger.

He knows he must be close, anxious to find out what it was that crashed. He decides to climb from the ravine and head over to a small rise of hill where he can get a better view. At the top he looks into an arroyo and is shocked by what he sees below.

An airplane. But it doesn't have wings. It has a crescent shape and a silver sheen to the fuselage, but not like the look of metal used in our airplanes. The nose is crushed where it smashed against the hard rock of the arroyo's steep wall. There is a long, open gash in the side.

A man is kneeling near the craft, bent over something — a small body. "Oh God, not a child?" He hurriedly works his way down the hill. He moves closer, then suddenly stops. "No, that's not...no, no, it can't be."

Chapter 1 — Arrival

We had no idea at the time that in just a few hours our lives would change forever. But that is the truth, and this is how it happened.

It was a Friday in June. We were just getting into the summer break of 1966 in the little town of Lake Oswego, the torture of homework well out of our thoughts. I could feel the Oregon sun beat down on us while my best friend Beanie and I sat on the grass trying to figure out one more way to harass Howie Howard. So, how could I not goof with a guy who has a name like that? I mean, it reminded me of the comic book, *Richie Rich*. I hated that kid and that comic. He was just too righteous for a kid with that much money. Same thing with H. H. He just asked for it all the time. What a jerk—thought he was God's gift, you know?

We were hanging out on the lawn next to the hedge between my house and the vacant one next door, close to where it ended at our road. This spot has always been the place where such devious plans are made.

I looked up at Beanie from a deep focus on the grass beneath me, as if that was where the next great plan would reveal itself. "I'm drawing a blank. I mean, what else is there left to do? We need to come up with something really awesome this time."

"Yeah," Beanie added, rubbing a newly formed zit on the side of his nose, "and the fact that we've pulled about four-hundred and fifty-thousand other pranks on Howie doesn't help. We're running out of ideas, well, good ones anyway."

"Wait a minute; I think I've got something." I leaned toward Beanie to share my plan. He liked the basics of it, so we huddled together to work out the details.

We were so deep into our plan, it wasn't until the moving truck had already pulled into the driveway next door and three brutally offensive men got out to unload it, that Beanie and I looked up from what was developing to be the ultimate Howie Howard prank to see what was going on.

Once we realized what was happening on the other side of the hedge, we knew this was something big so we dropped the Howie plan for now and took up positions. Strategy had to be struck. Our set-up was perfect. I took up a spot well worn into the hedge near the corner of my house, a successfully proven strategic position for hasty retreats. Beanie stayed down by the road, thinking himself more the risk-taker. We each held an Army surplus walkie-talkie purchased a year ago through one sweaty summer of mowing lawns.

I suppose if the walkie-talkies had worked right, they never would have been at the surplus store to begin with, or way too expensive for us to afford. Most people would have given up, but we spent good money to get them and through long hours of use, we came to feel they worked perfectly as we were able to recognize at least every third word.

The movers shuffled in and out of the house in a rhythmic pattern that blended magically with their swearing. The first items off the truck were odd boxes and wrapped items that didn't really tell us anything about the possible occupants. We sat anxiously waiting to read the first recognizable clue as to who the new intruders would be.

"Beanie, do you read me? Position One to Position Two, come in." At the other end this probably sounded something like "Beanie... you...meh? pos... own...to... two...me...in."

Without hesitation and with complete understanding, he replied in the affirmative.

"Let's hold our positions," I advised.

"Ten-four," Beanie answered, "awaiting more reconnaissance to form a plan."

We watched and we waited, but what finally appeared from that huge yellow truck was totally unexpected. Here we were, all primed to see the junk of a normal, everyday family with the usual allotment of a father, a mother, two kids, a dog, and maybe even a cat. What we expected were bicycles, a barbecue and lawn furniture. What came out of that truck was altogether different—women's things! Hundreds and thousands of things that were completely, unmistakably, and undeniably fluffy, frilly women's things. And not just the standard frilly like you might think of with a regular mother's influence either like, say for instance, pink carpeted toilet seat covers. These were classy and sophisticated goods, and just about everything the movers took into the house was pure white.

"Beanie, are you seeing what I'm seeing?"

"Affirmative, Kemosabe. Very interesting."

This was all pretty much overwhelming to Beanie and me, but the clincher was when they carried in the bed. What a bed! Of course, it was all in pieces when they carried it in, but I had no problem putting together in my head just how it would look in the bedroom. It was the biggest bed I had ever seen and took all three men just to carry in each individual mattress. When they unloaded the headboard and footboard, it was easy to see the corner posts would nearly reach to the ceiling. Next, they carried in a big white canopy trimmed in white lace, and I couldn't help but imagine what it would be like to lie on that huge bed, looking up at that canopy.

Wait a minute, what am I thinking? I quickly wiped the smile off my face and looked over at Beanie to see if he had noticed, but he was glued to that small world between the rear of the truck and the front of the house—a funny little smile on *his* face.

Then, just as quickly as they arrived, the men got into the truck and drove away. Beanie and I sat motionless for a minute. Slowly it dawned on me that we had been totally captivated for the better part of the last two hours by staring at, well, how else could I put it—at the dainty adornments of the female persuasion. Stuff that only a year ago would have made us retch in disgust, had just entranced us at an equal level to sitting in baseline seats during the fourth game of the '65 World Series with Sandy Koufax on the mound when he took down those despicable Minnesota Twins for the last and final count. I tried to ignore both the thought and the feeling.

"Beanie, what do you think? Should we check it out?"

"Ten-four," Beanie replied. "You go around back and I'll cut across the front. We'll meet at the far corner."

But just as Beanie was relaying this through the walkie-talkies, a white Thunderbird sports car pulled into the driveway. We receded deep into the security of the hedge until leaves stuck out our ears.

The driver's door opened and from below the door emerged a beautiful pair of legs. When the woman stood from the car, I could see that the legs were simply the point guard for a body that quickly placed them in a more minor role.

Then the passenger door opened and out stepped a girl. My heart pounded. I had never seen anything like her. She looked to be our age. Blonde hair — the kind that makes you think of a sunny day when everything is right in the world — hung down the curve of her back in great flowing waves. Any second now I thought she would look over to find the source of the resounding thump, thump, thump. I was amazed blood vessels could stand such pressure.

Regaining my cool, I popped my head over the top of the hedge just enough to get a better look as she walked from the car to the house. She was dressed in tomboy threads — faded blue jeans with the cuffs turned up, well-worn high-top Converse sneakers, and a sleeveless t-shirt — but even so, each step was art in execution. I studied her from head to foot. Somehow she had a confidence in her walk that both interested and intimidated me at the same time. I could hardly breathe just looking at her.

It was all so overwhelming, it took a moment to notice the slight turn of her head. I quickly ducked and looked between the leaves to see if she saw me. I felt relief as she continued to the house, apparently without notice of our surveillance. Then it was over. She had gone inside.

Beanie and I reacted simultaneously. We raced for the center of the hedge.

"Wow, man, did you see her, did you see?" Beanie asked, as if to convince himself that she really existed.

"Isn't she something," I added. "I've never seen anything like her. I mean, not even in my dreams."

"I'm in love," Beanie crooned, acting faint.

"Hey, hang on a second. What makes you think she's God's gift to you?"

"What?" Beanie looked at me as if he had just gotten back from vacation. "Wait a minute! I saw her first."

"I can't believe that even dressed like a boy she looked so good."

Beanie stared at me with his patented 'huh' expression. "What are you talking about? She was wearing a dress."

"A dress? You mean the *mom*? I'm talking about the girl!"

"What girl?" Beanie asked, again with the patented look. "I'm talking about the woman."

"You didn't see her?"

"Who?"

Just then we heard a grunt. Maybe it was a clearing of the throat or even an utterance of disgust. Whatever it was, we both swung around to see the girl standing behind us.

"What are you two *perves* doing gawking at my mom?"

We both froze: deer in her headlights.

I couldn't believe how pretty she looked, even with a scowl on her face. Her arms were wrapped across her chest, which I couldn't help notice not only existed, but seemed to be working on a reputation.

I looked over to Beanie for support but could see few resources existed there. I turned back to the girl. "I wasn't looking at your mom. I was looking at, I mean, well, Beanie, he was looking at...he was —"

"I saw who you were checking out."

I couldn't divert my eyes from hers, but swore I could hear her foot tapping, even though we were standing on grass.

"So, what are your names?"

"Why?" I asked, worried.

"So I can report you to the police."

Beanie and I looked at each other. The alarmed expression on our faces must have been obvious.

"I'm just kidding. What, you think you're the *first* boys I've ever caught gawking at my mom?"

It was our turn to tap the grass with our feet.

"My name is Franklin." I nodded toward my accomplice. "This here's Beanie. I live there." A hand flew clumsily from my side in the general direction of my house.

"*Franklin?* You actually go by Franklin? What, you into self-persecution or something?"

"I go by Frankie."

"I'm not sure that's any better. I think I'll stick with *Perv*. I'm Melanie, but you can call me Mel." Her frown broke to a smile and I melted.

Chapter 2 —King

Over the next month the three of us became good friends. Beanie got over her mother. I got to lie on the four-poster bed and look up at that canopy. Yes, it was Mel's and no, we didn't do it. And, although I could feel there was something more than friendship between Mel and me, nothing had happened yet to prove it. Summer wore on, but with a much more exciting influence than either Beanie or I could ever have imagined.

We called ourselves The Three Musketeers; partly because the movie had just shown at the Lake Theater a week earlier and we all wanted to be Gene Kelly's D`Artagnan, including Mel; partly because we became inseparable that summer—all for one and one for all—but mostly because 3 Musketeers bars were Beanie's favorite candy, always having one to share with us. So the expression, like the candy, stuck to the roofs of our mouths.

July passed and our adventures carried into August. We had just come through nearly a week of rain so were now down at the lake celebrating the Oregon sun.

We were at the neighborhood easement, as it was called. It sat below the bridge over Springbrook Creek on the edge of Oswego Lake with a couple of docks for boats and one for swimming, and had nice grassy areas where we could lay out in the sun. It was a great place to just hang out.

Beanie had his new transistor radio with him and was dialing in KGW so we could listen to some tunes. "The reception on this thing is really awesome. Much better than my last one. And the sound isn't as tinny as the old one either."

The radio dialed in and a disc jockey came on. "...and you are listening to the Super 62 KGW, the place to go to hear the latest happenings in music. This is Kenny B spinning the platters for you. Now, here is a brand-new song hot out of the jacket by the Monkeys, *Last Train to Clarksville...*"

The song started playing and Beanie said, "Man, I've been waiting to hear this. I heard it was great."

"Beanie, you think all songs are great. I'm into music and all, but not even close to how much you are hooked on it."

"Yeah," Mel agreed, "it's a good thing that radio has a strap for your wrist because you would get a cramp in your hand as much as you carry that thing around with you."

"Funny, Mel. Who knows, maybe someday I'll be the one on the radio spinning the discs."

"That, I can believe," I added.

"Speaking of which, have you guys seen the new Beatles album that came out? *Yesterday and Today*? The cover is really something."

"No," Mel answered.

"Me either," I added.

"They are all in white smocks sitting on stools. The big deal is they have chunks of meat draped all over them, and even more than that, there are decapitated and naked dolls on them, but the dolls are pulled apart, so a head is sitting on Paul's lap, and a headless doll is leaning over his shoulder with George behind it.

"That just sounds really weird," Mel said.

"I was reading in my Billboard magazine about it. They think it is a protest against the Vietnam War. You know, with all the innocent people and kids getting killed."

"And with all the protests going on," I added, "lots of musicians are showing they are against the war."

"Well," Beanie continued, "there is also a group of us who think it's really that they are protesting how this album got butchered when released. The Beatles haven't liked how Capitol Records has been cherry-picking the songs that go on albums released here in the States. When they do an album, they plan out how the songs will go on it, so don't like having their work cut all up. This album has songs from three different albums they had released back in England."

"Ya know, Beanie," I said, "I really do think you'll make it as a DJ someday."

"Until then," Beanie said, "I'll just focus on being professional at cannonballs." He jumped up and ran to the edge of the dock, then turned to us. "You see, it all has to do with style. Tuck the legs and hold them with your arms." He jumped, demonstrating in mid-air, and then landed in a big splash.

While he was underwater I added, "I think mass could also have something to do with it."

Mel giggled, "Maybe just a little bit."

Coming to the surface Beanie spit out some water. "See, it's easy. Bet that was my best one ever."

Mel yelled back, "Man, that was perfect, knocked an airplane out of the sky at twenty-thousand feet."

She sat on a towel next to mine laughing at Beanie as he floundered in the water doing underwater handstands. Normally Beanie and I wouldn't ever consider a *girl* as a friend, but Mel was just different—almost like a guy. I smiled at the thought because it seemed so ridiculous every time I snuck a peek at her in that two-piece swimsuit. She really was something.

Mel turned out to be the risk-taker in the group. Her mom hated Mel's tomboy style and tried to make up for it with all the girly stuff around the house. But what her mom apparently couldn't see, though completely obvious to me, was that even when Mel wore blue jeans with a hole in the knee and had a smudge of dirt on her nose, there was a beautiful girl under it all.

I was sure Mel liked me more than just as a friend because sometimes when walking our hands would touch, or when contact was appropriate while playing a game or for whatever reason, that contact lasted just a bit longer than what might normally be expected. And there were the looks, often catching each other in a fleeting side glance. I tried to figure out how to go about kissing her. I'd kissed a girl once, but that was more because of a dare from my friends than because I wanted to. I knew this kiss would be different...*way* different. Isn't there a manual for such things? I mean, I got the whole deal about 'the birds and the bees', but this seemed kind of like knowing how to tear down an automobile engine and put it back together, yet never having anyone quite explain how to start the car.

14

Mel could see I was off in the ozone. "A penny for your thoughts."

I snapped out of it, blushing a little bit. "Oh, it would cost you a whole lot more than that to find out what I was thinking."

We sat and watched as Beanie continued to do underwater somersaults and handstands in the water.

"Mel, are you okay? I mean about losing your dad?" Beanie and I had found out not long after we met Mel that she had lost her dad in a car accident. I couldn't imagine what it would feel like to lose my father like that. She seemed a lot stronger at handling it than I would have been.

She looked over at me, I think a little startled by the question. It was then I realized I had kind of blurted this out from left field, not even sure why it came out myself.

"I really miss him," she finally said, "but it's been over a year now, so I've gotten through the toughest part."

"I hope you don't think I'm prying or something. I just care about you and want to know you are okay."

Mel gave a little smile, then leaned over and kissed me on the cheek, doubling my heartbeat in less than a second. "That's really sweet, Frankie. I just wish it hadn't hit my mom so hard. She's still having a really tough time."

I could see she was wrapped up in her thoughts. She was quiet for a moment, then looked over to me and said, "I'm trying to figure out what to do. I was hoping the move here would change things, but I'm not seeing much improvement."

She stood up. "Come on, this is too nice a day to be thinking of things like that. Let's take advantage of the sun before it disappears. I'm going to beat you at king-of-the-raft."

She yanked me to my feet and raced for the end of the dock. I followed and we hit the water about the same time. Beanie heard the call and swam for the raft. It sat out in the middle of our inlet and was about ten feet square, made of two-by-fours over empty fifty-five-gallon drums lashed under each of the four corners.

For some reason, mostly unfathomable, I seemed to be pretty good at staying king, which simply meant that I could throw or push the other two off the raft to be the only one left standing. And for a different reason, completely fathomable, it always took longer to get Mel off the raft than it did Beanie, even though he probably outweighed her by at least a couple-hundred Musketeers bars.

But this time Mel definitely wanted to be king. She was up on the raft in a second and as I tried to climb up, she waited just until I gained my footing and then pushed me back into the water. Beanie was next to me and she pushed him down each time he tried to get up. It was easy pickings jumping back and forth between us.

"Come on, Mel, at least let me stand up," I pleaded.

"I have, *Perv.* Quit making excuses. You know the rules."

"Rules? There are rules? *What* rules?" I asked as I tried to pull myself onto the raft.

"*My* rules!" she shouted, pushing my head back into the water.

Beanie and I went under the raft to form a strategy. There was just enough space under it to breathe while treading water.

"Beanie, what do you think? We can't let her keep winning."

"I know you guys are under there," Mel shouted. "Come on out. Chicken! Bawk, bawk, bawk, bawk. Chicken boys!"

Beanie answered me, spitting water, "We've got to do something. I'll go to this end and you go to the other. We'll both climb up at the same time."

"Good idea. Ready, go!"

We dove underwater in opposite directions. When we surfaced, we could see Mel in the middle, checking all sides, knowing what was coming. She ran to me, but as she was pushing me back down, Beanie grabbed her from behind and pulled her off. I clawed my way up and we both got hold of her. Mel fought hard but finally shouted, "I give, I give," and we all fell into the lake. The three of us came up for air together.

Beanie swam toward shore while yelling back to us, "Last one to the dock is a rotten egg!"

I started to follow, but caught Mel out of the corner of my eye in one of her side glances. When I stopped, she grabbed her nose, submerged and swam under the raft. I looked at Beanie already halfway to the dock, then followed Mel and surfaced next to her.

Treading water under the raft was a mystical experience. It's like a whole different world. Sunlight filtered through the gaps between the boards lighting the water underneath to an emerald green. The effect was eerie and beautiful all at the same time.

"What's the deal, Mel? You probably could've caught him."

She didn't answer, but just looked at me.

Self-consciousness took over. "You okay?"

She leaned toward me, put her hand behind my head, pulled me in and kissed me. Just as suddenly, she moved back and smiled.

All I could do was stare at her. Definitely not the reaction she expected.

The smile disappeared. "Perv!"

She splashed water in my face and dove out from under the raft. I wiped the water from my eyes and tried to absorb what had just happened, still tasting the softness of her lips.

Chapter 3 — Hoaxes

Over a week had gone by since *the kiss* and neither one of us had made mention of it. Now we were in the Lake Theater watching the movie, *War of the Worlds.* I always wanted to thank whoever invented the idea of bringing these old movies to our theater on Saturday afternoons: a good movie—usually sci-fi or swashbuckler—a bag of popcorn, and a candy bar (3 Musketeers for Beanie, of course), and it didn't even clean out our allowance.

When the movie first started and the lights went low, Mel and I seemed to touch hands more often than normal. During some of the scarier parts we actually held hands, and the feel of her grip as it tightened during the more frightening scenes sent goosebumps racing through my body.

We were now just at the part of the movie where Dr. Forrester and Sylvia had crash-landed a light plane trying to get away from the Martian spaceships and thought they were safe in a farmhouse they found, but a Martian meteor crashed into it. They were trapped, with alien spaceships all around them.

Then Sylvia sees an actual Martian scurry by a window and says, "Something moved out there."

Mel grabbed my arm and held on tight.

Dr. Forrester looks and says, "There's nothing out there now."

But as they try to get out, one of the UFO's camera eyes, on a long articulating arm, comes down through a hole in the roof, and Sylvia turns around to see it looking directly at her. She screams, "Look Out!" and Dr. Forrester takes an ax he was using and chops the eye off the arm. Then, when you think the scariest part is over, a Martian comes into the house and puts a three-fingered hand on Sylvia's shoulder when she doesn't know it is even there. Wow! What a great movie.

But that's not all. Later in the movie, as a last, desperate resort, they drop an Atom Bomb on the aliens. But it doesn't even faze them, so it looks like humanity is done for.

But the best part of the whole movie was Mel holding onto me tighter than she ever has and not just my hand, but was wrapped all around my arm. And, maybe, I was holding onto her just as tight, which didn't bother me in the least.

The movie just kept getting better from there, especially when Dr. Forrester and Sylvia got separated and he had to find her, all while the Martians destroyed the city, building by building, and she could have been in any one of them!

When the movie was over, we had to sit in our seats for a moment just to get back to reality. After all, the human race had almost become extinct!

Finally, we shuffled out of the theater and took in the fresh air outside, standing under the marquee.

Beanie said, "It's kind of creepy, don't you think?"

"What do you mean?" Mel asked.

"When the movie began, they were standing under the theater sign, just like we are now. Then they saw the meteor fall to earth. That's how it started."

We all looked up, relieved to see nothing but blue sky and clouds above. Normally the idea of seeing a spaceship would be cool, but in *War of the Worlds* the Martians pretty much destroyed the earth, so our perspective in this regard was momentarily askew.

"You're always so dramatic," Mel told Beanie.

"I thought the special effects were really neat," I said, "especially for a movie made back in 1953."

"Oh, the movie was okay, but why do they always have to make the woman freak out and scream?" Mel pointed out. "I mean, Sylvia had a Master's Degree and was a teacher, but whenever things got tough, all she could do was scream and fall into the arms of Dr. Forrester. Why can't the woman be the hero for once? I sure wouldn't act that way."

"I think Frankie would just as soon faint into your arms," Beanie swooned. He fell into my arms and fluttered his eyes at me.

I pushed him away. "Flake off, Beanie. You're such a weirdo."

"Do you think there really are aliens on Mars like in the movie?" Beanie asked Mel.

She gave him a sour look. "You know, Beanie, 'War of the Worlds' *is* just a movie. Do you sleep through *all* your classes?"

He looked at her as if it was a real question. "No, just some of them."

21

"Mars doesn't have any life," I told him. "Aliens would probably come from some other galaxy."

We walked across the street to the Rexall drugstore for our ritual after-the-movie ice cream sundae. I reached over and touched Mel's hand. She wrapped hers around mine and I felt a jolt go up my arm. It was an amazing feeling and I wanted it to last forever. I looked over at her and wondered if she was thinking the same thing. She smiled at me, but I couldn't tell for sure. Why would she? She's so beautiful and who am I? Do all guys question themselves in these situations? I sure was. But, why? Should I feel inadequate, or unworthy just because someone so special and beautiful is interested in me? I quickly glanced down at my feet, embarrassed that she might know what was going through my head. *Come on dummy, she kissed you under the raft and is holding your hand*. I had to get out of this line of thought.

"Do you think UFOs really exist?" I asked as we walked into the drugstore and headed to the back where the soda counter was.

She didn't say anything at first. I don't know if she had read my mind or not.

We sat down at the counter. She finally answered, "How couldn't they? I mean, there have been so many sightings of them lately."

We each ordered hot fudge sundaes. What else is there to order when at a Rexall soda counter? When they arrived, we dug in with our spoons and savored the hot and cold.

Finally, Mel said, "Did you hear about the UFO sighting at Exeter? I just saw an interview on The Merv Griffin Show with the guy that wrote a book about it. It's called *Incident at Exeter*. Sounds like it's really stirring things up."

I was focused on my hot fudge, glad that the self-doubt had passed. "Do you think they have it at the library yet?" I looked over to her, "I'll check it out if they do."

She smiled at me. "That would be great."

We arranged a meeting two days later under the bridge at the easement. I had called Mel and Beanie to tell them it had been at the library and I had the book.

I was already waiting there, sitting Indian style near some canoes by the bridge support. A stairway led down to the area. I looked up to see Mel and Beanie coming down the steps.

When they got to me Beanie looked at the books I was holding in my lap. "Did you get it?"

"Yeah, they had it. I also found this other one called 'The Interrupted Journey'. I've only had a quick look through them, but man, some weird stuff went on with these sightings."

"Like what?" Beanie asked, sitting down near me. Mel sat down so as to form a little triangle.

"Well, in 'Incident at Exeter' I guess they chased a spaceship all over the state, and you know what?" I stopped in mid-sentence to build the delivery.

"What, *what*?" they asked in unison.

"...the guys chasing it were cops!"

"Cops," Beanie said, realizing what that meant, "*they* aren't going to lie."

23

"Beanie's right," Mel agreed. "Policemen wouldn't make something up like that. It must be true. UFOs really do exist."

"That's only part of it," I added. "You've got to check out this other book!" Again I paused for effect.

"Come on," Beanie groaned, "enough with the dramatic pauses. Clue us in."

"Well, this book," I held up *The Interrupted Journey*, "is about a man and wife that were coming back from vacation. Barney and Betty Hill. He's a Negro and she's white." I showed them the picture of the couple in the book.

Mel and Beanie practically knocked me over trying to get a good look at the picture.

"Wow, they sure are," Beanie said. "I didn't know that, well, that a Negro could marry a white woman."

Mel looked frustrated. "Beanie, you are so out of it. Of course they can. It's just that some white people don't like the idea." Mel studied the picture again. "Boy, besides the difference in race, they sure look like a normal couple to me."

"They don't look like the kind of people who would make something up like this to get in the limelight anyway," I added.

"So, what happened?" Beanie asked.

"Well," I scrunched in closer to them, "somehow they arrived home two hours later than it should have took. And get this, they couldn't remember what happened during the two hours."

"You mean they were abducted," Mel reasoned.

"Just keep it in check, will you? I'm not there yet. The Hills both noticed that when they got home and looked at

24

the wall clock, it was much later than they expected. Thinking the clock was wrong, they looked at their wristwatches. Both of them had stopped working!"

"Just like in the movie we saw!" Beanie said.

"Yeah, and what's even weirder is when they eventually talked to this guy that knows about radioactivity, he said to put a compass near the car and see if it would do anything strange."

"They used a compass in the movie too," Mel pointed out quietly.

"The Hills had one. So Betty took it out to the car and at first nothing happened, but then she noticed some shiny circles on the trunk. When she put the compass on one of them it went all sorts of haywire!"

This really got Mel and Beanie going.

"So, *were* they abducted?" Beanie asked, unable to contain himself.

"Well, the Hills tried to forget about it, you know, just put it out of their minds. But it wouldn't go away. Betty was having nightmares of really weird things happening. They eventually decided to go to a hypnotist, but not one like you see at the carnival. This guy was some sort of doctor. Anyway, that's when things really came out. I guess the doctor tape-recorded them. Look, it's all here in the book." I opened it to the middle where I had it marked and showed them the transcript of one of Betty's sessions. I read a little of this. They were taken into the flying saucer and all sorts of experiments were done on them.

"Experiments. Like what?" Beanie asked.

"I guess they stuck a needle in her navel and did other kinds of experiments."

Mel let out a little shiver at that one.

"Well," Beanie said, "they wouldn't want to waste the trip without getting some good samples to take back with them."

"But, that's not all. There is this map."

I turned to the page I had marked.

Mel and Beanie leaned into me to get a good look at the map.

I continued, "Under hypnosis it came out that Betty was talking with the leader aboard the spaceship and asked him where they were from. He showed her a map. She was telling the doctor about it and said she wasn't good at drawing, but thought she could do a sketch of it." I pointed to the lines between the planets on the drawing. "She said she was told by the leader that the heavier lines marked regular trade routes."

"Like, between planets?" Beanie asked.

"I guess. I mean, you can see it right here."

"Wow!" Beanie exclaimed.

"And these broken lines are expeditions to other planets."

"Like to Earth, maybe," Mel said.

"Yeah, like to Earth," Beanie agreed, "and a little visit with the Hills for some experiments."

We all sat silent for a moment thinking about that.

"Anyway, I can't wait to read the rest."

Mel looked at me. "You know, I just don't get it."

"What do you mean?"

"How the things in these books can happen, especially to people like the Hills—"

"Don't forget the cops," Beanie cut in.

"…or to policemen," Mel continued, "and yet the government still denies that UFOs even exist."

"Wow, wouldn't it be neat if we spotted a UFO right here in Lake Oswego?" Beanie said. "I mean, I wouldn't want to get too close to one, but it would really be something else to actually see one!"

"That would sure stir up this sleepy little town," Mel said.

We all sat in silence, thinking about what it would be like. I could tell Mel's mind was clicking away.

Her eyes suddenly lit up. "Maybe we should come up with our own little UFO."

"What do you mean?" I asked.

"Yeah, clue us in." Beanie added.

"You know how they are always saying these sightings are hoaxes."

"They're just covering up the truth," Beanie said.

"Probably in a lot of cases, but I'm sure some of them are hoaxes." She sat silent for a moment. "You ever hear about the UFO crash that happened near a place called Roswell? That's in New Mexico."

I searched my mind but came up blank. "No, I don't think so."

Judging by the expression Beanie had, or rather lack of it, he was in the same boat.

"Well, after our talk at the drugstore, I did a little research myself. I remember my dad having some articles about the crash. He was kind of into all this before he died."

I looked over at her. "Your dad was into the whole UFO thing, too?"

Yeah," she continued. "Well, he was really interested in the Roswell deal, anyway. I think because he was going to school near there when the crash happened.

"So, where are you going with this?" I asked.

"Well, I went through some of his stuff Mom keeps in the garage—she just can't part with it—anyway, the crash was covered by the local paper. Check this out."

She pulled some clippings from the back pocket of her jeans. They were yellow and old. She unfolded them and handed one clipping to me and another to Beanie.

I looked at mine. It was from the *Roswell Daily Record*, dated Tuesday, July 8, 1947. It had a big headline that read: "RAAF Captures Flying Saucer on Ranch in Roswell Region". I read the first few paragraphs. It said the base intelligence officer, a Major J. A. Marcel of the 509th Bombardment group at Roswell Army Air Field, announced that the Field had come into possession of a flying saucer at a ranch in the Roswell vicinity.

Mel pointed to my clipping. "I read some other stuff my dad had collected about this flying saucer. It had crashed in the desert, and this army major went to the site and brought back all sorts of debris, none of it looking anything like it could be of earthly origin." Then she grabbed the clipping from Beanie's hands. "The very next day this article came out in the same paper."

I read the headline: "Gen. Ramsey Empties Roswell Saucer".

"The same day as the first story came out this General Ramsey put together a hasty press conference and said that the first report was mistaken and this material was from a weather balloon that crashed. In other words, there was no UFO. Kind of funny how quickly they changed their story."

"It does sound kind of like the fix was in," Beanie added. "How is this Marcel guy going to mistake a weather balloon for debris from a UFO?"

"I know," Mel said. She looked at Beanie and then to me. "I think they switched it on him. They had to cover up their original statement. I think the hoax, in this case, was on the public. I also think that's what my dad thought."

I could see Mel's eyes twitching back and forth.

"So where are you headed with all this?" I asked. Beanie and I had learned that whenever she got this look, she was working on a really good idea.

"I have a plan." She put her hand in the middle of our group, palm down. "Three Musketeers. Are you in?"

Even though I had no idea what her plan was, you don't question the code of the Musketeers. I put my hand on top of hers. "I'm in."

Beanie added his on top of mine. "Me too."

"Frankie, watch the weather report tonight on the news. I'll be busy getting ready and won't be able to. Shouldn't rain, but see if there will be any wind. Beanie, you just make sure you show up. I'm going to need you too. Meet me back here tonight, right after dark. You all okay with that?"

Beanie and I nodded.

She put her other hand on top of ours. "All for one..."

Beanie and I joined in, "...and one for all!"

She looked up at us and we immediately knew this was going to be good.

Chapter 4 — Evening

It was hard waiting for dusk. What could Mel be up to?

The local news came on at six-thirty. My dad always watched it, so I knew there would be no problem with having to fight over the TV to make sure I saw the weather report.

Mom was finishing up getting dinner ready, and it smelled like the dreaded tuna-noodle casserole. She was always trying some kind of dish from one of those magazines of hers where you just pretty much dump everything into a glass pan, toss it in the oven and, voila, out comes a meal fit for kings.

Yeah, right. I have no idea why she had such an obsession with tuna when it came to these single-dish recipes. But if there were ever a mother on the face of this planet or, when I think about it, any other planet, that felt she needed to be the expert on every possible variation of a single ingredient in a dish, it was my mother and a can of Bumble Bee tuna; purchased with double coupons, of course.

"Franklin, dinner's ready," Mom called. "John, come sit down."

She placed the target of my despair on a hot pad in the middle of the dining room table. As if this form of torture wasn't enough, a bowl piled high with Brussels sprouts sat next to it.

Sure, put me on the rack, crank it hard and then, to top it off, stick bamboo slivers under my fingernails.

I sat at the table and noticed the opposite chair empty. "Mom, where's Suzie?"

"She's eating over at Belinda's tonight."

"Figures." My little sister may be twelve, but she was born with an uncanny ability to anticipate the less than favorable meal plans and always, and I mean *always*, figured out a way to avoid them.

On casserole nights I just played with my food, pushing it around the plate until I could actually identify something worthy of eating. In most cases, as with tonight, I failed miserably at the task, finally giving in, holding my nose closed so I didn't have to add smell to the taste as it went down. I guess the positive in it all was I could close my nose without using my fingers. This really impressed the gang down at the lake, though I never divulged how and why I learned to do this.

I had a lot of respect for my dad. He worked hard, took care of the family, and never gave any indication of closing his nose on casserole nights. There he was at the head of the table wolfing down the stuff like it actually tasted good.

"What have you been up to today?" Mom asked.

"Went swimming with Beanie and Mel down at the lake."

"It was a nice day for it," my dad added between bites.

"I sure like that Melanie," my mom said. "She's a nice girl. I just wish she wouldn't dress like a boy."

Mothers must conspire together on such matters.

"I like the way she dresses," I said, and left it at that.

We finished dinner and Mom started clearing the table. "Franklin, give me a hand with these dishes."

Not only did Suzie get out of tuna-noodle torture night, but also the washing the dishes, which was usually her job.

"Sure." I looked up at the wall clock. It was nearly six-thirty. At least we should be done by the time the weather report came on.

I picked up some dishes from the table, holding the bowl of Brussels sprouts at arms' length while walking to the kitchen. Mom washed and I dried. Every so often I looked at the clock on the stove tick away a few more minutes.

If I remembered right, the weather usually came on after the big stories of the day. This was somewhere around ten minutes into the news. It would be close, but there were only a few more dishes to get done.

"Franklin, there aren't many Brussels sprouts left so you might as well scrape the rest into the trash."

I opened the door under the sink to see the trash container nearly overflowing. I pushed the few remaining sprouts on the heap, happy to get rid of them, but the last one rolled off the top and hit the floor.

Mom saw it fall, looked down at the container and said, "Oh, you better take that out to the trash can."

"Mom, I've got something I have to do. Can it wait?"

"No. It will only take a minute, so do it now."

I looked at the clock again and then out to the TV. It looked like the weather would be coming up next.

I grabbed the container and ran for the stairs. The trashcan was down in the carport. I raced down the stairwell, out the sliding glass door, and over to the trashcan. A few of the sprouts fell as I ran. *Boy, they just don't give up*. I back-tracked to pick them up, threw open the lid, dumped the trash, slammed the lid back onto the can, raced back into the house and up the stairs.

Dad was sprawled on the couch so I jumped into the chair next to him. I looked at the television. The weather guy was on so I listened intently.

"...so it looks like we have a storm that will be coming in toward the end of the week."

The image cut to the main anchor, "And now for the latest in sports. Andy, how are those Portland Beavers doing?"

My heart dropped when I realized I had missed it.

I looked over to my dad. "What did the weather guy say?"

"Huh?" Dad was absorbed in the report from the sports guy.

"What did he say?"

"Who?"

"The weather guy. What's it going to be like tonight?"

Dad looked over at me. "Why are you so interested in the weather?"

"Oh, nothing. I was just kind of curious."

I'd missed it. I trudged downstairs to my bedroom and spent the rest of the evening wondering what Mel was up to and how the weather had anything to do with it. In late August it doesn't get dark until around nine o'clock, so it was a long wait. Finally, I went up to the living room, announced I was going to bed, headed back downstairs, snuck out the basement door and down to the lake.

Mel called to me from under the bridge as I got to the bottom of the easement steps. Beanie wasn't there yet. She had a flashlight and was kneeling on the ground, going over some things lying there.

In the beam from her flashlight I could see birthday candles, some plastic straws, masking tape, and a pile of clear plastic of some sort.

"What's all this? We having a birthday party?"

"Funny, *Perv*," she answered, looking up at me with a big smile, "It's our UFO."

"How is this a UFO?" I asked, kneeling next to her.

"We have to build it first."

"Okay…I still don't see it."

"It's simple. Here." She handed me some straws. "We need to put these together. Take one and scrunch the side of the tip in so it fits inside the opening of another straw." She showed me how to do it. "Then add another straw to the end of that one so we have one long straw. We need three long straws made out of three straws each."

Mel had two done by the time I finished mine. Then she took the straws and fanned them out from the center so they were like the spokes of a wagon wheel with a total of six points sticking out.

"Here, hold it just like that."

I held the straws while Mel took the tape and wrapped them together in the middle where they all met.

She checked her work to make sure it would hold, and then laid it on the ground.

Next, she picked up a long candle I hadn't noticed. "I'm going to light this candle and drip wax on the straws at points along them. When I tell you, you need to take one of these birthday candles and stick it in the wax while it's still soft and hold it there until it hardens. Make sure the candles stay upright."

We did this until we had twelve candles securely set on the spokes.

Mel looked up to the steps. "Where is that Beanie anyway? We need to get moving."

"Oh, he probably ran into a little trouble getting out of the house. I'm sure he'll be here. He wouldn't miss this for the world."

"Well, in the meantime, help me with one of these canoes."

Mel headed over to the canoes stacked near the bridge support.

"What are we going to do?"

"Borrow one. We need to go out to the middle of the lake."

I looked at her like she was kidding. "We're what?"

"Come on," she said, setting the flashlight on the ground so it shined on an aluminum canoe. It was upside down on a set of sawhorses.

Mel walked to one end. "You take the other end. Let's flip it over and get it down from here."

I grabbed the other end. We wrestled the canoe toward the ground, but it was long and awkward. We lost control as we turned it. The canoe dropped with a crash. Mel ran over and flipped off the flashlight. We both looked around.

A moment later we heard footsteps coming down the stairs.

Chapter 5 — Incident

A flashlight flipped on and swung in an arc across the stairs and then around the easement. We jumped behind the canoe. We couldn't see who it was as the flashlight swung our direction and captured the canoe in its beam. We held our breath.

"Hey, you guys. That you down here?"

"Beanie, you S.O.B, don't scare us like that!" I whispered.

"Quit swinging that flashlight around," Mel warned him. "You want someone to see us?"

"You're sure making a lot of noise, you know. I could hear it halfway up the street."

Mel stepped out from behind the canoe. "Well, if you would've been here on time and helped us get this thing down, we probably wouldn't have dropped it!" She turned on her flashlight and shined it at Beanie.

Mel and I both broke out laughing, then caught ourselves and tried to stifle the sound with our hands.

I looked Beanie over from head to toe. "What are those? Your *pajamas*?"

I could hear Mel behind me still trying to contain her laughter.

"Stop it, you guys. Mom makes me put them on before bed and then comes in to check on me. I had to wear them. Anyway, by the time she finished checking on me, it was so late I didn't have time to change. I hurried as fast as I could."

"But, really, Beanie," Mel snickered, "*Porky Pig*?"

Her flashlight focused on Beanie's chest. The Warner Brothers logo filled the beam with Porky Pig smiling and waving from the center of it just like at the end of one of their cartoons.

"Th-th-th-th-that's all, folks!" I couldn't help saying it.

"Ah, come on, Frankie, give me a break. My Superman 'jamas were dirty. This is all I had." Then Beanie looked down and spotted the spoke of candles on the ground. "Wow, what's that? We having a party?"

Mel walked over, picked it up and held it out for Beanie to see. "This, Mr. Porky Pig, is the silent, but highly efficient power source for our UFO."

Beanie frowned at first and then smiled—a dim light apparently turning on in his head. He reached out to touch one of the spokes. "That's cherry. So, how does it work?"

"Best way to demonstrate is to show you. Let's get this canoe in the water."

Together we worked the canoe over the rock wall and down to the edge of the inlet, then lowered it into the water. We managed to get it all done without making too much noise or falling in.

Mel went back to the sawhorses and returned with two paddles. "You guys ever paddle a canoe before?"

We both nodded, but I added, "It was only once, when we got to borrow one for a little while."

"Well, let's be careful because they are really tippy." She handed a paddle to Beanie. "Here, you get in front and, Frankie, you're in back. Paddle us out while I get the UFO ready."

I noticed the bowline trailing onto the grass. "Beanie, make sure you secure that line. I don't want you getting all tangled up in it."

Beanie curled it up and set it in the bow of the canoe.

We got in, pushed off the wall and started paddling.

Mel turned off the flashlight. She sat so she was facing towards me.

Once my eyes adjusted, I could see her in the silvery moonlight, which only now appeared from the trees as we moved out past the raft and into open water. The moon was almost full and she looked eerily beautiful in the cold, blue light.

I felt a slight breeze across my face.

Mel felt it too. "What about that weather report? What did it say about the wind?"

I sat quiet for a moment, my paddle making the only sound, and then told her softy, "I missed it. I had to take out the garbage and when I got back it was over. I tried to hurry." It really hurt to disappoint her.

"That's okay." She gave me a smile. "Half the time they don't even tell you about the wind. It's like that isn't one of the aspects of weather in their eyes."

We paddled out past the raft and kept on going. Oswego Lake isn't real big, being only half a mile wide and three miles long. Our swimming easement was about center between the two ends. The lake was manmade and sat in a depression between hills on both sides. The hills were covered by trees, but we could see the lights of houses that lined the banks all around, and up into the surrounding hills.

Before we knew it we were out near the middle. The moon made it light enough to see without a flashlight, but not light enough that someone could spot our canoe.

"Frankie, help hold this bag out of the way while I light the candles."

Mel had been getting the UFO ready while Beanie and I were moving into position. The plastic was a dry cleaner's bag, and she had taped the spokes into position inside the opening so the spoke setup was about four inches up the inside of the bag. The flap at the bottom would keep the hot air in. Real genius.

I looked around to see if anyone else was on the lake. "It looks all clear, but Beanie, keep an eye out for the Lake Patrol or any other boats that may be out. I won't be able to do it while I'm helping Mel." The police had a boat they used on the lake. We certainly didn't want to run into them just now.

"Will do," Beanie answered.

Mel lit the long candle first, and then carefully inserted it into the bag to light the birthday candles.

I tried to hold the bag at just the right angle to make it easy for her, but at the same time keep from melting the plastic. The bag began to puff up and take on a peculiar glow.

Mel worked diligently. "These candles will put off enough heat to make the bag rise. Not only that, but the bag will light up and glow like no flying saucer you've ever seen."

Of course, we had never seen a flying saucer, but her point was well taken.

She lit the last birthday candle and blew out the starter candle. She grabbed the UFO by the center of the spokes and held it high in the air at arms-length for a moment.

The bag swelled with hot air and radiated a glow that was definitely of UFO quality. She let it go. It rose slowly at first and then gained speed.

"Oh, man, that's bitchin'." This, from Beanie, who only now saw it for the first time since he was turned away from us.

"Mel, you've outdone yourself," I added. "It looks so real!"

"It's even better than I thought it would be. Look at it glow. Do you think anyone will see it?"

The UFO was now above our canoe about forty feet and rising rapidly.

"How could they miss it?" I answered.

It was Beanie who gave the first indication our plan was about to take a very bad turn. "Hey, guys, look!"

At first I turned toward the city side of the lake, but saw nothing so I looked in the other direction. When you grow up on a lake you know how to read it. Around the canoe the water's surface was like glass, but off in the distance I could see chop on the water. That meant wind! And it wasn't a slight breeze either. It was moving toward us at a fairly quick pace and coming across the lake at an angle I didn't like.

"Mel, the wind's coming up. Beanie, let's get this canoe turned around and head back to shore."

We paddled recklessly because neither of us had much experience with canoes. Instead of getting turned around, all we managed was to work our way farther out.

"Beanie, hold on. Let me get it turned around."

I back-paddled on one side and the canoe tip slowly turned toward shore. Just as we were facing the easement, the wind hit us.

"Mel, keep an eye on that UFO. Come on, Beanie, let's high-tail-it for the bank."

The wind came in at an angle that helped drive us toward shore. We battled to keep the canoe pointed at our easement because the wind also wanted to push us down the bank. We turned the nose upwind to correct our approach, but the wind kept trying to knock it back.

"Oh, God, no!" It was the tone of Mel's voice more than the words that sent a chill through me.

I looked in the direction of the UFO to see it suddenly burst into flames just as it hit the upper part of a big fir tree. There's nothing like melting plastic and pine needles to get a good fire going.

We stopped and stared for a second, the wind only an afterthought to what was happening about a hundred yards down the lakeshore. I could tell it was old lady Crowley's tree, easily identified because it had two tops, rumored to have been caused by a lightning bolt a long time ago.

"M-m-man, we'd better get out of here. I d-d-don't want to g-get caught," Beanie shouted. He had just done a perfect imitation of Porky Pig, but none of us were in the mood to laugh.

We paddled frantically toward shore. I looked over at Mrs. Crowley's place every few seconds to see a towering blaze light up the sky.

The first rule of canoeing was never lean to one side, particularly with the wind blowing from the other, but we were too distracted to remember such valuable information. One moment we were dry and scared, and the next we were in the lake—wet, cold, and terrified.

I reached for Mel who was bobbing like a cork in front of me. "You all right?"

"I think so," she said, spitting out lake water. "I might have hurt my wrist a little when we tipped."

I pulled her over to the canoe which, to my surprise, floated. "Hold on. I'm swimming up to the front." I tried to get a decent swim stroke, what with sneakers on and an air bubble in the back of my shirt. "Beanie, you okay?"

"This is great. Boy, are we in trouble!"

"Just take it easy. You got the rope?"

"Yeah, it's right here."

"Give me the end. I'm going for the raft. It may be long enough so I can get up and pull the canoe in."

Luckily, during all of our efforts paddling, we had managed to keep the canoe pointed in the right direction. It had tipped over just outside the easement.

I looked over Beanie's shoulder, "Mel, make sure to hold on."

The sound of sirens faintly appeared over the flailing of the wind and waves. I took the line and put it between my teeth, tasting the bitterness of the rope and our situation. I did a breaststroke to the raft. There was just enough line to climb up and pull Mel and Beanie in. I helped them up.

We righted the canoe, getting as much water out as possible and were ready to get back in again when a fire truck rushed across Springbrook Bridge. We had been so involved in saving ourselves, we hadn't noticed the sirens growing closer.

I looked at Mel and Beanie huddled on the dock, shaking like wet puppies. I put my arms around their shoulders. "This is my fault. I should have gotten that wind report."

Mel looked at me with a half-smile, water dripping from her chin. "We don't even know if it would have been on the news, and if it was, they probably would have gotten it wrong and said it was going to be calm as can be."

"Thanks for trying to make me feel better, anyway." I leaned in and gave her a kiss on the cheek. "Well, let's put this canoe away, and try not to get caught sneaking back to our bedrooms. You can bet it'll be pretty crazy on the street when we get up there."

"We'll know more tomorrow," Mel said.

Another fire truck and a police car raced across the bridge, their sirens blaring. I looked up to see red lights strobe across the trees above us.

"We'll know a lot more tomorrow," Beanie added, watching the fire truck disappear from the bridge, "like how long we have to live."

Chapter 6 — Aftermath

The next morning, I lay in bed staring at the ceiling. I had hardly slept. All night my dreams switched between UFOs causing forest fires and my father standing over me yelling about how it was all my fault.

I looked at the radio alarm clock on my bed stand. It was still early, but I rolled out of bed anyway and crept upstairs to see what was going on.

I found my mom tooling around the kitchen fixing breakfast. Suzie was already up and talking to Mom in excited tones. She was sitting on one of the tall stools at the breakfast counter that overlooked the kitchen area.

Dad was on the couch hunched over a cup of coffee and the morning edition of the *Lake Oswego Review*. Smoke from his cigarette curled through the rays of sunlight filtering into the room from the morning sun. He was in mid-sentence, "...Fire Department's not sure how it started."

Mom saw me standing in the hall. "You're up early."

"What's with the Fire Department?" I asked, realizing a slight shrill to my voice, but at the same time trying to act innocent of all facts.

Suzie cut in. "Boy, did you miss it last night!"

"Miss what?"

"Just the most exciting night ever in Lake Oswego—there was a UFO sighting over the lake, Mrs. Crowley's tree caught fire, and what's more, she's been abducted!"

"She's what?" Not sure I heard her right.

Mom answered over bacon on the griddle, "Now, we don't know for sure what happened to Mrs. Crowley. She just wasn't there, so the firemen had to break down the door."

"Broke down her door?" Weakness overtook my body.

"Well, *yeah*," Suzie added in a tone indicating the standard brotherly stupidity of my comment. "That's what they do when they have to put a fire out on her roof!"

"Her roof was on fire?" By this time I had slumped into a stool at the counter just to keep my legs from giving out. *So, this is what it feels like going into shock.*

Dad laid his paper down and a big headline stood out on the front page:

Special Edition: INCIDENT AT OSWEGO LAKE.

Below that read: UFO Sighted – Woman Missing. He looked up from the paper. "Some of the embers fell from the tree onto her roof and caught it on fire. I don't think it would've been too bad except the fire department had to hack a hole in the roof to make sure the fire was out. Probably caused more damage than the fire did."

I leaned into the back of the stool hoping it would hold me together.

"I'm gonna run over right now and see what's happening," Suzie said, jumping down from her stool.

"Not until you have a good breakfast. Then we can all go over," Mom told her.

Suzie climbed back up on the stool and dropped in a huff onto her seat. "Okay!"

Dad grabbed the sports page from the paper and headed for the bathroom, his usual time for the morning constitutional.

I waited for him to disappear down the hall and then headed for the couch and the paper. Below the headline was a picture of Mrs. Crowley's place with firemen on the roof holding axes. More were below spraying a long stream of water on the fir tree, which now looked like a poster for Smokey the Bear. The picture made me sick, but I forced myself to read the article anyway.

Lake Oswego, OR (AP).

AP? Even I knew that meant Associated Press. This article went national! I kept reading:

By Steve Sumpter.

In an evening of mystery and intrigue last night, the Lake Oswego Fire Department responded to a fire at 2554 Summit Drive at 9:45 PM to find the upper half of a large fir tree ablaze. Realizing embers had fallen on the roof igniting it, firemen attempted to awaken the resident, a Mrs. Evelyn Crowley, with no success. Concerned for her safety, and in order to access the interior of the roof, they broke down the door. Fire Chief Del Williams said they had responded in time to prevent the fire from penetrating the interior of the home so there was minimal damage.

When asked about Mrs. Crowley, Chief Williams indicated that she had not been located in the home even though it appeared that the house had been recently occupied. He then said that any further questions regarding Mrs. Crowley should be addressed to the police department who is currently conducting an investigation.

We located Captain George Thornton of the Lake Oswego Police Department on the scene. Captain Thornton stated, "It appears at this time that Mrs. Crowley is missing. Having conducted a thorough search of her premises, we are unable to locate her. In addition, her car is still in the garage. The investigation is in its early phases, but interviews with next-door neighbors indicate they have no knowledge of her whereabouts, or of any plans to be out of town."

Captain Thornton also told us they did not see any form of forced entry into the home other than that produced by the fire department, or notice anything of value gone. He would not speculate as to how she may be missing.

Further investigation by this reporter through interviews with area neighbors revealed that a UFO had been seen at the lake and may have been the cause of the blaze. Bill Spencer, a nearby neighbor stated that he had spotted the UFO hovering over the lake just moments before the tree caught fire. "I went out on the deck to have a smoke and next thing I know there's this UFO moving over the lake. I watched it for a minute and then ran inside to grab a camera. When I came back out the UFO was gone and the fir tree was on fire, so I called the police. What was really strange about this whole thing is the night was calm as can be when I was standing out there taking my smoke, but only a moment later, when I came back out, the wind was blowing like the dickens." Asked to describe the UFO he stated, "It was long, kind of like a cigar, but it wasn't on its side like you've heard of. The long ways was up and down. It had a real bright glow to it and kind of hovered there."

We were able to confirm with Captain Thornton that UFO sightings had been reported in the area of the lake. No less than a dozen calls were received by the police department during the short period of time just prior to the fire.

A follow-up article will be forthcoming in the next edition of the Review when we are able to further our investigation into this very bizarre night.

I sat back from the paper, as if by getting away from it I would be able to remove myself from this whole unbelievable situation. Could it get any worse? Of course it could, once our parents found out we started the fire!

I suddenly thought of Mel and Beanie. Were they up yet? Had they seen the paper? Did they have any idea what all we had done? And this Mrs. Crowley thing? What was that all about? Her missing sure threw a whole new twist into things.

Chapter 7 — Crowley's

Breakfast may as well have been tuna-noodle casserole. My stomach had so much going on inside, there wasn't any room for food. I knew if I tried even a minuscule bite, it would have launched back up with the force of a Saturn rocket blasting into space. So I spent most of the time pushing eggs and potatoes around my plate waiting for the rest of the family to finish, which seemed an unbearably long time.

Our house was up the hill where Springbrook Court and Summit Drive met at the entrance to the easement. Summit Drive followed the hillside above the lake. Mrs. Crowley lived just up and across from us on the lake side of the road.

It didn't take long to get there and see that the place was swarming with people. Little groups stood in half circles, some of them with their noses buried deep in the *Review*, and no doubt, the article I had read. The rest were staring at Mrs. Crowley's house and up at the tree.

A few firemen were there, I guess to wrap things up with the fire, though it looked more like they just wanted to be in the center of things. Officer Thompson, the most minor player in our grand police force of three, stood by the front door trying very much to be the power of authority; probably for the first time in his entire career. He strutted around reminding the curious to keep back from the house, regardless of whether they were intruding on the space or not.

"Careful, this is a crime scene," he kept repeating, as if there was a dead body inside.

Suzie raced to the front where some of her equally evil girlfriends were collected, all immediately talking at a hundred miles a minute, not an ear between them to hear what the others were saying.

Mom and Dad blended into the crowd, mingling with neighbors they hadn't spoken to since the last great neighborhood catastrophe. It's amazing how a good fire and abduction can draw out even the most devoted homebodies.

I tried to find Mel and Beanie, but neither was to be seen. I looked at Mrs. Crowley's place. The front seemed about the same as always, poorly kept and in need of serious maintenance. My eyes moved to the roof where loose cedar shingles mingled with burnt insulation around a bright blue tarp covering what probably was the hole the firemen had put in the roof. My eyes moved up to the fir tree. The upper third was bare of any needles, like some giant-something had felt it his duty to strip the upper half of foliage. The split tops of the tree stood naked in the morning sun. I caught a whiff of acrid smoke and it made me a little sick, or at least gave me something to blame the feeling on.

A familiar voice sounded from my side. "Boy, can you believe it?"

I turned to see Mel staring up at the tree. "Not in my worst nightmare." I thought about that for a second. "Actually, last night it *was* my worst nightmare."

She gave a little smile and put her hands around the crook of my arm and leaned her head against my shoulder. Things suddenly seemed a little better.

"What are we going to do?" she asked. "This is the worst."

"I don't know. Did you hear about Mrs. Crowley?"

"Yeah, and what's that all about? How can she have disappeared?"

I looked at Mel. Real concern showed in her eyes.

"She's fine. Beanie and I know Mrs. Crowley better than anyone, and for her to disappear is nothing new. She's always been like this. Her next-door neighbors don't even have a clue about how much of a kook she is. Now, with this happening, they all jump on the bandwagon as if they had tea together every day and Mrs. Crowley shared her most intimate life moments with them. Timing is everything, and this timing just sucks!"

Mel's eyes searched mine to figure out if I was just trying to make her feel better, then they shifted to look down the street. "Here comes Beanie."

I turned to see Beanie slugging his way up the hill, an obvious burden weighing him down. I grabbed Mel's hand and led her toward him.

Beanie stopped when he saw us coming. "I think things would have ended up a whole lot better if I'd just drowned at the lake last night."

"Oh, I doubt that," I told him. "Someday I'm sure you'll look back at this and have a real laugh, but of course, that's only if you live through what your parents do to you once they find out."

Mel elbowed me in the side. "Look, Perv, we really don't need to make this any worse than it is. Ignore him Beanie."

"Ignore who?" Beanie questioned, giving Mel a weak smile.

The touch of humor helped to lift our spirits.

"So you know about Mrs. Crowley?" I asked him.

"You mean that she's missing? Yeah, I heard. Who hasn't? It's all over the place that she's been abducted by our UFO. I know she likes her little disappearing acts, but why did she have to go on one of her kooky adventures right when this happened?"

We all turned as a white truck coming up the street caught our attention. The side had a big logo with the number six. A news team from one of the Portland television stations was here.

Beanie watched it pass. "Oh, great! Now it's going to be all over television. It wasn't bad enough that it made the *Review* this morning. Now the whole world is going to know."

"Did you see that article?" I said. "I thought that maybe a couple of people would see our UFO, but the police got dozens of calls."

"Yeah," Beanie added, "Why is it that when things work out well, it happens to be just at the time when you really don't want them to?"

We walked up the road toward Mrs. Crowley's. The crowd was gathering around the truck as a reporter and cameraman got out.

The cameraman immediately moved to the house and shot footage of it and the tree. I recognized the reporter from television. He was with the news station my parents always watched at six-thirty just after we ate dinner. He seemed to be trying to find anyone to interview who would have a new angle on what happened last night.

Mel, Beanie and I hurried past the crowd gathered around him, a little uneasy that he would suddenly swing his microphone in our direction. We stopped at the upper edge of Mrs. Crowley's lawn and sat on some railroad ties. They made a retaining wall on the up-hill side of her property, and now became the perfect observation point for a higher and less populated view of the event.

We watched the obsessed crowd below us. The reporter was now interviewing Officer Thompson. I wished I could hear what was being said, but we were too far away.

There was the neighborhood crowd, the reporter and cameraman, Thompson, the firemen, and what looked like a bunch of people I didn't even know. Word was getting out and more and more people were showing up. They were like ants swarming around their hill. The whole thing was taking on a life of its own—consuming its own energy and building bigger and bigger.

"Man, this is getting way out of hand," I finally said.

Beanie looked worried. "No kidding. What are we going to do?"

Mel answered. "I know what we're not going to do, and that's jump into the middle of all this and tell them it was a terrible hoax. As wacko as they are right now, they would either eat us alive or just think we were trying to take the limelight and not even believe us. We'd better just cool it for a while."

I jumped down off the railroad ties and turned to them. "I don't think we should do anything until Mrs. Crowley turns up again so everyone will know she wasn't abducted."

Mel agreed. "You're right, and we need her back so we can at least tell *her* what happened."

"And hopefully the extra time will also quiet down the frenzied masses," Beanie added, looking over the crowd. "So, I'm good with waiting a day or two, or three...or forever."

Mel punched Beanie in the arm and locked in our eyes. "You know we have to tell her."

I couldn't argue with those eyes. "Yeah, we know."

"Are we going to end up in jail?" Beanie asked. "You know what they do to guys in there, don't you?"

I rolled my eyes at yet another typical Beanie observation. "You watch too many movies, Beanie. We're not going to jail."

Mel jumped down from the retaining wall. "Whatever the outcome, we're going to tell her, right?"

Beanie and I reluctantly nodded.

Chapter 8— Landing

"Kids, it's time to get ready for bed."

"Okay, Mom," I answered.

Suzie and I were plopped on the carpet in front of the TV watching *Gilligan's Island.* I was glad, because I needed the distraction to get my mind off of this whole mess we were in.

It was rare to find something I enjoyed watching since Dad always managed to dominate the TV in the evening. Every time Suzie or I tried to change the channel and lobby for a program we wanted to watch, he would mention something about being the breadwinner in the family and paying for everything—which pretty much put an end to any of our attempts.

So, most of the time I was bored to death watching *Gunsmoke* or *Bonanza* (Yeah, he was into Westerns), but at least tonight it was Gilligan.

I think the only reason my dad liked this show was because of Ginger and Mary Ann. But then again, I couldn't blame him. They were hot! Me, I'm a Mary Ann guy. Maybe that's why I like Mel so much. They are both beautiful and down to earth!

The show was right at a part where the professor wires a few coconuts together to create a battery for the radio. But then the show suddenly went black and just as quickly was replaced by a "Breaking News" headline.

The local newsman came on. "We interrupt this broadcast to bring you a breaking news bulletin. We have just received a report of another UFO sighting near Lake Oswego. As you know, this follows yesterday evening's sighting in the same area which is being associated with a house fire and the possible abduction of its owner. We will have more information on tonight's evening news. We now return you to our regularly scheduled program."

Gilligan had somehow knocked over the table the professor was working on, but I hardly noticed. Dad, Suzie and I were all headed out the sliding glass door to check it out.

Our house sat a little ways up the hill and overlooked the lake, so we had a pretty good view of the sky above. We walked out to the edge of the front deck to get out from under the branches of the big oak tree that grew near the house. Our necks craned to the darkness above as we scanned the night sky, and even though I knew this couldn't be true, the hairs on the back of my neck were standing on end with the same rigid attention as a Marine squad at morning inspection.

"See anything?" Suzie asked.

"Not a thing," Dad answered. He looked down at us. "Kids, I don't want you to make anything of this. I don't know what happened over at Mrs. Crowley's, but I'm sure there is a more worldly answer than what everyone believes."

Mom came outside, having discovered the house empty of family content. "John, what is going on?"

"There was a news report about more sightings." He went over to her and put his arm around her waist as she walked out to where we were. I'm guessing because her motherly instincts made her want to be in arms reach of her children under such circumstances.

"Now, Betty, don't get all worried over this. It's just too inconceivable to be true. And what would UFOs want here in Lake Oswego anyway? There could be absolutely nothing of interest to them, and I say that under the wild assumption that UFOs even exist to begin with."

I looked over at my dad to see that even with what he just said, his eyes had gone back to their search above.

"John, I'm worried. What with the fire, and Mrs. Crowley disappearing. Now this? Should we do something? Go somewhere safer?"

"Everything is going to be fine, honey. We are perfectly safe here. Let's all go back inside. The news will be on in a minute and we'll know more then."

Mom, Suzie, and Dad headed back in.

"Franklin, come inside," Mom coaxed.

I could see she was concerned. "I'll be right there. I just want to look a while more."

"John?" she pleaded to Dad.

"It's okay, honey. Frankie will be fine." He turned to me. "But not long, Frankie. It will worry your mother."

"Okay, Dad. I'll be right in."

The sliding glass door closed behind them and Dad dropped into his lounger while Mom and Suzie took up spots on the couch. Their eyes were glued to the television screen as if all the answers would appear there in just a matter of moments. But I knew the answers were anywhere but there.

What were the answers? I looked up. The stars were shining bright overhead. I double-checked to make sure none were moving. It just didn't make sense. How could there be more sightings when it was all a hoax to begin with?

Unless UFOs *had* actually come. Could they be here because of what we did? Were they monitoring our broadcasts and had come to check things out? Or was it something else? We know Mel's dad was into the Roswell thing. Could that have something to do with it? But, how? All this suddenly made it seem like standing outside by myself wasn't a very good idea. I hurried back into the house.

The credits for *Gilligan's Island* were just finishing up. Even with the breaking news, I would have to wait for the lousy commercials to finish before I found out anything. I dropped onto the carpet. My eyes were on the TV, but my mind was a million miles away traveling a hundred miles a minute going over the same questions I had just asked myself.

I wanted to call Mel, but it was too late. Just talking to her would have made me feel better, though I knew she wouldn't have any answers. I would call her first thing in the morning.

We sat in silence as a television model smiled at us holding a bottle of Palmolive dish soap and explaining how this was the only product that could keep a woman from having dishpan hands. That was followed by a man who informed us, while lighting up, "L.S.M.F.T. Lucky Strike Means Fine Tobacco". It seemed so strange that they acted like nothing was going on. I know they're just people in commercials, but it added a freaky quality to what was already a very bizarre day.

The news finally came on. Following the program's introduction 'News Six, the News You Need to Know', the camera focused on the newsman behind a desk, his manner serious, almost anxious.

"Good evening, I'm Eric Sandler." He paused for a moment and then said, "Lake Oswego, a small hamlet just twenty miles south of Portland, has become the focus of the nation today."

The nation! Could this get any worse? I leaned into the television.

"We have a special report coming up regarding Unidentified Flying Objects and last night's events, but first we will cover this recent sighting.

"A few moments ago we received word of a new flying saucer sighting in the area. As you know, this follows a sighting last night which has been tied to a house fire and the disappearance of its occupant. Details on the new sighting are still coming in, but this is what we know so far. At approximately nine-fifteen this evening we received word that the Clackamas County Sheriff's Office dispatch took a phone call from a farmer in the Stafford Road area reporting another UFO sighting at his farm. The Sheriff's Office has responded to the call, and we have dispatched a News Six team to the area. Additional information will be provided as it becomes available.

"We will begin our coverage on today's events with a story filed earlier today by Robert Wright, our field reporter, on the sighting last night and the disappearance of Mrs. Evelyn Crowley."

The scene cut to a newsman standing in front of Mrs. Crowley's house. "I'm standing on Summit Drive in front of the home of Evelyn Crowley. As you can see, the house has sustained fire damage to the roof, and behind it a large fir tree also caught fire."

The camera panned from the reporter to the roof of the house and then up to the tree. As the camera widened out to take in the whole scene, it also took in the crowd of people gathered there, inclusive of my sister and her delusional sisterhood.

"Look! There I am!" Suzie shouted, as if she were the focus of the story.

The reporter continued, "Late last night the Lake Oswego Police Department received dozens of calls reporting a UFO sighting in this immediate area. Only moments later the fire department received a call reporting a fire at this address. They responded to the location and found a fir tree ablaze and the roof of the house on fire. The fire department was able to quickly extinguish the fires with minimal damage to the roof of the house. In the process they needed to gain entry to the home by breaking down the front door after multiple attempts to contact someone inside without response. Based on our inquiries from neighbors, Mrs. Crowley lived alone and is somewhat of a recluse. On an initial search by the police last night, it appears that she was not away on a planned trip. We bring in Officer Earl Thompson of the Lake Oswego Police Department to comment."

In stepped Thompson, obviously absorbing every moment of his short-lived fame.

"Officer Thompson, what can you tell us about the events of last night?"

"Well." He shifted his stance, threw back his shoulders, and looked directly into the camera. "Last night we received calls about an Unidentified Flying Object in this area, so we were investigating those reports when the fire department received the call about the house fire at this location. Feeling it could have something to do with the sightings, Captain Thornton made the decision to investigate. On arrival and working in hand with the fire department, we conducted a search of the house, but found it empty, even though the car was still in the garage. We also observed that the home had been recently occupied—evidenced by such things as dirty dishes on the kitchen counter, an unmade bed, and open toiletries in the bathroom—such things a person would normally have taken care of before leaving on a planned trip."

I couldn't believe it. Didn't anyone know Mrs. Crowley? All you had to do was look at the yard to know how the house would look inside. Great detective work!

"So, Officer Thompson, does this lead you to believe she had been at the residence, is now missing, and could have been abducted by the UFO?"

"We will not say for certain, though with the fire and sightings appearing in close proximity, we will not eliminate that as a possibility. We would like to ask that anyone with knowledge of her whereabouts contact the Lake Oswego Police Department."

"Thank you, Officer Thompson." The camera slowly panned to the other side of the reporter. Officer Thompson leaned along with the camera until he was out of view.

"Now, we would like to bring in Mrs. Crowley's next-door neighbor, Stan Francis."

Stan stepped into the picture, smiling.

"Stan, what can you tell us about your neighbor?"

"Oh, well, Evelyn, she's a great woman. We didn't spend a whole lot of time together because she was pretty much a homebody, but it seems unusual that she would be gone right now. We were close enough that I would have known if she was leaving, and I had no word. Just strange, you know."

Mrs. Crowley hated this guy.

"So you find her disappearance to be unusual?"

"Oh, yeah, absolutely. It just doesn't make sense. I think she must have been abducted by the UFO, which set the tree and house on fire in the process of grabbing her."

"Thank you, Stan."

The camera zoomed in on the reporter again, with Mrs. Crowley's place in the background. Suzie and her friends were huddled together behind him, whispering, snickering, and nodding in the direction of the camera. I looked over at Suzie on the couch. She was totally engrossed in seeing herself on television.

The reporter continued, "Late last night the police department received over a dozen calls reporting a UFO over Oswego Lake in this very location. Moments later the fire was reported and the house's occupant missing. Coincidence? Was she abducted by the UFO last night that caused this fire, or is there some reasonable explanation for these events and her disappearance? News Six will continue our investigation and bring you the latest on the UFO sighting and her disappearance as new information is made available. This is Robert Wright reporting for News Six."

The screen cut back to the reporter at the studio. "That report was filed earlier this morning. Further investigation has revealed no new information regarding Mrs. Crowley's disappearance." The reporter shifted in his seat, obviously excited about what he would say next. "We turn now to tonight's sighting. New information has just been received and although we can't confirm it at this time, we can report this sighting apparently includes an actual landing in the area. Our news team will be arriving at the location shortly. We will have a full report on tomorrow morning's news." He paused to let it sink in. "Now, in other news tonight, there was a riot in Waukegan, Illinois as racial tensions continue to escalate…"

"A landing!" Suzie barked, "An *actual* UFO landing. I wonder where?"

I couldn't believe it: first we set fire to a house, then Mrs. Crowley comes up missing, and now a UFO has landed somewhere in Lake Oswego! *So what's next?*

"Well," Dad said, "I think that's enough excitement for tonight. You kids go get ready for bed. Mom and I need to talk. When you're done, come and say your good-nights."

"But, Dad," Suzie exclaimed, "how can we sleep tonight with all this going on? What if a UFO did land? There could be aliens around!"

"Suzie, this whole thing is impossible to believe. Even so, I doubt they would be headed to our house, so I'm sure we are safe. Now, go ahead, both of you get ready for bed."

I headed downstairs not knowing what to think. Just when it looked like it couldn't get any worse, it did. How could this landing have anything to do with our hoax? It didn't make sense. I needed to meet with Mel and Beanie in the morning and try to figure this all out.

Chapter 9— Longmore's

I waited as long as I possibly could before I dialed the phone. It was obviously still too early when a flustered mom answered.

"H-hello."

"Hi. Mrs. Simpson? Is Mel up?"

"Frankie?"

"Sorry I'm calling so early."

"Hold on. Let me check."

I could hear her shout, "Mel, it's Frankie on the phone. You want to talk to him?"

Silence, then Mrs. Simpson's muffled voice, "Why is he calling so early?" Followed by an equally muffled, "Oh, Mom."

Muted sounds came from the receiver. "Hi Frankie, hold on."

I could tell she was taking the phone outside. It was a Princess phone mounted to the wall near the kitchen door. It had an extra-long spiral cord, which allowed her to take it outside for privacy.

She whispered, "Did you see the news last night?"

"Why do you think I'm calling so early?"

"I know. I've been up for a while, just lying in bed thinking."

"Man, this just doesn't make any sense. We need to get together, to watch the morning news. Can we do it at your house? My dad's going to work, but Mom and Suzie will be home, so my place is a no go."

"Mom will be leaving for work in a while." She paused for a moment, probably thinking about whether we could pull it off at her place, then said, "I guess we can do it here, but she doesn't like it when I have friends over while she's gone."

"We can't do it at Beanie's. You know how his mom would be all over us. We have to do it at your place."

"I guess you're right."

"When is she leaving?"

"I think soon. She has to be to work at eight."

"Good, because that's what time the news comes on. I'll call Beanie. We'll be over at a quarter till."

"Okay."

"Bye."

"Bye...Frankie?" I could hear the concern in her voice.

"Yeah?"

"What do you think this landing is all about?"

"I don't know. Hopefully we'll find out soon."

"I'm glad you'll be here."

"Me too. Bye."

I heard a click as she hung up. I stood there holding the receiver against my ear with nothing but a dial tone to keep me company. All I could think was how lucky I felt to have Mel right now.

I rounded the corner of the hedge between Mel's place and mine when I saw her sitting on the front step of her house.

She came running down the driveway. "Mom didn't go to work. She's staying home because of the UFO reports and is too worried to leave me alone."

"Great. Now what do we do?"

"I don't think it would be a good idea to watch at my place." She paused for a second, as if deciding if she should continue with her train of thought, then went on, "I don't like talking about this much, which you know from when I cut you off down at the lake..." She held her thought, looked down and kind of shuffled her feet before continuing. "Remember when I told you she hasn't been the same since my dad died, and how even the move here hasn't helped as much as I had hoped? Well, all of this is setting her off again and she's getting even worse."

I reached out and took her hand. "Wow, Mel. I'm sorry to hear that."

"I think there's even more to it though. My dad used to go on expeditions to archeology sites as part of his work. But I also remember other trips he made, where when he came back, he acted different. I could tell that even though he led me to believe they were regular work trips, I knew they weren't. It was like he didn't want me to know what he was doing. I'm now thinking they had something to do with the UFO crash at Roswell. Remember the clippings I showed you?"

"Yeah, and how we decided it was a cover-up," I said.

"Well, he had all sorts of stuff about the Roswell crash. He was really looking into it. I hadn't thought about it before, but I'm thinking those odd trips had to do with that crash."

"Oh."

"And now I'm starting to wonder if my mom knew about them too. I mean, that could help to explain a lot about how she's acting."

"Do you think she was part of it, or just noticing the difference in how he acted, like you?"

"I'm not sure. Maybe she was involved. It's hard to tell because I just don't know what he was doing. But if it did have to do with the crash at Roswell, and she knew about it, then that would go a long way to explaining how all of this is affecting her and why she is acting this way."

"Wow! I didn't know it was this bad. I'm sorry, Mel."

"Thanks, Frankie. Anyway, it's pretty obvious that having the news on at my place isn't a good idea."

"I guess we'll have to watch at my house."

"I have to let my mom know. I'll be right back."

"She'll let you come over?"

"Yeah, I'm pretty sure since your mom will be home. It should be okay as long as she knows where I am."

"Okay. I'll wait for you here."

I felt a tinge of guilt as I watched Mel head back up the drive. Even with everything going on I still couldn't take my eyes off her as she walked away, or divert my mind from the associated thoughts a teenage boy gets in such a situation.

"You're obviously focused on the crisis at hand."

I jumped at the voice right in my ear. "Damn it, Beanie, do you have to sneak up on me?" My face burned red in all its possible hues. "Give me a break, will you? How can I *not* watch?"

"If I knew how to admit that I'm jealous I would, but I don't."

"I thought you went for older women."

"Real funny. You're the *perv* here, remember?"

I ignored the direct hit.

"I guess we're going to have to watch over at my house," I told him. "Mel's mom is staying home because of everything going on."

"Sounds good to me, just as long as it's not my place. You know the deal there."

"Yeah, I know. Why is your mom so...involved all the time?"

"I guess she thinks it's just part of being a good mom, with probably a little single-child phobia mixed in. Sometimes I wish I had a little sister or something."

"Believe me, if you did, you wouldn't."

Mel came out of the house and hurried down the driveway toward us.

"Hey, Beanie."

"Hey, Mel."

I looked at Mel and then at Beanie as they just stood there silently. "Well, now that you two are all caught up, we'd better get going. It's almost eight."

We rushed over to my house and made it inside just in time.

71

Mom and Suzie were already settled on the couch with the television on. I could see the news hadn't started yet. Mom was in the middle of a sip of her coffee.

"Hey, Mom. Okay if Mel and Beanie watch the news with us?"

"Hi, Mrs. Strickland," Mel said.

"Yo, Mrs. Strickland," Beanie added.

She set her cup down on the coffee table, giving Beanie a 'mom look' over his form of greeting, before answering. "Well, your little club sure is meeting early."

"Yeah, uh, it's just all the excitement of the UFOs," I told her. "We want to see what happened last night."

"Okay. Find a seat. It's about to start. With all this going on, I'd just as soon know where you are anyway."

"Sounds like my mom," Mel whispered.

We all plopped down on the rug.

The usual 'News Six' intro happened and then the news anchor came on. "Welcome to the morning edition of News Six, I'm Graham Northern. Our top story is the sighting and alleged landing of a UFO in Lake Oswego last night. We have gathered our news team to bring you the latest coverage of the situation. We will start with News Six reporter, Tom Wilson, who has a background report about UFOs. Tom, what have you put together?"

The camera switched to another newsman at the studio. "Thank you, Graham." He turned to the camera. "Throughout history there have been reports of Unidentified Flying Objects all over the world. In the United States, the first widely reported UFO sighting occurred right here in the

Northwest on June 24th, 1947 when Kenneth Arnold was flying his airplane near Mount Rainer in Washington State." A picture of Arnold appeared on a screen behind the reporter. "He sighted nine flying objects between his plane and the mountain. The UFOs stayed within sight long enough that he was able to get a good look at them, which he described as 'saucer-like'. Ever since then, the term *flying saucer* has been used to describe these aircraft.

"Just days later, around July 4th, a flying saucer was reported to have crashed north of Roswell, New Mexico. The story was carried by the Associated Press and created quite a stir nationally, but the very next day the Air Force held a press conference and reported it was nothing more than material from a weather balloon." A picture of Major Marcel holding pieces of a weather balloon came up on the screen.

Mel nudged me with her elbow and whispered, "That's the one my dad was checking out!"

The newsman continued, "Yet reports persist that this crash actually occurred and, in fact, alien bodies were recovered from the scene. Since that time there have been hundreds of reported sightings, landings, and abductions, including reports by respected state and government officials. One such example is depicted in the recently released book, *Incident at Exeter*; about a close encounter involving two police officers that took place on September 3rd, 1965 in Exeter, New Hampshire."

"That's the book we looked at," Beanie blurted, "when we made our UFO."

Mel and I immediately stared him down. I shot a quick glance in my mom and Suzie's direction, but I don't think they overheard him.

"Another well-known event was a sighting last year on November 9th at Niagara Falls, New York which coincided with the largest power outage in United States history, blacking out nine northeastern states and parts of Canada. Even today the cause of this blackout remains a mystery, although power officials are skeptical that it was related to the flying saucer reportedly seen by dozens of people in the area of a large transformer station just prior to the outage.

"And finally, we can't finish our report without mentioning the photographs taken by Paul and Evelyn Trent at their farm near McMinnville, Oregon on May 11th, 1950." The photos appeared on the screen behind him. "These photographs are some of the most famous images of a UFO in existence, and have appeared in publications all over the world, including Life Magazine.

"There have been so many UFO reports across our country over the years that the government has set up a special task force called Project Bluebook to investigate these sightings. We have put their phone number on the bottom of our screen if you have seen anything and wish to file a report. Now back to you, Graham."

"Thank you, Tom. Let's turn to the big story at hand regarding last night's events. At approximately nine-fifteen yesterday evening we received word of a possible UFO landing in the area of Stafford and Johnson Roads, just south of Lake Oswego. Through sources at the Sheriff's Department we were provided the location and immediately dispatched a crew to investigate. Our coverage continues with this re-port from the scene filed late last night by Robert Wright, our field reporter."

The picture switched to the reporter standing in front of a white, two-story house. It was dark out, but the lights from the camera showed the house in the background and the out-line of a barn.

"I'm standing outside a farmhouse near Stafford Road about a mile from the crossroad with Southwest Borland. Mr. Burt Longmore, owner of the farm, was getting ready to settle in for the night when he noticed a glow in the distance coming from his wheat field. Mr. Longmore grabbed a gun from the house and headed into the field thinking some kids might be ruining his crop by racing through it with their car. I have Mr. Longmore here with me to describe what hap-pened next."

The camera view widened to include Mr. Longmore. He looked pretty old. His face had a few days' growth of white stubble on it and his eyes were tired and ringed. A beat-up baseball cap with a 'John Deere' logo on the front sat tilted on his head. His long-sleeved shirt was torn, dirty, and mostly covered by bib overalls of identical condition.

"Mr. Longmore, what was your intention when you went into the field?'

"Oh, I wasn't going to shoot no one if that's what you mean. I just wanted to scare the kids 'cause my wheat is money and it's like stealin' from me when they ruin it. It's happened before, so I figured they was doing it again."

"And what did you find when you entered the field?"

"First thing was I couldn't hear no car or nothing. It was real quiet, not even a motor idling. I figured they was parked with their lights on, so I kept headin' toward the lights."

"And what did you see?" the reporter asked.

"It wasn't no car, that's for sure. As I got closer I could tell they weren't headlights at all, but a row of lights that glowed along the bottom of a circular-like thing. Then it started to rise up off the wheat field and hovered in the air for a moment."

Mel, Beanie and I all scooted closer to the television and focused intently on his every word.

"Can you describe it?"

"Like I said, it was round. The lights were bright and had colors whippin' through them. It was hard to see the whole thing, but it was taller than it was wide."

"Was it cylindrical?"

"Cylindrical?"

"Cigar shaped?"

"Oh, yeah. But pointed up and down."

We all looked at each other.

"That was an awful lot like our UFO," I whispered.

Mel and Beanie both nodded.

"What happened next?" the reporter asked.

"When it started to move, it had a glow all over, but the bottom was the brightest with those colored lights moving all around. It started to move toward me as it rose higher into the air. Soon it was right over my head." He motioned with his hand, looking up. "I got real scared at that point and didn't know what else to do, so I shot it. I thought it was gonna get me or something."

"You fired your shotgun at it?"

"Yep. And it wasn't that far off, so I know my buckshot must've hit it. But nothing happened. It was as if it didn't even notice. Next thing I know is the thing shoots off faster 'en I've ever seen, and was gone."

"Would you take us to where you saw it in the field?"

"Sure."

The cameraman followed the reporter and Mr. Longmore into the wheat field. The camera lights danced around the two men and reflected off the wheat, giving an eerie feel to the scene.

After a while Mr. Longmore stopped and pointed, "That's the spot, right there."

The reporter and Mr. Longmore stepped aside and the camera focused on the ground at their feet. A circle could be seen where the wheat was obviously crushed. There was an outer rim to the circle and then inside three smaller circles as if made by landing pads. The outer circle had a dark tinge to it like it had been burned.

I studied the circle and could see the wheat wasn't just crushed straight down and spread in all directions, but was crushed all in the same direction, as if laid out in a pattern.

The reporter stepped into the scene. "As you can see, it is indisputable that something has made these marks. Something that appears to be of an intelligent nature. Could they have been left by a UFO? A question we hope to have an answer to soon. The Clackamas County Sheriff's Department just wrapped up their initial investigation tonight and has closed off the area until a full investigation can be conducted in the morning with better light. This is Robert Wright reporting for News Six."

The news anchor in the studio came back on the screen. "Again, that report was filed last night and the Sheriff's Department is continuing their investigation this morning.

"It is hard for all of us to digest the events that have occurred during the last few days. Many questions remain unanswered. Are these sightings real, and if so, why in the Lake Oswego area? And there is also the question of Mrs. Crowley's disappearance. Our News Six investigation has turned up no fresh information as to her whereabouts and the local police department has been unable to shed any new light on the situation.

"On a final note, we finish our report with the announcement that Lake Oswego Mayor Stewart Reynolds notified us this morning there will be an emergency town meeting today at eleven-thirty at the City Hall to address the concerned citizens of this community. Our News Six team will cover the meeting and bring you the latest on these extraordinary events." The program continued with other news stories.

Mel, Beanie and I sat there for a moment trying to absorb what we had just seen and heard.

"Let's head down to my room," I suggested. "We need to figure this out."

"Sounds good to me," Beanie agreed, "but I don't know how we are going to come up with an answer."

"Well, one thing is for sure," Mel said. "We're going to that town meeting."

Chapter 10— Basement

We headed downstairs to my bedroom. The basement was my personal haven from family, school, and the world in general when it all got too much, so obviously I spent a lot of time there.

I used to have the room upstairs across from my sister, something I was able to put up with during the formative Wonder Bread years of my life, but once I outgrew tricycles and advanced to the freedom of full-fledged bicycling, there was a whole new world to discover, and my little sister had become a dead weight attached to my pedaling legs.

My mom and dad had finally renovated the basement into usable space and it didn't take long to figure out who the ultimate beneficiary of their sweat would be.

The basement was what people call 'daylight'. The side opposite my room sat at ground level and had a carport where we kept the cars. There was a sliding glass door that provided an entry into the house on that level when exiting the family car or coming in from the driveway. But since we were on a slope, the other side of the basement, with my room, was tucked into the hill so the ceiling sat just below ground level on that side of the house. It created a dark, dank room with only one small window centered in the back wall near the top of the ceiling. The window faced nothing but a small concrete hole sunk into the cement patio that ran along the side of the house. Only the smallest amount of light filtered into the space—perfect.

It was a room no one would want anything to do with, let alone live in, unless of course, you were me and seeking what little freedom my small world could cough up. So, when I suggested moving down there, I found no resistance within the family: not from my mom because she would gain a sewing room, or from my sister because I would be removed to the nether regions of the house, and my dad, well, he simply didn't have an opinion. But they were all generous in their help with the move, including my sister, who worked her little heart out. Hmmm?

But really the best thing of all about moving into that room was when I showed Beanie my new pad. I could see he was jealous...and he's an only child!

I hurried ahead of Mel so I could kick the errant pair of dirty underwear beneath the bed before she saw them.

Mel walked in and looked around. "You still keep a real tidy place."

She said something like this every time she came into my room, which hadn't been a lot, but enough to where she had formed an unfailing opinion.

I looked things over. There was an unmade bed, clothes on the floor, a chair by a desk that was covered with more clothes, a bookcase with a few books and more junk, and a tiny table in the corner piled high with model airplanes, tanks, and cars in various stages of incompletion. I found absolutely nothing wrong with the room. "Thanks," I answered.

Mel swept the clothes from the chair onto the floor and sat down.

Beanie went over to the table by my bed and turned on the radio. "I think better when I have music." He dialed it to his favorite radio station and The Beach Boys' song *Wouldn't It Be Nice* played across the room. "Yeah, wouldn't it be nice," Beanie said, "if this could all just go away." He tossed himself onto my bed, which bobbed repeatedly in the hopeless effort to toss him back off.

I went to the door to make sure no one was there and then closed it. Heading for the bed I found Beanie spread across it, his dirty shoes propped on my pillow. I shoved them off and sat down.

Beanie spoke first. "I'm sure there's a logical explanation as to why one night we launch a plastic bag into space, and the next night that apparent *same* plastic bag lands in a farmer's field and makes the national news."

"That's what I don't get," Mel said. "How could his description be so close to our UFO? I know there are cigar-shaped UFOs, but most of the descriptions I've heard about are the saucer-shaped ones."

I nodded. "Yeah, and the ones that are cigar-shaped aren't up and down."

Beanie sat up. "Maybe he never saw what landed in his field and just used the description that came out from our UFO?"

"That sounds possible," Mel said, "but it still doesn't answer why a UFO would land in his field the very next night after we pulled our little stunt."

We all thought about it for a moment.

I looked over at Mel. "Last night, when they said on the news there was another sighting, I went outside to look. Then I wondered if maybe the UFOs had been monitoring our television and radio broadcasts, and that's how they knew about our fake UFO. Could they? I mean, they're obviously advanced enough to come millions of miles to get here, so you'd think being able to pick up our broadcasts is a piece of cake for them." I decided it wouldn't be a good idea to tell her what I had been thinking about her dad and Roswell last night.

"And maybe they just didn't like the idea of us taking their glory by making a fake UFO and getting all this attention," Beanie said.

I could see Mel working on an idea. "There are just too many questions and not enough answers, and we haven't even added in the Mrs. Crowley deal yet."

"Well," Beanie said, "Frankie and I were pretty sure yesterday she wasn't abducted. We've both hung around her enough to figure out just how wacky she is, but now I don't know what to think."

Mel stood up. "I know one thing. I'm tired of asking questions and ready to get some answers. Something screwy is going on here and we need to find out what it is."

She came over and sat down on the bed between Beanie and me, her serious and seemingly patented 'Mel' look on her face. "Frankie, you and I are going to that town meeting today, and we are going to keep our eyes open for anything, or anyone," she added after a thought, "that looks suspicious." She turned to Beanie, "And you are going to head over to Mrs. Crowley's and check out any news on that front."

"Man! Can't I go with you guys?"

"No, we need you to be there," Mel answered. "Somehow we're going to figure out what this all has to do with our hoax."

Just then we heard what sounded like a light scrape against the door. I motioned for them to keep talking and tiptoed to the door.

Beanie followed my cue. "Yeah, we need to figure it out."

I yanked the door open and Suzie fell into the room.

"You little snitch. How long you been there?"

"Long enough," she struck back, regaining her composure and her legs at the same time.

"What did you hear?"

"Oh, I think you'll be doing my share of the dishes for a long time."

"Get in here. We need to talk to you."

She backed toward the doorway. "No, I don't think so. I prefer to live."

I grabbed her arm and tried to pull her in.

She wedged herself in the doorway and screamed, "Stop it! Mom, MOM! Frankie's hurting me!"

I let go of her arm. "Look, we'll cut you a deal."

She rubbed her wrist, checking it for damage, and then stared at me while obviously considering her options. "Only if you tell all."

I looked to Mel and Beanie.

Mel gave a small nod. "What else are we going to do, kill her?"

I thought about it for a minute, but couldn't come up with a good way to dispose of the body.

"Get in here," I told her.

She inched inside and I closed the door.

Suzie backed against the wall, surveyed the room and then each of us as if she had just been lured into a den of hungry cobras ready to strike. To a certain extent she was right, because although we didn't have fangs, we definitely had venomous stares.

"You guys are in big trouble." Obviously she said this from the position that the best defense was a good offense. A fairly impressive strategic move, I must say.

"Thanks for the breaking news," I answered, being sure to stay in front of the door so she couldn't bolt. She eyed the door and considered the angles, but knew she was cut off.

"Look Suzie," Mel said, "this is pretty serious stuff. We need to know that what we tell you will be kept secret."

"You're kidding, right?" Beanie broke in. "You've got to be kidding me, Frankie. This will be all over in about two seconds the minute she leaves this room. You don't really expect her to keep her word, do you? She's a little sister, and a *girl*." Realizing what he just said, he diverted his eyes from Mel to avoid her look.

It didn't matter; her glare came through the tone of her voice. "I'm going to ignore that Beanie, *only* because we still need you."

"Actually, Mel, I think Beanie's right. And I'm not sure how long we can, or *should*, keep this a secret anyway. This has all gotten way too out of hand. I think we need to go to the police and tell them."

"Wh-what!" Beanie blurted, his voice breaking in mid-word.

"They at least need to know about our hoax—"

"What hoax?" Suzie asked, a peaked interest noted in her voice.

"I thought you heard us?" Mel questioned.

"Well, kinda, but not really."

"See," Beanie said. "I told you she couldn't be trusted."

"Look," I kept going, "the police have plenty to do as it is, what with Mrs. Crowley's disappearance, and the landing. They at least need to know we made the UFO that caused the fire."

Suzie was astounded. "You guys did that? How?"

"Shut up Suzie," I told her, "we're trying to figure things out."

"Yeah," Beanie moaned, jumping up from the bed and pacing the room, "like do we just plead guilty in court and throw ourselves at their mercy, or do we plea bargain for a shorter-than-life sentence?"

"I think Frankie's right," Mel added, ignoring Beanie, "no matter what they end up doing with us. The town meeting is less than two hours away. The police should know what we did so they can at least explain that much to everyone. We can ride our bikes over. Captain Thornton should be there since the police station is right in City Hall."

"Well," Beanie said, "I guess the bright side of all this is we won't have to worry about your little sister tattling on us anymore." Then he looked at me. "And you won't have to do her dishes since you'll be in jail."

Suzie took a few steps toward Beanie. "No wonder you're an only child. If I was your mother I'd kill myself before having another one like you."

I grabbed her arm to keep her from the possible brutalization by a giant Musketeers bar. "I suppose I can't stop you from telling Mom about this if you want, but it won't matter anyway since she'll find out soon enough."

She turned back to me, forgetting about Beanie. "Aw, you're kind of taking all the fun out of it anyway," she answered. "I mean, I may hate you because you're my stupid brother, but I don't know that I want to see you in *this* much trouble."

"Thanks."

Suzie left, and for the first time ever I actually felt I could believe her.

I shuffled over to Mel and Beanie. "I guess we'd better get going."

"What about Mrs. Crowley's?" Beanie asked hopefully. "You still want me to hang out at her place, right?"

"No sense in it. We should all be at the police station when we meet with Captain Thornton."

"Oh, sure, now you *want* me to go. Share in the pain, huh?" He headed for the door. "I'll just race home to grab my bike."

I called after him as he was closing the sliding door to the carport, "Meet us at the bottom of the driveway."

"Can't wait," he yelled back, then closed the door.

I sat down next to Mel.

She slumped against me. "This is my fault."

I put my arm around her. "Hey, we were all in on it so quit blaming yourself. Besides, I remember something about someone who screwed up checking on the wind that night."

"But it wasn't *your* idea."

I had never seen her so down.

Chapter 11— Confession

We rode into the underground parking garage that served Wizer's Grocery and the JC Penny department store. This was the hub of downtown Lake Oswego. Or, at least it sure seemed that way to me. Sure, there was a fancy Safeway store a ways up 'A' Avenue, but Wizer's Grocery had been here ever since I can remember, and this was still where we did most of our shopping.

Mr. Wizer seemed to always be there to greet his customers, and you could count on finding what you needed, even when it wasn't available at the 'chain' grocery stores. That's because he just knew his customers in Lake Oswego and what they wanted.

There were a couple of other little shops in the building— a barber and small bookstore were there—but it was mostly because of Wizer's, and probably more importantly, Mr. Wizer. Sure, the JC Penny store took up most of the rest of the building, and maybe could have been part of the reason people thought of this as the shopping nerve center of the town. But as far as I was concerned, clothes shopping was about the most boring thing there ever could be, so I kept my distance from that store.

Another neat part of the building is it actually had an escalator. A pretty big deal for a small town like ours. We put the bikes in the rack by the lower entrance and jumped on the escalator. While riding up Beanie insisted on stopping to get a Musketeers bar or two. Whenever he got nervous, he got hungry.

"We'll wait for you across the street," I told him when we reached the top.

"Don't you guys want anything?" he asked.

"We're good," Mel answered. "I don't see how you can possibly eat anything right now."

"I told you, it settles my stomach." He rubbed the roundness of it.

"You do look a little queasy," I said.

"I feel it, too," he added. "You don't want me to spew all over the captain, do you?"

I chuckled. "I'm sure that wouldn't go over real well. Hopefully it works, because spewing chocolate nougat would be even worse."

Beanie headed into Wizer's. Mel and I walked across Second Street to City Hall. The building was a combination of the police station on one side and a town hall on the other.

We waited for him on the lawn. The police entrance was on the far side of the building on First Street, while the town hall entrance was facing 'A' Street.

When Beanie finally showed up, Musketeers bar in mouth, we walked up to the doorway and took a few deep breaths to steady our nerves.

"You guys ready for this?" I asked them.

"As much as we can be, I guess," answered Mel.

Beanie just took a big swallow of nougat and nodded.

We opened the door and went inside. We all stood there for a second. Having never been in here before, we were a little taken back by the scene.

Beanie was the first to comment. "So where's the high, massive counter with the disgruntled, burly police sergeant behind it?"

That's what we expected because that's what we had always seen on the cop shows. Instead, a little old lady sat off to the side of the door behind an office desk. Her appearance made me think she had taken a wrong turn some sixty years ago, having planned to apply for a job at the library, but went through this door by accident and never came out.

She looked up from what she was doing, gave the three of us a once over through horn-rimmed glasses, and then asked, "Can I help you children?"

"Where would we find a copy of *Treasure Island*?" Beanie asked, obviously thinking the same thing I had.

I quickly stepped in front of him. "Sorry, ma'am. We need to see Captain Thornton."

She absorbed this for what seemed like way too long before answering. "He's a very busy man. Can I tell him what it is about?"

"The UFO sightings," Mel answered. "It's important." The librarian opened her mouth as if to ask us for more information, but Mel broke her off. "Honestly," she pleaded, "he'll want to hear what we have to say."

She considered this for a moment. I'm not sure if it was because she wanted to figure out if what Mel said was true, or if it was because she just didn't want to walk all that way to the captain's office. But she finally gave a big sigh, took off her glasses and set them on the desk, got up, slowly, and shuffled down the hall, disappearing through a door near the end.

We waited for what seemed like forever before she reappeared from the door, shuffled all the way back to the desk, and slowly sat down. She picked up her glasses, put them back on her nose and adjusted them until they apparently were sitting just right. She looked up at us. "He's very busy you know. He's getting ready for a town meeting, but if this is as important as you say, then he can give you a few minutes."

"Oh, it is, believe me," I answered. "Thanks."

She motioned down the hall. "It's the last door on the right."

Beanie led the way, mostly by default because he happened to be the closest. He looked back at us as we walked down the hall. "Ever have your life pass before your eyes? You know, like just before you die?"

"Let's get this over with," Mel said, "whatever happens."

We came to the doorway and stood just outside it as if someone had drawn a line in the sand and made a dare. Captain Thornton sat at his desk, a phone to his ear and a pen in his hand flying furiously across a yellow, legal-sized notepad. It was easy to figure out what had happened to the burly police sergeant we expected to see at the front desk. He had been promoted to captain.

I tried to size him up as to how this would go. He had stubbly, graying hair that started above his ears and wrapped to the back of his head, but the top was bald as a cue ball and just as polished. Lines ran from the corners of his eyes in all directions, none of them looking like they had been created by smiles. His uniform shirt showed buttons strained to their popping point from a combination of massive shoulders and the one-too-many-jelly-donut ritual; the evidence of which sat off to one side of his desk in a partially eaten condition. Overall he didn't look like a particularly friendly and understanding person. I could only hope my impressions were immeasurably wrong.

His expression showed that there had been too many phone calls just like the one he was on now. "No, Mrs. Sinewald. Uh-huh, yes, Mrs. Sinewald. At eleven-thirty...yes...yes. Thank you, Mrs. Sinewald. Yes, I appreciate the fact that the Women's Auxiliary Club has confidence in the police department. Goodbye."

He hung up the phone, checked his watch, grunted, looked down at the legal pad, scratched something out and began writing furiously again. He didn't notice we were standing there.

I cleared my throat to get his attention.

"Oh, yes. Kids, come on in. Have a seat."

We took two steps into the office and looked down at a single wooden chair across from his desk. It was an easy decision to stay standing.

"Now what's this about the sightings?" he asked, as he looked about his desk for something. "I haven't got much time. There is a town meeting in half an hour and the mayor and I need to go over a few details before it starts."

"That's why we're here," Mel said, "because you need to know this before the meeting begins."

"Well?" the captain said, looking up at us, tapping his pencil on the legal pad impatiently.

"It was us," Mel told him. "We made the UFO that first night."

"Out of drinking straws and birthday candles," Beanie blurted.

Captain Thornton's busy-look morphed into a blank stare. "Drinking straws and birthday candles?"

"And we burned Mrs. Crowley's roof and tree," I continued, as if that would tie everything together and allow him to make sense of it all.

He paused for a minute, set his pencil down, sat back in his chair and said in a very solemn tone, "This is very serious. You kids could be in real trouble."

"We know," Mel agreed, her voice a little rattled.

"So, what about the body?" he asked.

"Body?" I questioned. "What body?"

"Mrs. Crowley's, of course. After you made the UFO and burned everything down, you must have gotten rid of her to cover your tracks and did something with the body. And what about Mr. Longmore's field, did you use straws and birthday candles to make the landing marks there too?"

"We didn't have anything to do with those things," I exclaimed.

Captain Thornton leaned forward over his desk on two massive forearms and looked intently at us. "Kids, this is no joking matter. I'm sure that you and whatever friends provoked you to come in here and pull this little prank, think it is funny, but if you hadn't noticed I have a crisis on my hands."

"But it's the truth!" Mel pleaded.

"Listen. I don't have time for this. And if I hear you've been spreading your story around to anyone else, I'll have you arrested and thrown in jail for obstruction of justice. Yeah, just like in the police shows you've obviously been watching. Now get out of my office."

We walked down the hall, out the front door, and sat on the lawn.

"What happened?" Beanie asked. "Did we just get off the hook?"

"Apparently so," Mel answered.

"At least we tried," I added. "What else can we do?"

"Nothing I can think of," she answered, "other than go to this meeting."

"Check out all those people," I said, looking around. We had been too focused on what just happened to have paid much attention to them until now. There were all sorts of cars pulling into the City Hall parking lot and all along both sides of 'A' Street. People were flowing into the front doors of the town hall.

"Well," Mel said, "let's stick with our original plan. We may not be able to get the police to believe us, but there is still something happening here and we're the only ones that know this whole thing got started as a hoax."

"Does that mean you want me to head back over to Crowley's?" Beanie asked.

"That was the plan," I reminded him. "Mel and I can cover the meeting. You still need to see if anything is up over there."

"I always get the dirty work. Geez, if we actually *had* killed Mrs. Crowley, it's not hard to guess who would be picked to dispose of the body."

I smiled at him. "Someone would have to do it."

"Right."

"Let's meet back under the bridge in an hour," Mel suggested. "We can compare notes and figure out what to do from there."

Beanie gave Mel a look of frustration. "If I have time, I'll try to bake up some Tollhouse cookies for our meeting. I wouldn't want you two to starve to death."

"Come on, Beanie, focus here. We all need to do our part." She put her hand out.

I put my hand on top of hers.

Beanie sighed and said, "Don't you think this is kind of corny?"

I looked over at Mel.

She thought for a second and then said, "It was good enough for the Musketeers, so it is good enough for us. Or, if you prefer, we could get a knife and slice our palms to blend our blood in a ritual handshake?"

Beanie's eyes widened. "Naw, this is good!" He put his hand on top of ours and together we chanted, "All for one...and one for all."

Chapter 12 — Outburst

Mel and I headed into the hall. Most of the seats were already taken, but we didn't want to sit anyway. We walked behind the back row of chairs and up the side wall about halfway. This seemed like a good spot to keep an eye on everything.

The town hall served a lot of purposes. The mayor and his town council held public hearings here, but it also had a stage where the local theater group put on plays. Velvet curtains hung in their retracted positions on the sides of the stage. The floor was also lined to be a small basketball court for GRA-Y youth basketball games. It had two basketball hoops that were raised up against the ceiling on either side of the room. A table, two chairs, and a speaker's stand with a microphone were set up in the middle of the stage.

The room buzzed with the chatter of everyone already in the hall. There was a row of arched windows along the far wall that faced Second Street. Daylight streamed in through the windows, filling the room. Now the chairs were completely full and more people lined the walls and stood in layers at the back of the room.

Over in one corner a platform had been erected where three television news cameras now stood. They were big and bulky things. Each camera had three lenses of different focal lengths on a turret that could be spun to select the best lens for the distance to their subject. The cameras stood on sturdy tripod legs, spread out to hold the massive cameras.

I could see the mayor at the front being interviewed by two reporters. They looked new to me. I hadn't seen them at Mrs. Crowley's over the last few days, so who knows where those articles were going to end up. They were hastily taking notes as he spoke. He kept shaking his head and waving his hands as he answered their questions, or more likely from his manner, avoided them.

The mayor wore a light blue suit that I swear was on a rack at the J. C. Penny's store a couple of years back when my mother had caught me off guard one day and dragged me down to shop for my back-to-school wardrobe. Everything ages, but that suit looked like the process had accelerated to the highest degree by having to support a large butt that depended on an equally proportioned stomach to keep itself upright. The mass of humanity in the room amplified our typical Oregon humidity, and there was no better example than provided by the mayor. His forehead was beaded with sweat, and if it hadn't been for his shirt and jacket acting as a sponge, a torrent of perspiration would have flowed from his body.

"Maybe we should have gone to the mayor," Mel said.

I took another look at him. "I doubt the outcome would have been any better. At least we tried with the police. Right now, I guess we're in a wait and see mode."

"No kidding."

Captain Thornton walked into the hall from a door on our side of the room near the stage. I didn't realize the door was there, but obviously it connected to the police station. He went to the mayor and whispered in his ear. The mayor nodded, shook the reporters' hands, excused himself and then walked with the captain to the steps onto the stage. The captain sat at the table while the mayor moved to the speaker's stand to call the meeting to order. He tapped the microphone and it reverberated through the hall, hushing the high murmur that had dominated the room since we first walked in.

"Thank you for coming. Most of you know me, but for anyone new to our community, I am Stewart Reynolds, the mayor of this fine town. To my right here is our Chief of Police, Captain George Thornton." He waited for a moment as if expecting applause at these announcements. When none came, he moved on. "We have all been," he paused, looking for the right word and then finding it, "*distracted* by the last few days' events."

"Understatement," Mel whispered under her breath.

"These recent UFO sightings and the reported, but *unconfirmed,* landing of a UFO—along with the national news coverage it has fostered—have this community quite stirred up. Captain Thornton and I felt it necessary to address these events, and your concerns, before things got too out of hand."

"So what are you going to do about it?" someone yelled from the seats.

The mayor looked in the direction from where this came. "Now, Don, I know how you get. We all have your same concerns, but it's important that we keep our heads. This has been of the highest importance for Captain Thornton and myself since the first sighting. We are investigating these reports to find out if they have any basis in truth at all."

"Well, Mrs. Crowley is missing and that's the truth!" someone else shouted.

"Yeah, what about Mrs. Crowley?" another man stood and yelled. "And what are you doing to make sure no one else gets abducted?"

The mayor pulled a handkerchief from his pocket and wiped his brow. He didn't expect this, but neither did I. It was easy to see he was flustered by the outburst. "Now, we don't know where Mrs. Crowley is. She could just as well be visiting at relatives, or sitting on a beach somewhere sipping on a Pina Colada and taking it easy. We have no proof that she was abducted."

"Her tree and house aren't proof enough for you?" the man shot back, "when a UFO was sighted right there at her place?"

The crowd erupted in support of his argument.

Mel and I cringed at what we had started. I wanted to yell out that it had been us, but knew that would not go well with Captain Thornton. And the way this crowd was acting, it scared me even thinking about telling them the truth right now, not that they would believe it.

People stood and shouted: "They're landing right here," and, "Why aren't you calling out the National Guard?"

Another man added, "Do we need to patrol the streets ourselves to keep our families safe?"

Mel and I looked at each other. We were mesmerized by the frenzied horde.

Captain Thornton swaggered to the speaker's stand. The mayor happily stepped aside.

The captain leaned into the microphone and I expected uniform buttons to fly off and wipe out the entire front row of spectators. "Everyone calm down. We aren't going to accomplish a thing if you don't. Now sit down and let's conduct this meeting with a little courtesy and some common sense."

I don't know if it was the uniform, or the concern for being hit by a button from it, but he seemed to have some effect. Eventually the room became quiet and everyone took their seats.

"The police department has been conducting an investigation into the sighting over the lake, and we are working closely with the Clackamas County Sheriff's Office regarding the marks in farmer Longmore's field. We have yet to uncover any evidence that proves UFOs were in fact sighted, or created those marks. Yes, Mrs. Crowley is missing and her roof and tree caught fire, but again we have no proof that UFOs were involved. We are also doing everything in our power to locate her, and have every confidence that we will find her safe and sound."

Mel leaned over and whispered to me. "Frankie, I think we're being watched."

"What?" I asked.

"This guy has been looking at us more times than could be coincidence. Everyone's attention has been focused on Captain Thornton ever since he started talking; everyone except this one man on the other side of the room. I noticed him earlier, but that's when everyone was looking around. Once the meeting started, I caught him watching us a couple of times, and then quickly turn away when I looked in his direction."

"What does he look like?" I asked.

"He's an older man with short, dark hair, some gray at the temples. He's dressed in a yellow button-down shirt and blue jeans. I've never seen him before."

"Where is he? I'm not seeing him."

"I'm worried he might catch on to us and take off."

"Come on, I want to see him. Maybe I would recognize him."

"Across the room. Just to the right of that second window from the doors. But don't look now. He's looking our way. Hold on...okay, now."

I looked over and finally found him. "Oh, there he is, got him." He was kind of hidden behind a couple of other people. "I've never seen him before, either."

Captain Thornton had been droning on and was finishing up a point, "...and the department is doing everything in its power to get to the bottom of this."

A woman in the third row suddenly jumped up. "That isn't good enough!" she shouted.

Mel grabbed my arm. "Oh, my God. That's my mom!"

We hadn't seen her sitting in the crowd.

Mel's mom continued, "You have to do something. First Roswell, then Portland, and now here! We moved to Lake Oswego because it was supposed to be a good community...a *safe place!* Now it's happening all over again."

Mel and I looked at each other, shocked by her outburst. She was frantic. A woman sitting next to her grabbed her arm and tried to pull her down, but she just yanked her arm away.

"My husband died. He died because of all this."

Mel shook her head to indicate she had no idea what her mom meant.

"You have to do something. Now!" Mel's mom shouted. "My family's not safe. None of us are safe."

Captain Thornton broke in, "Ma'am, I understand you are upset, but you need to calm down. You are disrupting this meeting and creating unwarranted concern for everyone here."

"Everyone should be concerned," she answered. "They need to know."

He motioned to Officer Thompson who was standing near the stage. "Officer Thompson, would you please assist this woman to my office where she can calm down?"

Thompson moved into the row where Mel's mom stood.

"Hushing me up isn't going to stop any of this. That always seems to be your answer. Get us to shut up with bullying and threats, and it will all go away."

Officer Thompson reached for her arm.

"Don't touch me. I'm coming." She walked out of the aisle, escorted by Thompson, who led her to the same door Captain Thornton had entered by earlier. She turned to the eyes watching her. "None of you know the reality of what exists out there, and what your government will do to keep it that way." Then she disappeared through the door.

I looked at Mel. Worry and confusion covered her face.

"I've got to go to her," she said.

"I know. I'll see what else happens here. If you don't come back in, I'll wait for you out on the front lawn."

"Okay."

I reached out and squeezed her hand. "I hope she's all right."

"Thanks." She gave me a half-smile and then skirted along the wall and hurried through the same door where her mother had been taken.

Mayor Reynolds was at the microphone again. "I apologize for the disruption. This is a good example of what can happen if we do not keep our heads about us." He glanced over at Captain Thornton who nodded to him. "I think this is a good time to introduce someone who is better able to address this subject." He looked to the far side of the stage.

A man in military uniform walked out from behind the curtains, apparently having been there the whole time. He stood next to the mayor.

"This is Major Burnham with the A.T.I.C. He is a special investigator for Project Blue Book, a task force with the Eighth Air Force assigned to investigate UFO sightings."

While the mayor was introducing him, I glanced over at the mysterious man. He seemed startled by Major Burnham's sudden appearance because he quickly turned away from the stage and slowly moved to the back of the hall. He worked his way through the throng of people in the back and stood behind them as if he were hiding. *Why did he need to hide from the Air Force officer?*

The mayor continued his introduction. "Major Burnham has come to Lake Oswego to investigate these sightings and

I, for one, am grateful. Major Burnham?" The mayor motioned to the microphone.

I kept one eye on the stage and another on the man in the back should he slip out the doors.

Major Burnham stepped to the microphone. He looked out at the crowd with the posture of a parent about to reprimand an out-of-control child.

"There is no need to marshal the National Guard, or to form vigilante groups, and your government is certainly not out to get you." He paused, allowing the full effect of his authority to sink in. "The United States Air Force has investigated UFO reports ever since the inception of Project Signs back in 1947. In 1952 the Project Blue Book study was formed as a better method to analyze UFO-related data scientifically. First and foremost was the goal to determine if UFOs, in fact, do exist. To achieve this, we positioned trained investigators at USAF bases throughout the country to conduct first-hand interviews of eyewitnesses and perform field analysis on a scientific level. Detailed reports from these field investigations were then submitted to A.T.I.C., that's the Air Technical Intelligence Center, where they could be thoroughly analyzed. Utilizing this process, we have evaluated thousands of UFO reports. There are very few cases where we were unable to determine the origin of the sightings, with most of these attributable to hoaxes or such identifiable phenomena as airplanes, shooting stars, planets, clouds, ball lightning, and swamp gases.

"Having reviewed the initial details of these sightings, I have no doubt that with further investigation into their origination, we will be able to file them under the category of hoax."

Those last words hit me with a jolt. I was sure his investigation would eventually lead to us. We might have been able to handle whatever punishment our local police department handed out, but what would the United States Government do to us when they found out?

I couldn't dwell long on this fear. While Major Burnham continued on his quest to mesmerize the crowd, I shifted my attention just enough to catch the mystery man disappear through the doors at the back of the hall.

My feet were moving even before my mind told them to. I quickly hurried down the side aisle and thrashed my way through the crowd at the back. Once out the doors, I looked in all directions and found him jogging across the street to a car parked on the other side. I ran after him. When he reached the car, he looked back toward the hall. I quickly jumped behind a tree. I was pretty sure he hadn't seen me. He got in, started the engine and drove up 'A' Street.

I raced to the sidewalk to try and get a good look at the car and its license plate. By the time I got there, the numbers were too small to read, but it didn't have yellow letters on a dark blue background—the colors of an Oregon license plate. It was from a different state. I had no idea which one. But the car looked like a late model Ford Fairlane, Baby Blue in color. Between the out-of-state plate, model and color of the car, I would know it again if I saw it.

Chapter 13 — Merriweather

I couldn't do anything else about this mystery man, and I really didn't want to go back inside the meeting hall to face *that* problem, so I sat down on the lawn to wait. Things must have still been at full swing inside because no one was coming out of the town hall yet.

I was surprised when Mel showed up as quickly as she did. She plopped down next to me, avoiding eye contact.

"Is your mom all right?" I asked.

"Yeah," she answered, staring at the grass where she sat, pulling little tuffs out of the ground, studying them and then tossing them aside. She didn't say anything for a while. I felt like it was best to just sit and wait for when she was ready.

Finally, she looked up at me. "Mom's still really upset. She keeps saying the same things over and over again, just like in the hall. They've got her in a room across from Captain Thornton's office. They let me in to see her for just a minute. I think they thought it might help calm her down."

"Did she give you any explanation at all, you know, about your dad's death?"

"No. I tried to ask, but she just hushed me up. I couldn't get a word out of her. I'm not sure if it was because she didn't want to tell me or because we were at the police department and they might overhear. Maybe it was both."

"Do you know if Captain Thornton mentioned our little meeting to your mom?"

"I'm pretty sure he didn't. I don't think it even entered his mind after what my mom pulled in the meeting. But he must imagine my family is just outright crazy, what with how she acted and the story we told him."

"Is he going to arrest her?"

"No. I asked Captain Thornton when I left the room. He said there was really no reason to, but they want to keep her there until she calms down and the meeting is over. You know, just in case. They'll let her go home then." She reached out and touched my hand. "Frankie, don't take this wrong, but can we be done with the twenty questions for now? I really don't want to talk about it anymore."

"Sure, I guess I'm prying again."

She gave me a little smile. "That's okay. I know you just want to help."

I felt so sorry for Mel, to have lost her father in a car crash and now to be going through all of this. What could she be thinking of her mom right now? I tried to get her mind off it.

"You know that man you spotted in the meeting hall, the one that kept looking at us?"

"Yeah."

"Something really weird happened. Right after you left, an Air Force officer came out on stage to talk to the crowd about the UFO sightings, and as soon as he appeared our mystery man headed to the back of the room and stood behind a bunch of people. It looked like he was hiding."

I filled her in on Major Burnham, why he was here, and my worries about finding us out. Then I finished up with how I followed the man to his car.

"Wow, I sure missed a lot."

"Mel, I just don't get it. Some really strange stuff is going on and it seems to just keep building. And somehow, we're in the middle of it all, and I mean a whole lot more than just our little UFO."

"I know. None of it makes sense right now, but we're sure going to do everything we can to figure it out." She stood up. "Come on. Let's head back and fill Beanie in on what we saw. But not about my mom, okay?"

"Sure, not a problem."

"We also need to see if he's come up with anything."

We walked over to Wizer's and took the escalator down to our bikes. They were in the bike rack at the far end of the underground garage. We grabbed them and pedaled out of the garage and onto 'A' Street heading up the hill toward Iron Mountain Boulevard. It was only a few miles from downtown Lake Oswego to home.

Both our bikes were Schwinns. I rode a Sting Ray, but we called it a Banana Bike because of the shape of the seat, which is long and curved like a banana. It had a small frame and high-rise handlebars, so was easy to perform tricks and jumps on. Mel's bike was no doubt picked out by her mother, because it was all girl—from the frillies on the end of the handlebars, to the woven white basket on the front, and right down through the pink on white frame.

Mel led the way, which was fine by me. Somehow watching her long blonde hair flow in the breeze managed to keep my mind off of things, at least for a little while.

When we reached the top of 'A' Street we cut over to Iron Mountain and coasted down the hill past the entrance to Lake Oswego Golf course. The sky was clear and although the meeting hall had been hot, the temperature outside wasn't too bad. The air flowing past us while we rode cooled us right off. At the bottom of the hill some train tracks curved in on our left to parallel the road.

I shouted up to Mel, "You want to take the back way or stay on Iron Mountain?"

There are two ways to get home. The first would be to continue down Iron Mountain for another mile, take a left onto Lakeview, and from there it was just a short ways to where we would drop down onto the road across the bridge at our easement. The other way was what we called 'the back way' onto Summit Drive, which was just coming up. It crossed the railroad tracks, and then went up to the top of our hill and paralleled the lake.

Before she could answer her peddling became erratic, she swerved to the side of the road and stopped.

I pulled up next to her. "What happened?"

She looked down at her bike. "My chain broke. Great, just great! What else is going to happen to us today?"

"Well, for one thing, I guess we'll have to walk the bikes home." I smiled with my little joke. From her expression I could see it didn't take. I looked behind us. "I'll go get your chain."

I laid my bike down on the side of the road and went back to where the chain had fallen. I picked it up, getting oil on my hands from examining it on the way back.

When I got to Mel I said, "This chain is in good shape. I don't see how it could break."

Mel looked at the chain. "I don't get it. This bike isn't very old. Here, let me have it."

She put her hand out expectantly.

"You'll get oil all over your hands," I warned her.

She gave me one of her looks and took the chain from me. She worked it through her fingers to the broken link, turning it in the sun back and forth, studying it.

She looked up at me as if she just figured something out. "Look. See this pin that's hanging out where it broke? See how the end is all shiny?"

I moved closer to her to get a better view. "What do you mean?"

"Look at these other links. They have oil and grime all over them. I think someone did something to this link."

"Like what?" I asked.

"Like tampered with it or something."

"How would they do that?"

"I don't know." She studied it closer. "Wait. Look here." She pointed to the end of the pin. "There is a hole here, like it was drilled out."

I looked closely and could see the hole.

She went on. "See how these other pins stick out from the chain links? Well, the one with the hole was drilled out so it would eventually fail."

"And," I added, "it wouldn't have been that hard to do since our bikes were way in the back of the underground garage."

She thought for a minute. "Someone *wanted* my bike to break down!"

"Why would someone...the mystery man from the hall. He had been watching us. I bet he did it, but why?"

"It's a set-up."

I could see her mind working through all the possible reasons. She looked over at me and said, "This has something to do with my dad."

"Your dad?"

"Because of what my mom said back at the hall. I mean I just don't know, but it keeps repeating in my head. She said he died because of this—whatever *this* is? Maybe that man had something to do with his death. It can't just be coincidence that he shows up at the town meeting at the same time as my mom says that."

"But, Mel, how could that be? You said he died in a car accident."

"I don't know. It's all so confusing. I think we had better get off this road. If he tampered with the chain so my bike would break down, then it could only be for one reason. He wants us stranded."

A chill ran through me. "You may be right or you may be wrong, but whichever it is, I say we get out of here. We'd better take the back way. He'll probably look for us on Iron Mountain. If we get over the railroad bridge and down the other side of it, he won't see us."

Mel and I picked up our bikes. She tossed the chain into her basket. We were just getting to the top of the bridge over the tracks when an old, white pickup truck came down Iron Mountain and turned onto our road.

"Is that him?" Mel asked, concern in her voice.

"No, he's driving a car."

"Maybe we can get a ride," she said. "It would be a lot better than walking the bikes all the way back."

"Sure, good idea." I held out my thumb.

The pickup slowed as it approached. The guy driving looked us over real good as he passed, but kept going. The bed of the pickup was full of boxes.

"Jerk," I said. "Can't he see we need a ride?"

"Maybe he just has to get somewhere."

We continued to walk our bikes as we watched the truck rumble up the hill. About halfway up it stopped.

"What's he doing?" Mel asked.

Before I could answer, it slowly backed down, the old truck grumbling all the way, not used to going backwards. When it was even with us it stopped. The man inside seemed pleasant looking, in a middle-aged sort of way.

"You two in trouble?"

"What do you mean?" I asked, alarmed that he could know what was going on.

He gave me a strange look. "The bikes. Most people ride them, not hitchhike with them."

"Oh, her chain broke," I explained, covering my slip.

"Could you give us a ride?" Mel asked.

Now that he was sitting there, I wasn't so sure. I leaned into Mel and whispered under my breath, "Maybe this isn't such a good idea. After all, we don't know this guy."

Mel looked at me and whispered back. "But he's better than the one we *do* know."

"Good point."

The man thought for a second, then nodded. "I'm obviously in the middle of something and pretty loaded down, but we can probably make this work. Sure, why not."

He turned off the engine, jumped out and came around to our side. "Let me make some room. We're good if I can fit the bikes in back." He adjusted what looked like moving cartons around.

Mel and I leaned against the bridge railing while we waited. I could see the intersection just below us where Summit Drive ended on Iron Mountain Boulevard. A car appeared. A Baby Blue Fairlane. It was him! It slowed as it neared the turn-off.

I elbowed Mel in the arm. "Hey, that's the car."

The man inside stared at us. I think he would have turned up our street, but saw the truck and took off. He kept watching us until the car disappeared from view.

"Are you sure that's him?" Mel asked.

"Yeah, it was the same kind of car with the same out-of-state plates."

"Then we were right. He *was* after us."

We heard a clang from the pickup. "That should do it." The man had just finished putting my bike in the truck and was walking over to us. "My name is Mike Merriweather."

"I'm Frankie and this is Melanie," I told him.

113

"Nice to meet you." He opened the door on the passenger side. "Hop in."

Mel got in first and I followed.

"You're a life saver," Mel told him when he jumped in on the driver's side.

"I wouldn't go so far as to say that," he answered.

"Oh, I would," Mel confirmed. She looked over at me with relief.

He started the engine, put the truck into gear and headed up the steep hill. It was a tight fit on the bench seat. The truck bounced along and I could feel Mel's body rub against mine. I looked down at her hand on her knee. I reached over and cupped her fingers in mine. She had been deep in thought, staring out the windshield, but turned to me at my touch and smiled.

At the top of the hill Summit Drive curved right to parallel the lake far below us on our left. I looked across the valley that held the lake. A heavy growth of deep, green fir trees covered the far hillside. A few houses dotted the lake's edge and up along the crest where South Shore Boulevard ran in a parallel course on that side.

"Are you students at the high school?"

"Will be," I said. "Freshman."

"Oh, so you'll be joining the big leagues! I bet that's an exciting thought. And who knows, you might even end up in my class. I just moved here. I'll be teaching English and Theater Arts at Lake Oswego High." He glanced over at us and smiled. "Yeah, you're stuck in a truck with a teacher."

"I like theater," Mel said. "I just moved here too, from over in Southeast Portland. I was in a play back at my last school. It was *The Red House Mystery*, a who-done-it."

I looked at Mel. This was news. I had no idea she liked acting.

"I know the play," he said. "It's a good one. What part?"

"Angela Norberry."

"That's a good role."

"So, how long have you been teaching, Mr. Merriweather?" I asked him.

"Call me Mike. Using my formal name makes me feel too old. Not long. It's kind of a fallback role for me. I tried acting, but got real hungry trying to make a go of it."

"Were you in anything?" I asked.

"You ever see or hear of the movie *A Bucket of Blood*?"

Mel and I looked at each other. I answered for both. "No, we haven't."

"See. That's why I'm a teacher now and not an actor. I not only never made it into a major movie, I never even got past minor roles in the Grade B ones. So, teaching it is. I've always been something of a free spirit anyway, so teaching lets me stay that way and helps pay the bills."

I heard the gears shift as we went around a curve.

He looked over at Mel. "I saw you duck through the door back at the meeting after they took the woman out. I guess that was your mom."

"You were there?" Mel asked, shocked at the sudden change in subject.

"Even though I'm in the middle of this move, I couldn't help but go. I figured it would be good theater, and a good way to see what this community is all about, what with being new and all. It didn't fail me in either regard."

No one said anything for a while.

"Is she okay?" he finally asked.

"She's fine. I just don't know why she did that. We lost my dad a while back and she just hasn't been the same since. She's taken his death really hard."

"I can understand that," he told her. "But the whole conspiracy thing. Bullying and threats, blaming the government. And something about *Roswell?* What was that all about?"

We were heading down the other side of the hill, winding through curves that would soon take us past Mrs. Crowley's place.

Mel looked at him. "I have no idea. This is the first I've ever heard of anything like that from her. I know my dad and mom lived down near Roswell when he went to school, and he was really interested in..." She stopped. "Anyway, I don't have any idea why she is blaming the government."

We came around the last sharp curve in the road and onto the straighter section that ended at Springbrook Bridge. Mrs. Crowley's place was about halfway down and groups of people stood by the side of the road. A news truck was parked across the street in a neighbor's driveway.

"What's this?" Mike asked.

"That's Mrs. Crowley's," I answered. "You know, the woman who's missing."

"Oh, yes," he laughed, "abducted."

"What, don't you believe it?" Mel asked.

116

"I don't believe any of this, especially about the UFOs. I said I'm a free spirit, not a fool spirit. In fact, I'm going to check the night sky this evening; it must be a full moon. It's a proven fact that people get really weird during a full moon."

"Never heard that," I commented.

"It's true," he assured.

We passed Mrs. Crowley's place and I looked for Beanie, but couldn't spot him in the crowd. We approached the bottom of the hill.

Mel said, "Take a right there," pointing to Springbrook Court.

He turned onto the road and drove down a little ways.

"This will do," she told him. "That's my driveway on the right."

He pulled in and stopped the truck. We all jumped out and went to the back. Mike took out the bikes.

"Melanie, I'm sorry about your mom," he said.

"Thanks, Mike. I'm sure she'll be all right."

"Hold on." He went to the driver's door, opened it, and got something out of the pocket in the side panel. He closed the door and came back with a notepad and pen in his hand.

"I'm writing my number down. It's got to be hard enough moving to a new neighborhood, just being the two of you. And then with all this going on, well, I just want you to know you can call me anytime. I'd be happy to give you and your mom a hand if you ever need it. I'm not that far away, so it wouldn't be a problem." He tore off the page and handed it to Mel.

"That's really nice of you."

"Honestly, I mean it. If you need help with anything, let me know."

"Thanks again," Mel said. She took out her coin purse and put the paper in it.

"Yeah, and thanks for the ride," I added. "That would have been a long walk."

"No problem." He got into the truck, backed out of the driveway, waved to us and disappeared across Springbrook Bridge.

"Drop your bike off and meet at the bottom of my drive-way," I told Mel. "We'll head down to the lake and see if Beanie's there."

"Okay, I'll see you in a minute."

I watched until she disappeared around the side of her house. I hadn't realized until just now how much Mel meant to me. She had somehow become my whole world. I wanted to do everything I could to protect her, what with everything going on and what's happening with her mom. I've seen tons of movies where two people fall in love, but this is the first time I'm actually beginning to understand how they felt. I thought about this while I walked my bike to my place.

Chapter 14— Back

Mel met me at the bottom of my driveway and we held hands as we walked down the wooden steps to the easement. I loved the feel of her fingers intertwined with mine. Just this simple act created sensations I had never experienced before.

"It doesn't look like he's here," Mel said.

He wasn't on the lawn so we checked under the bridge.

"Maybe the cookies aren't out of the oven yet," I joked. It made Mel smile and I liked that. "Let's hang out at the picnic table 'til Beanie gets here." I was glad to see we had the easement to ourselves.

The easement had two levels. A rock retaining wall separated the upper lawn from the lower one. We walked down the stone steps that split the wall into two sides.

Mel pointed to the wall on our left. "I've always meant to ask how come it has that weird spot in it."

The wall was really well done for most of its length, but then in one section, about a third of the way along, the stonework became erratic and jumbled before it returned to the tight and well-laid form of the rest of the wall.

119

"The neighborhood had a big party a couple of years back to build the wall. Mr. Wilson is an architect. He lives just above the bridge. Anyway, he was in charge of the project. It's not hard to tell when he took some time off for lunch. We now call that section 'The Lunch Hour'. Mr. Wilson wasn't real happy when he came back, but the cement had set so we were stuck with it."

Mel smiled at that.

The picnic table stood in front of the boat docks, which were on the inlet side of the swimming dock. We sat on the bench seat facing the water. I rested against the edge of the tabletop, put my arm around Mel and stroked her side. She leaned into me and I felt her body relax. It was nice to have this quiet moment together after everything that had happened today. The lull after the storm...or was this just the eye?

"I've never had a boyfriend, you know," Mel said.

"Is that what I am?" I asked, hopefully.

She turned to me, her blue eyes filling mine. "Of course you are." She leaned in and kissed me to prove it. Not a long one, but definitely a boyfriend kiss.

My body temperature shot up a few degrees. "And that makes you my girlfriend, which I think is really cool."

She snuggled in closer to me. "So that means we can share feelings, right?"

"Yeah, that's what relationships are all about...other than the great sex, of course."

Mel sat up and turned to me. "What? You *are* a perv."

I grinned. "Just kidding, kinda."

"Frankie, I'm serious."

"Sorry. I couldn't help it."

She turned back toward the water and nuzzled up to me again, her head on my shoulder. "I'm really scared, Frankie."

"I am too."

"I'm so worried about my mom. She just isn't making it. Not since Dad's been gone. And now this thing about his death and what she said. I just don't know what to think."

"And our hoax, and the fire, and Mrs. Crowley, and the Air Force Major, and the mystery man, and who knows what else."

She sat up so she could see me. "I never told you, but back in Portland our house was burglarized."

"What? Oh, so that's what your mom meant about Portland back at the meeting."

"Yes, it was terrible. The whole place was trashed. We felt so violated."

"And you moved here to be safe. Boy, that really worked out."

"Frankie?" She looked down at her hands. "My mom's been drinking a lot ever since Dad died. I was hoping moving here would help, but you know how that has gone. I tried to ignore her drinking at first, but now I think she's becoming an alcoholic." Her voice had a slight tremble to it. She twisted a ring on her finger.

"Wow. I didn't see that coming." I put my leg over the bench to straddle it so I could face her better. "Do you think she was drinking before the town meeting?"

Mel slumped a little. "I'm sure she had been, but she hides it really well. I guess that's what they do—alcoholics. I got a book at the library. It's by a group called Al-Anon." She looked up at me. "It's for families who have this...problem." Tears welled in her eyes; little pools forming on her lower eyelids ready to spill over.

This was a whole new side of her, a vulnerable side she had hidden too well. I scooted in close and wrapped my arms around her. She buried her face into my chest. I pulled her in close and kissed the top of her head. My nose touched her hair and the scent of this astonishing girl filled my lungs and flowed to my heart.

Her body shuddered as she broke down and cried. "She's all I have and I just don't know what to do. She's losing it. I feel so alone."

I tried to think of something brilliant to say, something that would fix everything and comfort her, but I was completely lacking in experience when it came to things like this. Everything I thought of just sounded stupid in my head. But I did know how I felt about her and hoped sharing that was enough. "I'm here, Mel. You know how much you mean to me. You're not alone."

She grabbed me tight. I held her until she finally stopped shaking, and then lifted her face to look into her eyes. Tears flowed down her cheeks. I wiped one away with my thumb, leaned in and kissed the spot. A gentle kiss tasting of salt. I brushed a strand of hair away from where it had matted to the moisture. We were so close her warmth radiated against my face. I leaned in and then hesitated, but she finished the distance and we kissed: a real kiss—deep, long, and wet—a movie kiss.

"Uh-hum."

We broke the kiss off, startled by Beanie standing on the other side of the picnic table.

He shook his head. "I just can't leave you two alone, can I?" Then he saw Mel's red, swollen eyes. "Kiss was that bad, huh?"

"Mel's just worried about her—" I stopped, remembering my promise. "Worried about all this stuff going on."

"Yeah, I see that. Anyway, while you two have been busy necking, uh, worrying, I have been keenly focused on my assignment."

Mel wiped her eyes with her sleeve. "Mrs. Crowley?"

"What else? You don't see any Tollhouse cookies, do you?"

"You've got news." I could see it in his face.

Beanie looked down and kicked at the grass with his foot. "Oh, just a little."

"Come on, Beanie, stop with the torture," Mel pleaded.

I was glad to see her thoughts redirected.

He smiled. "Hmmm...naw. I've finally got something over on you two. I need to savor the moment. Yeah...this feels good, really good."

Mel wasn't going to be outdone. She looked at me. "Did he just use the word *savor*? I didn't know a word like that could possibly be in his vocabulary."

I gave a little chuckle. "It's a food word. Of course, he knows it."

"Oh, that makes sense."

Beanie didn't like our bursting his bubble. "Hey, this is my moment, remember?"

I rolled my eyes at him. "Fine! Then enough already."

"Okay, okay. It's just that Mrs. Crowley," he paused long enough to draw one last groan from us, "is back!"

"What?" We jumped up from the bench.

I had a hard time believing what he said. "She's home?"

"Yeah, just a little while ago."

"But how?" Mel asked.

"By cab."

Mel looked at him in disbelief. "She took a taxi?"

"Yep. You think it would have been something a little more dramatic, like, say, getting beamed down from a space-ship." He gave us a wry little smile. "Want to go check it out?"

"Are you kidding," I answered, "let's get up there." I grabbed Mel's hand and we headed for the stairs.

Mrs. Crowley's house was a beehive of activity. Another news truck had somehow appeared since we had driven by, and most of the neighborhood had shown up, gossip travel-ing fast in our little neck of the woods.

We walked past the crowd to our usual spot on the retain-ing wall.

"It's like déjà vu all over again," I said.

Beanie looked at me. "Hey, that's what that Yankee player said. What was his name? Oh yeah, Yogi Berra."

"Wow, Beanie, I'm really surprised," I told him.

"Why, because I know Yogi Berra said that?"

"No, because I thought you were going to say Yogi Bear."

Mel laughed. "Well, in case either of you want the latest update, Berra isn't a Yankee anymore. He played for the

Mets last year, but only four games before switching over to coach for them."

Beanie and I looked at each other in amazement.

"Oh, and one more thing, they actually have more in common than you think. The Yogi Bear character was named after Yogi Berra."

"Beanie, you got anything to add to that?" I asked.

"No-sir-ee, Mr. Ranger, Sir, not a thing," he answered, mimicking Yogi Bear in a half- decent attempt.

Beanie and I laughed at his effort.

Mel could see we were thinking her knowledge of baseball a little outside the realm of normal. "Look, you guys, my dad always wanted a boy, but I came along and then Mom couldn't have any more kids, so I kind of had to fill that role for him. Our house in Portland sat next to Berkeley Park. The baseball diamond was practically in my backyard. Dad gave me a baseball glove on my eighth birthday. Ever since I was six my dad would take me to watch the Portland Beavers at Multnomah Stadium when they were in town. Then, on Sundays, we would toss the ball around in the backyard. In the evenings after he got home from work and whenever the field was free, we would go over so I could pitch to him and practice my batting. He had pitched in college and showed me all the grips. I took to it naturally. He taught me how to read box scores, and believe it or not, I actually came to like them. Dad may have never gotten his boy, but he had a girl that could chuck a really good curveball."

If we were amazed before, now we were flabbergasted.

"Actually, Mel, that's pretty cool," I finally said. "I know one thing's for sure, I would much rather have had you for a sister than what I got stuck with."

"Thanks, Frankie," Mel cooed, snuggling up against me, "that's really a very sweet thing to say, but it isn't going to save you from trying to hit against my pitching."

I knew I'd better change the subject. Behind the retaining wall I had noticed a pile of 3 Musketeers wrappers. I gave Beanie the look.

He smiled weakly. "I had to keep myself busy. There wasn't much going on until Mrs. Crowley showed up."

At least it got us back on the subject.

"Has she talked to anyone?" Mel asked.

"I don't think so," Beanie answered. "She didn't when she showed up anyway. She was kind of startled by the attention when she got out of the cab and just hustled inside."

I looked at Beanie in disbelief. "Hustled? Mrs. Crowley?"

"Well, you know what I mean. So, what happened at the town meeting?"

We filled Beanie in on everything that happened at the hall, minus her mom's outburst, and then about the broken bike chain on the ride home.

"So now I suppose we're going to have the Air Force after us, only if this mystery guy you're talking about doesn't get to us first. If there was a corner around here somewhere, it would sure feel like we were being backed into it."

"Do you think that maybe we can focus here," Mel offered. "We need to see Mrs. Crowley as soon as we can."

"Why?" Beanie wanted to know. "You curious to ask her what the interior of a spaceship looks like?"

126

"No. It's because we need to tell her we caused the fire, remember?"

I gave Beanie a startled look and found the same on his face. We had completely forgotten what Mrs. Crowley's coming back meant. The last time we sat in this very spot, we had agreed to tell her.

"Do you think she'll call the police?" Beanie asked.

I thought about it for a minute. "Mrs. Crowley is hard enough to figure out. I have no idea, but I doubt it. I think she likes us too much for that."

It doesn't really matter," Mel told us. "It's the right thing to do."

We all turned at the sudden clamor from the crowd in front of Mrs. Crowley's. Then someone said, "She's coming out." The reporters shoved their way to the front of the crowd, cameramen in tow.

I looked at Mel and Beanie. "This should be interesting."

"Any time Mrs. Crowley opens her mouth it's interesting," Beanie agreed, "so this ought to be especially good."

Chapter 15— Explanation

Mrs. Crowley stood at her door, surveying the mass of humanity gathered in her front yard. After a moment she stepped out, closed the door and shuffled to the edge of her front porch.

The two television reporters, their cameramen, and what must have been a half dozen newspaper reporters ran up to her, jockeyed for position, and shoved microphones in her face. They were all shouting questions. The crowd swarmed in behind the reporters. The police were nowhere to be seen, or anyone else of authority who might stem the hordes from washing up onto her shore.

Mrs. Crowley just stood there for a moment watching what was taking place before her, perhaps a little taken back by it all. She was wearing her best muumuu; the one from Halloween nights when Beanie and I came to trick or treat. It was her idea of dressing up. We were the only treaters to ever show up at her place, but it was still a big deal because we were company. The muumuu had been purchased many years and too many meals ago. It now covered her immense body the way a casing covers a sausage. A cigarette hung from the tip of her lower lip, a wisp of smoke curling from the long ash.

The people pressed in and a frown formed within her sagging eyebrows. "Now you-all be careful of my flowers there," she bellowed, the cigarette flapping with her jowls as she pointed toward a withered mass of green foliage I took to be the subject of her remark. If there were flowers in there somewhere, I couldn't see them.

The reporters started to shout questions again.

"Now hush. Just everyone hush up." She looked over the throng of people like a school teacher quieting a disruptive class, waiting until they had taken their seats and settled down. Satisfied, she continued. "I guess you've all been pretty concerned about me, so I best let you know first of all that I am just fine."

One of the reporters barked, "Where have you been?" Another shouted, "Were you abducted by aliens?"

She shifted her weight in an offish sort of way. "Well, if you'd all just jam those gums of yours together and keep them that way for a moment, you just might find out something." She waited to make sure no one had missed her point.

"So that's Mrs. Crowley," Mel commented, having never met her before.

"Yeah, that would be her," I answered. "She put on her best threads for the event."

Mel gave me a quizzical look. "That's dressed up?"

I nodded.

Mrs. Crowley started in again. "I'm not interested in any questions when I'm done saying what I got to say, so you might as well just keep them in your pockets. Got that?" She waited to make sure the reporters understood.

Finally, one of the reporters answered, "Yes, mam." I think more to get her kick-started again, rather than out of respect.

Mrs. Crowley continued. "All I can tell you is that about an hour or so ago I found myself on Stafford Road over near Johnson Road. What a heck of a thing, I thought, because I had no idea how I got there. I was walking to the Mercantile down at the Crossroads to use their phone when along comes Mabel Swenson. Mabel lives down that way, you all know. Soon as she spotted it was me, she pulls over and asks if I'm okay. She is all kinds of concerned and I couldn't understand why. So, she offers me a ride into town and it is while on the way that Mabel tells me all about what has happened, that I had been missing for a couple of days, and my house had caught fire."

She could see some mouths gape open, so raised her hand to stop them and gave the reporters a stern look. Once again satisfied they wouldn't interrupt, she continued, "Well, Mabel had a doctor's appointment in Portland that she just had to be at, so dropped me off in town. She felt so terrible about it, but she just couldn't miss that appointment. I told her not to worry and that I would be all right. She dropped me off at the Rexall by their outside payphone. I figured I could give Abe a call and he would come pick me up."

I leaned over to fill Mel in. "Abe Shuster is the only cab driver in Lake Oswego. Mrs. Crowley uses him a lot because she hates to drive."

"Well, bless Abe's heart, when he heard who it was, he just about died. He said he would drop everything and race right over to pick me up. And sure enough, that's what he did because he made it there in a jiffy. He didn't even charge me for the ride, he was so happy to know I was okay. So, that's how I got home. Now, as far as this whole UFO abduction thing, I just don't know what—"

The sudden blare of a siren broke her off as a police car rounded the corner. People scurried out of the way when it whipped to the side of the road and ground to a stop in front of the house. Captain Thornton and Major Burnham jumped out and hurried up the walkway to Mrs. Crowley.

"That must be our Air Force officer," Mel said.

"That's him," I confirmed.

Captain Thornton stepped in front of the reporters while the major pulled Mrs. Crowley aside to talk with her.

Thornton addressed the crowd. "That will be it for the interview. Mrs. Crowley is part of an ongoing and active investigation. Major Burnham and I will need to debrief her before she gives any more comments to the press."

"Come on, Captain!" one of the reporters shouted, "She hasn't finished her statement yet."

Another said, "When will you be releasing her?"

The rest of the reporters burst out with a slew of questions.

Captain Thornton put his hands up. "We will not be taking questions at this time. Thank you."

He went over to where Mrs. Crowley and Major Burnham stood, nodded in response to whatever the major told him, and then escorted Mrs. Crowley inside her house.

We watched as the two television reporters took up positions in front of their cameras, obviously all abuzz with these latest developments and anxious to get their reports onto their respective television stations. The newspapermen were dashing to their cars so they could race back to their papers in hopes of publishing the next Pulitzer Prize winner.

The crowd of spectators started to disperse, though I am sure having set up a way to get the word out should Mrs. Crowley come out again.

It was all just crazy. "Can you believe it? It sure sounds like she's going with the abduction story," I said.

"You don't think she really was abducted, do you?" Beanie asked.

Mel answered, "No way. How could she? This all started with drinking straws and birthday candles, remember?"

"Well, we're going to find out, that's for sure," I told them. "But we'll need to come back later tonight. After everything calms down."

"Meet at the easement after dark?" Mel asked.

"That's the plan. Then we'll head up to her place. I'm going to be real interested in what she has to say after we tell her about our hoax."

"Oh, and Beanie," Mel added with a little smile. "Think you can show up in street clothes this time?"

Chapter 16— Decision

Oregon weather can be a real pain sometimes. One minute it can be sunny and the next pouring down rain. I think we have more types of rain than anywhere else in the world. Worst of all is our famous Oregon Mist. It's rain so tiny you can't even see the drops. The thing about an Oregon Mist is that one moment you notice a little moisture in the air, kind of like a light fog, and the next you are absolutely dripping wet, even when wearing a really good raincoat.

I stood under the bridge: cold, soaked to the bone, and shivering. I was waiting for Mel and Beanie to arrive, and it seemed like a long time for them to get down here.

Finally, they came running down the steps, sopping wet in just the short time it took to get from their houses to the easement.

"What's the deal anyway?" Beanie asked. "We've only been here twice at night, and each time we end up drenched."

Mel twisted the sleeve of her sweatshirt. Water dripped in little beads from the tip. Her hair was matted to her head and shoulders. She looked at us and said, "We're only going to get wetter the longer we stay, so we might as well not worry about it and get going."

I told them, "I checked out Mrs. Crowley's place on the way down; looks like the mist has driven everyone indoors." Soon as I said it, I got the irony of the comment. "Well, the sane ones anyway."

Beanie splashed a wet foot in a puddle that had pooled under the bridge. "I don't think it's gonna get any better, so I'm with Mel. We may as well head out."

"Okay," I said, "but we better be careful anyway, just in case I missed someone."

We snuck up to the top of the stairs and looked both ways before we ventured onto the road. I knew that pretty much the whole time we were going up Summit Drive toward Mrs. Crowley's house, we would be exposed. One side was a big bank with a hedge on top of it. On the other side, the lake side, all the driveways dropped down the hillside to houses below. Mrs. Crowley's place was one of the first ones to be at road level, so we would need to be careful until then. Who knows when a car could come from either direction, or some nosey neighbor come wandering out of their house? Half-way up a car did come down the road, slowing when it got to Mrs. Crowley's place. Which was good for us because it allowed time to ditch down a driveway far enough to get out of the headlights as it continued by.

Finally, we were approaching her house. I stopped and said, "Keep an eye out for anything that looks out of place."

When we were satisfied that no one was hanging around, we ran across her yard and followed the retaining wall along the side of her house to the kitchen door. I knocked.

"Who's that?" we heard her call out.

"It's me, Mrs. Crowley, Frankie. I've got Beanie with me."

She opened the door wearing a shapeless housecoat we had come to know as her usual lounging attire. "Thought it might be one of those nosey reporters. They've been bothering me all afternoon, knocking on my doors, trying to shout questions through them when I don't answer. Pretending to be flower delivery men. The gall of them!"

Then she checked us out and saw our condition. "And what are you poor souls doing out on a night like this? Just look at you!" Then she saw Mel. "And who is this wet little thing? She's like a little kitten left out in the rain."

"That's Mel, ah, Melanie. She's with us."

"Hi, Mrs. Crowley," Mel said, in a bit of a shivery voice. "Okay if we come in?"

"Oh, my goodness," Mrs. Crowley said, swinging the door wide open. "Well, I can't just leave you out in this mess, now can I? Get on in here."

We shuffled inside and stood just far enough into the kitchen so she could shut the door. Pools of water were already forming at our feet on the linoleum floor.

"Hold on now, hold on. Let me just get you some towels." She waddled off to a hallway and disappeared.

From the kitchen, we could see into the living room. Flower bouquets filled the room. There were ones that stood on little pedestals, and others in glass vases. Some were in little teapots or other types of containers. One was even in a little UFO saucer vase. *Where did they get that?*

In the kitchen, the breakfast table had assorted plates of cookies, cakes, and pies spread across its surface. And the kitchen counter was covered with different baked breads, rolls, and pastries.

Mrs. Crowley came out of the hall with a stack of tattered bath towels. Seeing our eyes glued to the table of goodies she said, "I tell you, this town has some wonderful people in it, now don't it? I've been getting this stuff all afternoon. You should see my refrigerator." She handed us each a towel and set the rest on the sill of the banister by the door. "Get off what water you can, and get rid of those shoes. They aren't doing you any good in here other than tracking up my floor." She wandered into the living room to wait for us, saying as she left, "And be sure to grab some of those treats over there. I can't eat them all myself."

I fought over the improbability of that statement for a lot longer than it took Beanie to kick off his shoes and make it to the table.

I grabbed a towel and started to wrap it around Mel's hair, delicately patting it between the layers, carefully drying it out. She smiled at me, took another towel off the banister, threw it over my head and roughly rubbed it against my hair and face. I pulled it off and we both giggled.

An utterance of disgust came from the kitchen. Beanie had been watching us. "Stop, or you will ruin my appetite."

We all laughed as Mel and I joined Beanie in the kitchen. All this food made me realize I had hardly eaten a thing all day. Every time my family had a meal, my stomach always seemed to want to be somewhere else. Until now anyway. These treats brought back my appetite. Same with Mel, from what I could see.

"Wow," Beanie said, "check this out. That's Mrs. Lawson's triple-layer cake." He grabbed a slice and shoved a chunk into his mouth. "I remember it from the easement party."

Mel asked, pointing to some cookies, "What are these?"

Beanie answered, "Those look like Mrs. Miller's famous cookies. They have oatmeal, raisins, *and* chocolate chips."

Mel picked one up and took a bite. "Oh, they are good!" She finished that one and grabbed another.

I followed Beanie's lead and took a big piece of Mrs. Lawson's cake.

Beanie kept talking and pointing to various plates and their creators while we snacked, but I could hardly understand a thing that came out of his mouth once he started shoveling treats into it. Only Beanie could identify the neighbors through their baked goods.

Mrs. Crowley called to us, "Come on into the living room. Bring some of that with you, if you want."

Beanie grabbed the plate of Mrs. Miller's cookies to keep us company.

Mrs. Crowley was tending to some flowers in a vase, leaning over to smell them. Not a pretty sight. Once we came in she waddled to her chair and settled into it, fidgeting just so in order to get all her considerable parts nestled into their appropriate and familiar depressions. She looked us over for a few seconds then said, "Well, don't just stand there, have a seat!"

One look around the room showed us the hopelessness of such a request. Junk covered every possible part and piece of furniture in the house. Cigarette ashtrays were on every table stacked high with butts. An odor permeated the air, which seemed to be a combination of stale cigarettes and the many fragrant flowers throughout the room.

Beanie, Mel and I looked at each other and then crumpled to the floor right where we were, sitting Indian style and looking up at Mrs. Crowley. We each grabbed another cookie.

"I suppose you battled this weather because you were worried about me and this whole UFO abduction thing."

Mel and Beanie looked at me. I guess they thought I should be the spokesperson of the group. I stalled at the idea, but then Mel nudged me with her elbow to confirm my nomination, should there have been any doubt. I looked up at Mrs. Crowley. "Well, actually it's because we have to tell you something."

She was a little startled by my comment. "Tell me something? I figured you were here to get the low-down on what happened to me."

I tried to think about how to get into this whole thing, looking around the room in case an easy way to do it was just standing in the corner waiting to be used, but it wasn't. Nothing smooth came to mind, so I just let loose. "We know you weren't abducted."

Mrs. Crowley squirmed in her chair, absorbing what I had just said. She looked at me, and then to Beanie, and finally at Mel. "You boys haven't been gentlemen at all. Other than this cutie pie's name, I know nothing about her. Now, first of all, which of you two boys is lucky enough to call her your girlfriend, and more importantly, how did you manage to hoodwink her enough to get her to fall for you?"

She was obviously avoiding my comment, but before I could say anything Mel answered. "I just moved here a few months ago. We used to live in Portland. And Frankie's the lucky guy, if he still wants to call it that." Mel's face had apology written all over it for what we had gotten into.

"Mel's great, Mrs. Crowley. And I do feel lucky." I reached over and took her hand, looking directly at her while I said this, reassurance in my eyes to back up my words.

"Well, you should." Mrs. Crowley swept her hand across the room. "See all these flowers? Everyone has been so wonderful. That one there is from your mom and dad, Frankie," she pointed out. "And those two big ones on the stands in the corners of the room, well, they're from the news stations. I guess they think they can bribe their way into an interview."

She looked like she was going to do anything to avoid what I had told her, so I broke in real quick. "Mrs. Crowley, we were the ones that burned your roof and tree. That's how we know you weren't abducted."

She blinked a few times, as if just now realizing that something solid before her eyes had suddenly disappeared. Her lounge chair had white doilies on the arms and she rolled the edge of one back and forth in her fingers. "Know what it's like to be lonely? You boys used to be the only ones who ever came by. Now it's like I'm a celebrity or something."

I knew I was going to expose her lie, but the truth was the truth. I kept going. "That night, the one where your roof and tree burned, we were pulling a little hoax. We built a fake UFO with candles and a plastic dry cleaner's bag. We went

139

out on the lake to release it. We didn't know the wind would come up and blow it into your tree, but it did. And then it caught fire." I paused for a minute remembering that night. "We had no idea it had burned your house until the next morning."

Beanie had actually stopped shoving cookies into his mouth so he could speak. "Yeah, we're real sorry, Mrs. Crowley. You know we'd never do something like that on purpose."

Mel kicked in. "Then you were gone and everyone saw our fake UFO and reported it, and they put two and two together. Next thing we know, everyone thinks you've been abducted."

"Yeah, where were you Mrs. Crowley?" I asked.

She looked at us for a long time, as if trying to read us as she fought over whether to come clean or just try to stick to her abduction story. It was obvious she never considered that anything other than a UFO had caused the fire.

Finally, she let out a small sigh. "I was staying with a friend. I had left that morning you kids pulled your hoax, to go over and help her for a few days. I never get to see her much anymore, so was excited to get her call. She needed help with some things since it's hard for her to get around."

Knowing what Mrs. Crowley was like, this made me really wonder about the condition of her friend.

"So, I agreed. She picked me up pretty early in the morning. That's probably why no one saw her come by. Wasn't till the next evening, when I was doing dishes in her kitchen, that I heard my name on the news. I stopped and watched the story about the fire the night before, and me being missing. I didn't know what to do. Thought about it all night. Wasn't till the next day, after watching the morning news and seeing that everyone seemed settled on my being abducted, that I decided I'd better call the police to let them know I was all right. Then I realized things would stay the way they were. I get lonely, you know. I didn't want to go back to that if I had a chance to change it. I decided right then and there that this happened for a reason. I needed friends and the UFO...I guess *your* UFO, gave me a chance to get them. I didn't think my little fib would hurt anyone. I certainly didn't think it would involve anyone else, other than my friend who agreed to keep silent. So, I arranged to be dropped off on Stafford Road because that's where the other sighting took place. Seemed to make sense. I made my friend promise not to say a word about where I had been." Her eyes scanned the room. "Just look around this place. I tell everyone the truth, and this is all gone."

"But we burned your house!" I said.

"That's what insurance is for. It will still cost me some out-of-pocket money for the deductible, but I don't care. Besides, I'm sure we can work something out where you kids can pay that back. I'm to where I can't get around in that yard so well anymore, so could use some help with it. You know—mowing, weeding, planting."

Mel brightened up. "We'd be happy to help you."

At first I was in with Mel, but then it hit me that this still wasn't right. "Mrs. Crowley, but what about the police, and the way everyone is so stirred up? We can't just let this go. We need to tell."

Mrs. Crowley leaned forward in her chair, her eyes suddenly focused on the significance of what I suggested, and on us. "Tell, and then what? You kids get in real trouble with both your parents and the police, so where does that leave us? I lose my only really good friends. And yes, I know that everything you see around here—the flowers, desserts, food—are not from people who care because of who I am, but because of what they think happened to me. Someday, and probably much sooner than I would like, I will be old news. So, again, where does that leave us? With lots of trouble and no friendships, maybe even between ourselves. We will be labeled as liars and hoaxsters. I'm sure your parents will demand that you never come over again." She let us absorb what she had just said.

None of us knew what to say. Even though it was wrong, we knew she was right.

She leaned back in her chair. "Why don't we just keep our little stories to ourselves?" She winked and gave us a smile. "You know it's for the best that way."

We stood on the front porch, Mrs. Crowley having just closed the door behind us. I stared up at the streetlight across from her house and could see the Oregon Mist still in full form, passing through the light in waves like floating fog.

Mel leaned against me. "It sure seems like we're getting off easy with this whole thing; first with the police not believing us, and now with Mrs. Crowley not wanting us to tell."

Beanie looked at her like she was crazy. "You've got to be kidding. Take a look at this yard, and if you think this is bad, wait until you see the back. I'm not sure that spending the rest of our lives tending to this jungle is a better option to complete and total humiliation and community expulsion."

We all laughed. We needed it.

I bumped Beanie with my shoulder. "You know, you sure have a way of putting a different spin on things."

We stepped into the dark and stormy night to head home.

Chapter 17— Deeper

Suzie had answered the phone. "Frankie, it's Melanie. She sounds really strange."

We were in the middle of breakfast when she called. I quickly swallowed the bacon I was working on and ran to the phone, grabbing it from my sister and getting a dirty look in return.

"Mel—"

"Frankie! You've got to get over here right away!" She sounded frantic.

I quickly pulled the phone down the stairwell as far as it would let me go, sat on a step and hunched against the wall so I could get a little privacy. Luckily, we had a long phone cord for such situations. "Why, what's happening?" I whispered.

"It's that Air Force officer. He just got here. My mom told me I had to go to your place so they could talk, but I snuck back in to call you."

"Can't they hear you?"

"No, I'm outside with the phone. They're in the living room. He's interrogating her! You've got to get over here!"

"I'm on my way."

"Come up the side of the house to the sliding door in back so they don't see you. And hurry!"

I hung up, ran back up the stairs, set the phone on the counter, raced back downstairs and threw on my street clothes. I grabbed my shoes and was going to spring back up the stairs when I realized I'd better slow down so I don't throw up any red flags to my mom. I took a deep breath as I put my shoes on and tied the laces. All I could think about was what Mel had just said to me over the phone. *The Air Force Major was interrogating her mom!* I went back upstairs, taking two at a time, trying to make sure it didn't sound too rushed. I walked to the door, looking over at my mom in the kitchen as I went by.

"Mom, I've got to go. Mel needs me." I opened the sliding glass door.

"But, Frankie, your breakfast?"

"It's an emergency." I tried to think of what that could be. "Her bike chain broke. I need to fix it."

"Bike chain? Why is that an emerg—"

The door cut off the rest of her sentence. I raced down the front steps and onto my driveway. At the bottom, I rounded the hedge and saw a dark blue sedan parked at the Simpsons. It had government plates. I snuck up the side of the hedge and around the house to the back door. Mel was waiting for me there.

"Hurry, they're in the living room," she whispered. "We can listen from the dining room." She grabbed my hand and pulled me through the sliding door, closed it softly, and then snuck over to the corner of the kitchen. As soon as we came inside, I could hear Mrs. Simpson and the major in a heated discussion.

The dining room had a half-high wall that was open to the living room. We crouched low so we wouldn't be seen, worked our way to the wall, and sat down with our backs to it. The major and Mel's mom were already well into it.

"You and your husband have *always* been on our radar, Mrs. Simpson. Ever since Roswell. You think the Air Force would send a *major* up here just to investigate a UFO report?"

"Oh, I know exactly what the government is capable of," Mrs. Simpson retorted.

We heard the major's footsteps come close to our wall. We scrunched up against it, hoping he wouldn't see us over the top. His voice sounded like it was directly above us.

"I've been in the service for quite a while, Mrs. Simpson. Long before my attachment to the Air Technical Intelligence Command, or involvement in Blue Book, or even Project Signs. Do you have any idea where I was stationed twenty years ago?"

She didn't answer.

"Where were *you* twenty years ago, Mrs. Simpson? Or better yet, where was your husband?" He didn't wait for an answer. "He was going to college at Texas Technical College, wasn't he?

"Yes," I heard Mel's mom answer.

"Well, I was a lieutenant based at Roswell Army Air Field at that time. I was there in July of 1947. And I happened to be the officer that interrogated your husband."

Mel grabbed my arm and looked at me. Neither of us could believe what we were hearing or quite understand what was going on.

"I know all about his interrogation," Mel's mom answered. "I'll never forget that day. Roger came home white as a sheet and scared to death. And it makes me sick to be looking at the man who did that to him."

"He was at the crash site, Mrs. Simpson, but of course you are well aware of that." The major moved back to the center of the living room. "We had to interrogate everyone who was there."

"What crash site? Wasn't it a weather balloon? Isn't that what your brilliant minds came up with? I still feel sorry for Major Marcel. You threw his whole life away just to cover everything up. Made him a laughing stock!"

"You obviously don't understand just how serious that event was, Mrs. Simpson. We couldn't let the world know we had recovered a crashed spacecraft. The public wasn't ready for it, and they still aren't. I won't even go into what such information would mean to our enemies."

"And just who are your enemies, Major Burnham? I really do have to wonder. I know what you did to people there. How you threatened them. How you threatened us!"

"When it comes to national security, we do whatever is necessary."

Mel was staring at the clawed foot of the dining table, seemingly for no other reason than a point of focus for whatever reality she could hold onto. Tears formed in her eyes. She squeezed my arm so hard it was cutting off the circulation, making it tingle. I pulled her forehead over against mine and stroked her hair, trying to give her some form of comfort.

"Oh, and we were such a threat to you." I heard Mel's mom jump up and start pacing the room. She must have been sitting on the couch. "I'll never forget what he was like after he got home from your *interrogation!* He was frantic. He told me all about it. How you had treated him, and threatened him. It scared me to death. And then that next evening," she paused as if to try to collect herself. "That next evening, just after it got dark, we got a knock at the door. Roger pulled the window curtain aside to see who it was. There were two men in black suits standing on our doorstep. We wouldn't let them in, but they forced their way inside anyway. They made us sit on the couch while they spent hours interrogating Roger again, asking him where he had hidden the package from the crash site. Then they started with the house, going through everything, dumping out drawers and turning over furniture—looking for anything my husband might have saved from the spaceship. They threatened him. And when that didn't work, when they couldn't find anything, they threatened me. They told him *things would happen* if he didn't keep quiet about what he saw. And you know who they were looking at when they said that? Me! They were deliberately looking at me. He got the message, and so did I."

"We found out through interrogations of the other students who were at the site that your husband may have conspired with someone to get some of the crash material out. We know everyone there was collecting pieces of the spaceship. Your husband was seen putting some in a satchel. But when we arrived, that satchel was nowhere to be found. We recovered all the material from the other witnesses and cleaned up the crash site. But we still don't know what happened to that satchel, or the man your husband had been talking to. He also disappeared. We believe he managed to get away with the satchel and debris in it."

"Well then go find him. Just leave us alone. Haven't you done enough to my family?"

Major Burnham sighed. "I'm sorry if we put you under duress, Mrs. Simpson. We had to recover that material and stop any potential leaks. It had to be done."

"Duress. Duress! You have no idea what that did to us. We were young and in love. We had only been married a year. Roger was still in college, but we wanted to start a family right away. Were you aware I was pregnant at the time, Major? Five months! Well, those men knew. It was easy to see their threats weren't just against us; they were also against the baby!"

The math was easy. Mel and I were born the same year, 1952. *It wasn't Mel!*

She pushed her face into my chest to muffle the sobs, and I felt her grip tighten even more on my arm.

"They kept on us, following us, following me! Threatening phone calls late at night. It was too much. You probably don't know that I lost that baby only a week later. I began having problems. I went to the doctor, but they were no help. They said it was due to extreme stress; that my body couldn't handle carrying it and rejected the baby in order to save itself!"

I heard her fall to the couch and break down crying.

Mel kept sobbing against my chest. I put my arm around her back and felt her convulsions as she gasped for breaths between sobs. I stroked the back of her head, doing everything I could to keep myself together. The only sound I heard for a while was Mel's mom crying on the couch and Mel's stifled sobs.

Finally, Major Burnham spoke. "Yes, I was aware you lost a baby. I am very sorry. I hope you believe that. But it still doesn't change why I am here." He paused for a moment as if he was trying to shift gears. "You need to understand. We had to find that material. We had to be sure. When we didn't find it in our search of your house, we were satisfied he had not recovered the satchel."

I could hear him pacing back and forth in the living room working on his thoughts.

"But we believe now that your husband did get that satchel back, and has some of the debris from the crash site in his possession. It took quite a while to come to that conclusion. An eyewitness finally came forward. At the time of the crash he was initially too scared to admit what he knew, but two years ago he got into some serious trouble and offered up the information as a plea bargain. He knew how important it was to us. He told us he was at a restaurant in town not long after the crash. Two men were in the booth behind him, and although they were trying to keep their voices low, he caught some of their conversation. A package exchanged hands and from what he overheard, he knew it was from the crash site. Then he saw one man leave with a bag strung over his shoulder, which he did not have when coming in. He identified your husband as that man from pictures we had taken. There is only one conclusion. It was the satchel from the crash site and given back to your husband at the restaurant meeting. As for the other man, we are still trying to identify who he is."

I heard the major sit down on the couch. His voice turned softer. "It's imperative the government recover that material, Mrs. Simpson. It is evidence the crash actually happened and we need you to turn it over to us. I ask you to imagine what would happen if that material fell into our enemy's hands or became public? It would be a national disaster."

Her response came in a burst. "You want my help! You've got to be kidding! You've destroyed my family and you want me to help you!"

"I want you to help your government."

"And what, you didn't get what you wanted when you burglarized our house in Portland?"

"That wasn't us, Mrs. Simpson. So, you'd better give that a little thought, as to who it was. We also know the material wasn't there. We had already looked. Your husband must have hidden it somewhere."

"Get out of here. Get out of my house! I've never seen any *material,* and Roger has never mentioned a thing about it. Go fabricate something about some other victim to harass. Just get out of here and don't come back. Let me and my daughter live what little lives you've left for us."

I heard footsteps and then the front door opening. "I know you want this over. The only way that's going to happen is for you to turn the material over to the Air Force. We won't rest until then, and neither will whoever burglarized your house. So, Mrs. Simpson, this is in you and your daughter's best interest. My card is on the table with my local number on it. Call me when you come to your senses and realize what you need to do." The door closed.

I heard Mrs. Simpson get off the couch and the sound of her sobbing slowly disappear. She must have gone down the hall to her bedroom.

Mel suddenly jumped up from the floor next to me and ran into the kitchen. I heard the sliding door open and close. It took a moment to react. I raced after her and searched the backyard, but she was gone. I ran down to the lake. No good, she wasn't there. I wanted to wrap my arms around her. Hold her. She needed me right now. And I needed her!

I dropped onto the picnic bench, tilted my head back and stared at the dark clouds overhead. It started to drizzle. Drops hit my face. Little tears falling from the sky. I looked out at the lake, across the raft, and to the spot where we had launched our UFO. How could I have known back then that it would lead to this?

Chapter 18— Clue

"How long you been here?"

I turned to see Mel standing behind me. She had changed her clothes, probably because she had gotten as soaked as me from being out in the rain. She was wearing a heavy grey sweatshirt with a screen print of The Beatles album for *A Hard Day's Night* on the front, a pair of white shorts, and her patented Converse sneakers with ankle socks.

"I don't know...how long ago did you run off?"

She came over and sat down next to me. "I'm not sure? Maybe an hour. I needed time alone. Then I went back home, but my mom was gone. I changed clothes and came looking for you. I went by your place, but your mom hadn't seen you, so I came down here." She looked over at me and asked, "What's the deal with the bike chain anyway?"

I smiled at her because I had forgotten all about it. It seemed so long ago. "Oh, yeah. That's all I could come up with. What did you tell her?"

"That you fixed it. I rolled with the story. I don't think she knew anything was up."

"Are you all right?"

She didn't answer for a while and then finally said, "Would you be?"

Easy answer. "No."

We watched tiny raindrops hit the water, making little dimples in the gray surface. Neither one of us said anything. I reached over and held her hand. It felt so warm.

After a while she said, "Don't you think you should get out of those clothes? You're sopping wet."

"Hadn't noticed. We live in Oregon. It's status quo."

"Funny." She bumped me with her shoulder.

More silence. More raindrops. We were both in our thoughts but our hands kept us connected.

I turned to her. "Mel, I'm so sorry, about the baby."

"That's all I've thought about...that I could have had an older brother or sister. I've been wondering what it would be like. I feel this big, empty spot in me; like a hole that will never be filled."

I put my arm around her and pulled her into me. "You know, Suzie can be a real pain, but I've been thinking about what it would be like without her. And when it comes right down to it, I figure she's not so bad after all. We used to have a lot of fun together when we were kids."

"It's funny," Mel said, "how one thing can change your whole life; make you realize you'll never be the same."

"I wish I could change things back...to how they were before we pulled our hoax."

Mel turned to me. "Don't even think that. All of this stuff was just hidden, waiting for something to set it off. That's all we did. I'm actually glad we found out about the baby, and my dad, and what the Air Force did. At least now I know."

"What do you mean?"

"Because if you don't know, you won't know what to do."

"To do?"

"Yeah. I've been thinking about it. We need to find that debris."

"But how are we going to do that? From what I over-heard, experts were looking for it and they couldn't even find it."

"Because *my* dad hid it and they wouldn't know where to look."

My eyes opened wide. "And you do?"

"Not yet. But I'm sure going to try, and I bet I can figure it out."

"So, what do we do?"

"Well, you're going home to get into some dry clothes and then meet me at my garage. I'm going to call Beanie to come help. We need to do this right now because my mom's gone so we won't get a bunch of questions. We're going to look through my dad's stuff for clues."

I put on a pair of jeans and matched Mel's sweatshirt with one of my own, though mine had Batman's logo on it; the one with a black bat in a yellow oval. The dry clothes felt good. I didn't realize how wet and cold I had been.

I headed over to Mel's. The rain had finally stopped and that was a good thing. I walked up the driveway. The garage door was open and she was sitting on the ground in the mid-dle of a bunch of stacked boxes she must have pulled out from storage. She was focused on the inside of one, going through the contents.

"Find anything yet."

She jumped at my voice. "You scared me. I didn't hear you coming. No, nothing yet. Grab one of these boxes and start going through it. Show me anything that looks unusual."

I grabbed a box and sat down next to her. I opened the lid expecting stacks of paperwork. Instead, I was greeted by a bunch of pottery fragments. "What was it you said your dad did?"

"He was an archeologist. He studied ancient civilizations."

Since the first box had nothing but pottery fragments, I opened another. It held little statues of various sizes. All of them were women and all had rather large breasts. "And I'm supposed to know when I find something unusual? It all looks unusual to me."

Mel looked in my box. "Oh, those are fertility figurines."

"How do you know that?"

"Over at our other place my dad had set up a workshop in the garage where he could work with the things he brought back from his trips. He used to do a lot of his research there. I would go out and see what he was doing once in a while. He always had something interesting going on. He would teach me about whatever he was working—"

She never finished her sentence so I looked up from my box. She was frozen in thought.

"What is it?"

"He would teach me about whatever he was working on. And now that I'm thinking about it, above the worktable there was a big pegboard. It was covered with all sorts of stuff about the Roswell crash. I didn't know what it was back then, but the two newspaper clippings were there, and a picture of Major Marcel with the balloon, though I had no idea who he was at the time. I can't remember specifics, but it seems like the whole pegboard was covered with his research about the Roswell crash. Mom took it all down after he died."

She paused for a moment, focused on her memories, then looked over at me, her eyes wide. "I remember once, a while back when I think I was about seven, I came out to the garage. He had some weird stuff on his worktable. It's kind of hazy, but I think he was startled at first when he saw me because he quickly stuffed everything into his backpack that was on the table. I remember because most of this stuff was silver and shiny, not dull and brown like statues and pieces of pottery. Then he pulled up a footstool like he always did when I came out. He picked me up and set me on it so I could see better. His eyes were glowing. He told me he wanted to show me something and pulled out a little piece of silver foil from the bag. He put it in my hand. It was flat and smooth like water. He told me to make a fist and crumple it up as much as I could." Mel was going through the motions as she spoke, reliving the experience. "I did that. Then he said to drop it on the workbench. I opened my hand and it fell to the table. At first, it sat there in a little crumpled ball, then it slowly started to...I don't know how to describe it." She looked at me with excitement in her eyes. "It was like it melted. In seconds it was flat and smooth again. He told me it was magic."

"It had to be from the spaceship," I said.

Mel nodded. "I think we need to find that debris."

Beanie walked into the garage. "Looks like a scavenger hunt to me. So what's up? You were pretty mysterious on the phone."

"We're looking for clues. We found out my dad was at the crash site in Roswell. He took some of the debris."

Beanie stood there, dumbfounded for a moment. "Hold on just one minute. Did I hear what I think I just heard? You mean *the* crash site? The one with the spaceship?"

"That's right, Sherlock," I answered.

"So, let me get this straight, we're looking for actual...stuff...from an alien spaceship?"

Mel glanced up from her box. "No, we're looking for clues. The debris isn't going to be in these boxes. He hid it so it wouldn't fall into the wrong hands. We need to figure out where it is. I think there may be a clue in one of these boxes. Grab one and start looking for anything that appears unusual."

Beanie sat down and I scooted a box over to him. He opened the top and stared inside.

I looked over at Mel. "Like I said, *everything* is unusual. I'm almost thinking we need to look for something that isn't unusual."

Mel was rummaging through her box and stopped the instant I said that.

She thought for a moment and then said, "Frankie, I think you're right. If there is some sort of clue in here, he wouldn't want it to stand out like a sore thumb. I mean, he must have known that if anyone found out he had that stuff, he could be in danger. That's why he hid it. And why he would leave some sort of clue that only my mom or I could figure out, in case anything happened to him."

We spent the next twenty minutes working our way through the boxes with added energy. We went through box after box, and still nothing stood out. We had gone through most of them when we decided to take a break. Mel headed inside to get some soft drinks.

When she returned she handed an R. C. Cola to Beanie and one to me. She pulled off the tab from her can, took a sip and then said, "I just don't get it. The clue has to be here somewhere."

Beanie pulled a box out from the dwindling pile still to be searched and sat on it. The top crumbled and he barely caught himself from falling in. He looked over to Mel. "Sorry. I was tired of sitting on the ground. I hope I didn't break anything." He opened the lid to the box. He stared in it for a minute and then pulled out a baseball glove. "What's this doing in here with a bunch of pottery?"

Mel's eyes lit up. She put her soda can down and grabbed the glove from Beanie. "That's my dad's! I looked all over for it after he died because I wanted to have it. What was it doing in there?" Then it hit her. "He put it in here on purpose. This is the clue!"

"How can a baseball glove be a clue?" Beanie asked.

Mel's eyes told me her brain was working on the idea.

"Let me think a minute."

She stared off into space and then down at the glove. She put her hand inside it and worked the leather with her other hand while she thought, just like any ballplayer would work a glove.

"Okay, we always played catch in the backyard. It has to do with something back there." Her eyes suddenly narrowed and she smiled. "I know where the debris is hidden. We need to go to my old house to get it."

Chapter 19— Detained

It was late morning when we hooked up again in my room. Beanie was going through my 45 record collection looking for the next one to play while we waited for Mel. She was sitting in my chair trying to figure out the bus schedule she had grabbed from her house.

"What would you prefer," Beanie asked, looking over to me, "'Louie Louie' by the Kingsmen, or 'Like a Rolling Stone' by Dylan?"

I pushed a bunch of stuff aside and jumped up to sit on my desk. "Put on 'Louie Louie'. Dylan is too depressing for what we are dealing with right now."

Mel looked up from the bus schedule as *Louie Louie* droned out of the portable record player. "It's not like there's a direct route. We'll need to transfer at least three times, but we can get to the house."

Beanie had tossed himself onto my bed and was now sprawled across it. "That sounds like a real hassle." He looked over at me. "What about Mrs. Crowley? Did you ask her if she'll drive?"

"Yeah, but she barely even goes to Wizer's for groceries and that's only a couple of miles. She wasn't hot on the idea.

I tried to talk her into it, but when I told her the place was in Southeast Portland there was just no way she would do it."

Mel got up from her chair. "Then we have no choice. It's the bus. And we'd better get moving. The next one will be here in twenty minutes, and the stop is over on Iron Mountain near the Hunt Club."

I got off the desk and we headed for the door. We turned to see that Beanie hadn't moved from the bed. We stopped and waited for him.

He sat up, feigning surprise. "What? Oh, you want me to come. You sure you don't have some boring little task for me to do around here?"

"Funny, Beanie, of course we want you along." I gave him a wide grin. "Besides, if we come across a dead body, we'll need you along to dispose of it."

"Now, *that's* funny." Beanie jumped off the bed and followed us outside.

To get to the Hunt Club we headed down Springbrook Court. The road ended by Mrs. Miller's place and I could see Beanie looking longingly in that direction, no doubt in remembrance of her cookies. From there the road turned into a wooded trail to where we dropped over the top of a little hill. The trail to the railroad tracks cut through a thicket of blackberry brambles, which I pulled out of Mel's path so she wouldn't get stuck by a thorn, and in the process managed to get stuck a couple of times myself, ending up with a few scratches.

Once we made it onto the tracks, we followed them to where they intersected Lakeview Boulevard near Iron Mountain and the bus stop. Beanie and I had watched trains flatten a lot of pennies on these tracks, and we often went this way to go to the Hunt Club to hang out. The place hadn't been doing well lately. It hardly ever had anyone around, so we liked to goof off there a lot. It had a big building with horse stalls and an indoor training arena. Behind it was a horse track.

The overcast sky that brought rain in the morning had broken up to expose patches of blue. The sun peeked over the edge of a cloud and I immediately felt its warmth. It looked like it would be a good day after all.

We were nearing Lakeview when a police car crossed the tracks. I looked over at Mel and Beanie. "I think that's Thornton. Where is he going?"

Beanie answered. "Fast on the heels of our UFO, no doubt."

None of us laughed because the police car suddenly pulled into a turn-around on the side of the road and doubled back. It stopped by the tracks. Captain Thornton stepped out of the police car, closed the door, and leaned against it to wait for us.

I whispered to Mel, "What do you think this is all about?"

"I don't know, but I'm sure it's not good."

Beanie started singing the words to the Bobby Fuller Four's song, "I Fought the Law, But the Law Won..."

When we got to the car Captain Thornton opened the back door. "You kids just couldn't keep out of trouble, could you? Get in."

"What's going on?" Mel asked.

"Get in. You'll find out at the police station."

Bolting didn't seem like a brilliant idea, though it did enter my mind for a half-second. There was nothing else we could do, so we slid into the back of the car and he closed the door behind us.

We rode in silence. I had a ton of questions but didn't ask a single one because I knew I wouldn't like the answers. I looked around the back of the police car, never having ridden in one before. The first thing I noticed was the door handles were missing. I guess just in case we made a desperate move to escape at 30 miles an hour. A wire screen separated the back from the front, again so we couldn't overpower the captain and take control of the police car. And finally, there was a shotgun in a holder next to the police radio and Captain Thornton's right arm—only a quick grab away in case we pulled anything. All these amenities and accoutrements seemed like overkill for little old Lake Oswego, but that didn't make me feel any better.

Mel, Beanie and I glanced at each other every once in a while to share the fear on our faces. The trip only took about ten minutes, but it seemed like hours.

We walked in through the front door of the police station to see the librarian at her regular post. She gave us what I took to be a knowing smile. I tried to smile back like I was Mr. Innocent, but it just didn't take.

Captain Thornton led us down the hall to a room near his office. He motioned toward the room. "Inside, sit down, and keep quiet."

We went in and took chairs around a table in the middle. The door closed behind us.

I looked around the room. The walls were bare and a single light was attached to the ceiling covered with a wire guard. There was nothing else in the room other than the table, which was mostly metal with a laminate top, and the chairs, which were metal with vinyl cushion seats.

"This is the room they put my mom in," Mel said.

"What do you mean?" Beanie asked.

Mel and I glanced at each other. We never told him about her outburst.

Mel gave Beanie a look to shake it off. "Oh, long story. We've got bigger issues right now."

Beanie kind of nodded, maybe deciding it wasn't worth pursuing. "What do you think is up?" he asked. "I bet it's our UFO. They finally found us out."

"How could they?" I answered. "Mrs. Crowley and Suzie are the only ones besides us who know about it. I'm sure Mrs. Crowley isn't going to say anything, and if it was Suzie we'd sure hear about it from my parents long before ending up here."

The door opened. Major Burnham stepped into the room and closed it behind him. Right then and there I knew this would have nothing to do with *our* UFO.

"I didn't expect your two friends to be along with you, Miss Simpson, but it doesn't really matter. I'm sure that whatever you may know, you have conveyed to them."

He walked up to the table and stared down at us. It was like a scene from the movie, *Dr. Strangelove*, where General Buck Turgidson is in the war room, the overhead lights casting his face in shadow under the brim of his hat. I shrank back in my chair. He was a scary figure up close in his military uniform.

"As a matter of formal introduction, I am Major Burnham of the United States Air Force, 509th bomber group, attached to A.T.I.C., that's the Air Technical Intelligence Center. I asked Captain Thornton to locate you and bring you to the police station so we could have a little chat." He looked us over. "There's no sense in beating around the bush, so I'm going to get right to the point."

Beanie cut in. "Before you do, would you mind sitting down? I'm getting a kink in my neck."

I looked over at him hardly believing what he had just said, but then again, everything that came out of Beanie's mouth was unbelievable.

A frown came over the major's face. "And you are?"

"My name is Beanie; on account of one day when I was a kid I stuck a dried pinto bean up my nose. They had to take me to the doctor to get it out." This was said, of course, with the straightest face you ever did see.

Mel and I looked at each other, trying to stifle our snickers. She straightened out quickly but I couldn't stop, so she kicked me in the shin. The pain did the trick.

The frown disappeared from the major's face. He was dumbfounded. Beanie's comment had definitely put him off-balance. He didn't know how to respond. He finally said, "Interesting," then sat in a chair on the other side of the table and focused his attention on Mel again. "We believe your mother has information of vital importance to the United States government. I have tried to get through to her, but I am afraid that she is unreceptive and antagonistic."

Mel played dumb, which was the right thing to do. "What kind of information?"

He leaned forward on the table and looked at each of us in turn. "You are all old enough to know that when I tell you what I divulge in this room is of the greatest national security, you will understand the weight of that statement and its ramifications. There have been few citizens in our history who have before them the ability to help their government in the way that you can." He paused so that this statement could sink in.

We just stared at him with blank expressions to let him know his grandiose speech meant little to us.

Apparently giving up on that approach, he turned to Mel. "I don't know what your mother may have shared with you regarding recent events, or what your father may have revealed to you before his death." He paused again, but this time I think it was because he just didn't know how to put the right spin on what he wanted to say. He fidgeted in his chair, obviously not used to discussing national security with kids. "Look, we know your father had in his possession some sensitive material, and I need your help in recovering it."

Mel leaned back in her chair and crossed her arms. "I don't get it? You mean that the United States Air Force can't do this on its own, and you're asking a teenage girl and her two friends for help?" I could see Mel wasn't going to make it easy on the major, considering what he had done to her family. We had the edge. He didn't know we were in that dining room.

"Miss Simpson, I can assure you this is not the time to be flippant. You and your mother are in danger. And I am the person holding the key to your safety."

Mel stood her ground. "Then I think you need to explain what we are in danger from, and why it is you think you can get us out of it."

The major considered this for a moment. It seemed he didn't want to show his whole hand at once, but with a sigh he laid down his cards. "Your father recovered material from a crashed extraterrestrial spacecraft. He hid it somewhere. How we know this doesn't matter, but the fact that we do is what's important. I need your help to bring your mother to her senses. She knows where this material is hidden. You can help us obtain that information."

"That still doesn't explain how we're in danger."

Major Burnham sat back in his chair. It squeaked from the load. I could see he was wrestling over something. "I explained that I work for the Air Technical Intelligence Center. Everyone thinks we just chase UFOs, but that is not all we do. Our main function is counterintelligence."

Mel said, "You mean like spies?"

"Yes, spies. We are in the middle of a cold war. As important as this incident outside Roswell was, right now we have a more important task at hand—to keep our edge against the Soviet Union and their agents."

"So how does that have anything to do with us?"

"Your father's car crash wasn't an accident. It was staged. Someone was trying to get information from him. Our best experts investigated the accident, location, the damaged vehicle, and reviewed the autopsy report. Many of his injuries were not consistent with those that would occur from such a crash."

I looked over at Mel. She shook her head when she realized what he meant. "You're saying he was tortured?"

He nodded. "I'm afraid that's the only possible conclusion."

She stood up, walked over to the far wall and leaned into it with her back to us.

The major continued. "He was killed because they want that material. We also know your father never divulged the location."

Mel turned to him. "And how do you know that?"

"Because we have information there is still at least one operative in the area, and the only reason he would still be here is if the material hadn't been recovered."

I made eye contact with Beanie. We were both thinking the same thing—the mystery man.

"So now they're after Mel and her mom?" I asked.

"Yes, we think so. The Soviet Union would do anything to recover that material."

"You mean the KGB?" Beanie asked, startled.

"Yes, the KGB. Like I said, we are in the middle of a cold war. Do you have any idea what they could do with this material? It's called reverse engineering. The technology from this spacecraft could lead to advances that would take decades to develop otherwise. It is important to our national security that the Soviets do not recover these materials."

"What's reverse engineering?" I asked.

"Countries have been using it for years. During the Korean War our Sabre F-86 fighter had advanced gunnery radar which helped our pilots direct their fire against the Soviet's MiG-15s. It gave us air superiority. The Russians provided their planes to the North Koreans so they could see how they did against our fighters. They weren't happy with the results. Then a Sabre crashed in North Korea. It was secretly taken to the Soviet Union where they used reverse engineering to figure out how our radar worked. They were able to develop a warning device, and installed it in all of their MiGs. Once these planes were introduced into the war, they could detect when our radar tried to lock on their planes, letting them escape before our pilots could fire. Our advantage in air superiority was lost." He leaned forward, his face in shadow. "If the Soviet Union gets their hands on the material from that spaceship and they figure out the technology before we do, it could give them a tremendous advantage. It could change the shape of the world as we know it."

Mel returned to the table and sat down. "But you've had the whole spaceship ever since 1947. You should be way ahead of any country that might get some of this stuff."

"It isn't that simple. This material is beyond anything we have ever seen. It is so advanced, that although we have been working on it around the clock, we have been unable to reverse engineer it so far. It is, in fact, just now that our scientific advances have put us in position to make minor progress along that line. But eventually we will have the ability to comprehend and modify the materials for our use. For example, we recovered quite a bit of flexible, glass filament material from the craft, something like quartz, that we know was used for the transmission of information via light. We believe we will soon understand how this works and adapt it for the benefit of us all."

Beanie had to kick in. "Yeah, I'm sure that the betterment of mankind is your main intent."

Mel's eyes narrowed and her face hardened. "I have a question."

The major read the look and I could tell he was wondering where this would lead. "What would that be?"

"How long ago did you figure out my father might have some of the UFO debris?"

"That question has no importance to what we need to accomplish here."

"Hmmm...I guess if I were you, I wouldn't want to answer it either."

"I don't like your attitude."

"About two years ago. Am I right? When you found out my dad might have some of this debris?"

The major was shocked by her knowledge. "Where did you get that information?"

"Now *that's* what isn't important, but you know what is? The fact my dad died less than a year later."

The major sat in stone-dead silence. He knew where this was going.

She continued. "It's not a coincidence, but I'm sure you figured that out already. The leak came from your office, and it killed my dad!"

"That's speculation."

"And you want my mom and me to count on *you* for protection? I don't think so." She stood up from her chair and we knew to follow. "Come on you guys, let's get out of here." She walked out the door with Beanie and I hurrying to keep up with her.

I turned to see Major Burnham stand up and shout, "We're not done, Miss Simpson, get back here."

Mel just ignored him and marched down the hall and out of the building. I expected a large hand, uniformed cuff and all, military or otherwise, to grab my shoulder from behind to stop us, but it never happened.

Out on the sidewalk Mel pulled the bus schedule from her pocket. She studied it intently for a minute and then looked at a clock on the front of City Hall. "We can catch a bus in ten minutes down on State Street. Let's go get that debris."

Chapter 20— Game

The bus we caught at State Street in Lake Oswego traveled up Riverside Drive, across the Sellwood Bridge, and there we transferred to another bus to go down Milwaukie Boulevard. We caught a third bus at Bybee Boulevard and were now heading east on Bybee to where Mel said we needed to get off at 39th Avenue. This was the last leg of our longer than expected journey. The buses didn't have many people on them. We sat in the very back row so no one could overhear us.

Beanie and I spent the better part of the first leg reliving how Mel had handled the major.

"You were just like Perry Mason," Beanie said. "Just like he does in the last five minutes of any of his hundreds of TV shows, leaning over the witness stand, arm on the banister, staring into the eyes of the guilty." He jumped up from his seat and into the seat in front of us. He turned and leaned over the back as if it were the banister of the witness stand. In his best imitation of Perry Mason, he said, "So, Major Burnham, where were you on the night of the 13th?"

I jumped in. "Yeah, it was like you were grilling that episode's culprit while they sweated under your heat, finally squealing in the last minute."

"You were so cool in there, Mel," Beanie said.

Mel smiled at both of us. "Gosh, you're making me blush."

"Well, you sure didn't scream and faint like Sylvia did in *War of the Worlds*," I added.

Mel decided to turn things around. "True, but it was nothing compared to Beanie and his kinky neck-pinto bean moment and the way it threw the major off!"

We relived that moment and laughed over and over again about it. But Mel spent most of the time interrogating Beanie on how he could manage to stick a pinto bean up his nose, rather than dwell on how it had affected the tougher-than-nails Major Burnham.

But then the conversation turned serious as we got closer to our stop. We talked about her father's death, his torture, and how there was a Russian agent out there somewhere after the material, and probably us.

Mel battled with what to do. "Maybe turning it over to Major Burnham is the best thing. I don't like the idea, especially when I think about the smug look I will get from him when I do. But at least my mom will be safe then. I'm sure it would leak out to the Russians the same way it did that my dad had the debris to begin with."

I agreed with her. "Mel, this is your decision. I mean, Beanie and I are involved, but it's your family that's really in danger. I'm sure by turning it over, everyone will leave you alone."

174

"But not before I get a good look at the debris," Beanie added. "You know, it's just a guess on my part, but I'll probably never have another chance to goof around with some really cherry stuff from an alien spaceship."

"Don't worry, Beanie," I answered, "We all want to get a look at that debris."

"This is our stop," Mel said as she jumped up and pulled on the cord.

We waited for the bus to pull away and then crossed Bybee. There was a park on the other side, and at the far end I could see the top of the chain-link backstop for a baseball field.

Mel stood there for a moment, taking it all in since it had been a while.

"That's Berkeley Park," she told us.

I checked out the park. Houses lined it along Bybee Boulevard. There were trees everywhere, except the baseball field, of course. It looked like the park had an area at the opposite end from 39th with picnic tables, swings, and a play area.

Mel said, "My house is on the other side. The hiding spot is in the backyard. Come on." She led us down a path from Bybee past a tennis court and then across the park toward the baseball field. As soon as we cut off the path, we could see about eight boys playing a pick-up game of baseball. We skirted the field to 39th and walked behind the backstop.

"I don't like this," Mel said. "They'll be able to see me if I go after the debris. Let's sit on the other side and watch for a while until we figure out what to do."

We walked around the backstop to the other side. Some of the kids gave us the eyeball, most likely trying to figure out what we were up to. We looked at her old house. The side faced the park, with the front pointed to 39th Avenue. A long, thick hedge separated it from the next house along the park. It had a small yard in back, and other than a few shrubs was open to the park. I was glad to know we wouldn't have to sneak through a fence or fight through a hedge to get to the debris.

We sat down on a slope of grass between the house and the field. Most of the kids playing ball were our age, give or take a few younger and a few older.

"Do you know any of these boys?" I asked her.

"Not really. A couple of them look familiar, but this is the only park around here, so kids come from all over to use it. And since I'm a girl, I didn't get a lot of invites to come play."

"So, what are we going to do?" Beanie wanted to know.

"Sit and wait, I guess," she answered. "I don't know what else to do. I can't get to the hiding spot without these kids seeing, and I don't want to risk it considering what's in there."

"I hope it's not too long. I'm getting kind of hungry," Beanie added.

We sat and waited. It looked like the boys would be there for a while. Every so often one of them would look our way, probably wondering what we were doing watching them play. Then again, most of these boys are my age or older, and Mel is really pretty, so it's more likely their looks were directed at her.

One of the older boys, who had been glancing over more often than the others, put his hand up to stop the game and walked over to us. He was tall and thin, had long hair and wore a plain white t-shirt. I figured his age to be maybe six-teen. It looked like he was the leader because the rest of the boys came to a huddle near the edge of the backstop to watch and see what would happen.

"So, what, you got nothing better to do than watch us play ball?" he said.

"We're just waiting for the field," I told him, trying to be matter-of-fact about it.

"Well, we're going to be a while, so you've got a long wait." He looked me up and down. Mostly down, I guess, because I was sitting.

"No problem," I said.

"Why are you waiting for the field anyway? You don't even have any equipment with you."

Beanie had the answer here. "We prefer it that way. It's amazing how good we are at this game when we use an im-aginary bat and ball."

"Whatever." He gave us a 'you're crazy' roll-of-the-eyes look. "But like I said, you're going to have a long wait." He headed back to the field.

Mel watched him walk away. "With that kind of attitude, he'll probably keep the field all day just to spite us." She stood up and called after him, "What if we challenge you to a game? Three innings and winner gets the field."

Beanie and I looked at Mel like *she* was crazy.

I got up and smiled at the guy when he turned around. I whispered to Mel out the side of my mouth, trying not to move my lips, "What are you doing? We don't even have gloves, and there are only three of us against eight of them."

She put her hands on either side of my head and turned it so I could see her. There was this amazing confidence in her face. "Don't need them, and don't worry."

The boy took a couple of steps back to us. "You three want to play *us*?"

Mel nodded. "For the field. But we don't have any gloves, so part of the deal is we need one of you to catch for us. We'll even let you bat first."

Beanie and I looked at each other. We had our confirmation. She really *was* crazy.

The boy just kind of chuckled and said, "Sure, why not." He took a couple more steps toward us. Then he looked Mel up and down. "What's your name?" Funny how he didn't ask all of us our names. It must have had something to do with the long, tan, beautiful legs below Mel's shorts that spurred that question.

"I'm Melanie. This is Frankie and Beanie." She pointed us out.

"Well, Melanie, I'm Dodger. This will be fun. I'm going to enjoy watching you, your wimpy friend, and chubby boy over there, try to beat us." He flashed a little grin at her, and then walked back to the group of boys.

I looked over at her. "Mel, what are you doing? We can't beat these guys!"

"We need to get that debris and can't sit here all day waiting. I haven't seen anyone at the house, but that doesn't mean they won't be home soon. We have to do something." She turned to us with a sparkle in her eyes. "So how are you two at batting?" she asked, a big smile on her face.

I looked at Beanie who just kind of shook his head.

I answered. "Well, I'm not too bad, but I've played enough ball with Beanie to know when he gets a hit, it's only because the ball found the bat and not the other way around. Sorry, Beanie."

"No, that's pretty much true. I'm not real good at just about any sport."

"No problem," Mel said. "I've been watching these guys play, and there is nothing special about any of them. I have a good idea of who can hit, who can't and what pitch placement will make sure of it."

Beanie and I just stood there dumbfounded. Then it all came flowing back to me. How she had gone to ball games with her dad, had learned to read box scores, and worked on her pitching with him at this very ballpark. Mel knew more about baseball than most of the boys out there. She had basically been training all her life for this moment. A little smile formed on my face as the thought hit me. *But they don't know that!*

Mel saw me and said, "What's that look for?"

"Oh, nothing," I said.

She figured something was going on in my head but decided to drop it. "Okay, let's just try to get some hits. Frankie, you play between third and second, and Beanie, you're between first and second. I'm pitching." A glow came over her face.

We walked out on the field together. When Beanie and I headed for our spots and when the boys realized who would be pitching, a slew of catcalls came from them.

Dodger shouted, "You know this isn't a game of underhand pitching."

Mel was just getting to the mound, but turned at Dodger's slam and walked over to him. He held the ball in his hand. She took it, gave him her prettiest smile, spun on her heels so her long hair flipped across his face, and then walked back to the pitching mound. She stood on it and said, "Who's catching? I need a couple of warm-up pitches."

Dodger smirked and then pushed one of the younger kids out toward home plate. "I'm sure Billy here can handle it. He usually plays right field."

Billy was one of the smallest and youngest kids in the group. He was probably the worst player on the team because right fielders don't see much action. He looked out at Mel with all the self-doubt being in this situation could dig up.

Dodger shouted out to him, "Come on Billy. Easy-peasy. She's a girl, so you'll probably have more trouble digging the ball out of the dirt, than anything else."

It didn't look like Billy gained any visible confidence from Dodger's efforts. He headed for home plate, switching anxious looks between Mel and the group of boys who had moved into the dugout area.

Mel watched him walk out to the plate. "Well, I guess he'll do for the warm-up pitches."

Billy sat on his haunches behind home plate.

She tossed a couple of soft pitches to get her arm loose, just as any pitcher would do. Smirks and a few catcalls came from the boys in the dugout.

"Hey, she's a lefty," Dodger shouted mockingly. "Watch out."

Mel ignored him. She set up her stance to throw the first real pitch, went through her windup, and fired the ball. It zipped into Billy's glove, practically knocking him off his haunches.

Beanie and I exchanged wide smiles which, coincidentally, had disappeared from the boys' faces. She threw two more pitches of equal speed and accuracy.

"Well, that should be enough. I haven't pitched for a year but seems like I still have it. You might want to get someone a little better behind home plate though because those were just my warm-ups."

Billy didn't need the advice. He was already headed for the dugout. "You go catch for her," he told Dodger. "I'm not going to get killed out there."

Dodger swiped his glove off the bench and headed to home plate. "No sweat. Doesn't bother me."

"Then bring on your first batter," Mel told him.

The boys all looked at each other. No one wanted to come out to the plate and bat against a girl that could throw like that. I'm sure Dodger would have been happy to, but now he was catching, so couldn't. Finally, one boy grabbed a bat and walked toward the plate.

Dodger said to him, "Okay, Nate. Get a hit so we can dump these three and get back to a real game."

Nate stepped into the batter's box and looked back at Dodger with a slight nod that did not exude a ton of confidence.

"Come on Mel," I called, "put the heat on this guy."

Beanie chattered from the other side of the field, "Hey batter, batter, batter. Hey batter, batter, batter."

Mel looked back at us and winked. She turned to the plate, wound up and threw the ball. I'm sure Dodger would have liked to dodge it if he could, but the throw was way too fast for him to do anything other than protect his life by catching it. He winced when the ball hit his glove but immediately tried to cover up the pain.

Nate looked out at Mel, then back at Dodger behind the plate, letting out a low whistle. "Now that's some heat."

It didn't take long before we were up. Nate whiffed on the next two pitches. Neither of the batters up after him came close to connecting with the ball; every swing being a full-on whiff.

But we didn't fare much better. Dodger pitched and he wasn't too bad himself. It didn't help that he had a few years and a lot of size on us. I managed a ground ball but was put out at first. Mel popped out, and Beanie struck out.

The second inning mirrored the first. One boy managed a foul ball, but other than that, no one got close to getting a hit. But on the other hand, Dodger was gaining some confidence back, I think mostly because he had seen our batting capabilities in the first inning, and had realized they were desperately lacking.

After two innings we were still scoreless.

We took the field for the final inning. Dodger hadn't batted yet, probably saving his bat for when and if it was needed. Mel had been throwing mostly fastballs and a few sinkers just to change things up. But I couldn't forget what she had said when we were back at Mrs. Crowley's and she first told us about playing ball, "Dad may have never gotten his boy, but he sure had a girl that could chuck a really good curveball!" I couldn't wait to see it, and I knew I would when Dodger came to the plate.

Mel struck out the first two batters with her usual combination of fastballs and sinkers. One more out and we would at least end in a tie. Dodger walked to the plate. He kicked up a cloud of dust from the batter's box, which was a pretty good feat considering the soil still had a little moisture to it. He stared intently at Mel, trying to psych her out.

"Come on, Mel," I shouted, "bring on the magic. I know what you've been saving for him."

Mel was too busy staring Dodger down to acknowledge my shouts. She was going to do it. Throw the curveball. I could see it in her grip on the ball hidden behind her back. She held it just like Sandy Koufax did when he used it to help win the Series last year. And the really neat thing about it, both Mel and Sandy were lefties! Dodger didn't have a chance.

The ball headed to the plate like a fastball, but a little higher and slower. I could tell Dodger thought she had worn out. His eyes gleamed at the fat pitch. Just when he started his swing, the ball suddenly dropped and slid to the right. His bat flashed through the air nowhere near the ball. Dodger practically spun around in the batter's box. He tried to regain his composure, but it was easy to see the pitch had deflated his ego. Mel threw two more curveballs, each even better than the first. Dodger struck out and it was our turn to bat.

We huddled together in our dugout. "Mel, that curveball is unbelievable!" I told her.

"Thanks. But what we have to do now is get some hits. We need this field. I've been watching Dodger throw. He's all about fastballs, so don't expect anything else. He also tends to put them to the outside of the plate and just above waist level, so set your swing up for that. She put her hand out in the middle of us. We looked at her. We hadn't done this for a while with everything going on, but it sure seemed like the right time. We placed our hands on top of hers.

"All for one...," she started.

"...and one for all," we finished together.

Mel stepped up to the plate. I could see Dodger really wanted to strike her out. His first pitch was just where she said it would be. She swung and hit the ball right through Dodger and over second base. This time he dodged really well, ending up on his butt. Mel made it to first base easy.

I was up next. I knew if I hit the ball outright we might end up in a double play, and that would pretty much be the end of it. I stepped into the batter's box and took my stance. Dodger threw the ball and I let it go by so I could judge it. The next pitch came. I quickly lowered my bat to bunt and the ball bounced off it and trickled down the first base line. I sprinted for first and Mel raced for second. Dodger was just slow enough in his reaction. He didn't expect a bunt and I was counting on that. He got to the ball, but was too late for a throw to second, so tossed it to first. It made it to the glove just as my foot touched the bag. There was a big argument over whether I was out or not. I was sure I had made the bag before the ball, but Dodger was screaming and about ready to tip over the edge, so Mel stepped into the argument.

"Okay, okay! Frankie, forget it. Beanie will get a hit." She looked over to Beanie and said, "Right, Beanie?"

He just stared at her, unable to believe she could put it all in his hands.

The good part of it was that although I was out, Mel was on second base and in scoring position.

I ran over to Beanie, breathless. "Come on now, Beanie, you can do this." His eyes had a glaze over them. I shook him. "Beanie. You in there?"

He finally turned to me, making eye contact.

"Listen, just wait for the pitch where Mel told you it would be. Focus on the seams of the ball when it comes in. That will help you connect with it. Now get a hit!"

He picked up the bat. "Thanks, Frankie."

I gave him a pat on the back as he headed for the plate. I could almost see a sense of confidence in his stride. Or at least that is what I hoped it was.

"Come on, you can do it, Beanie!" I told him.

Mel shouted from second base. "Go get him slugger. You're the next Babe Ruth."

Beanie stepped up to the plate. Dodger was fuming. Both Mel and I had gotten hits off him. He wasn't about to let 'chubby boy' do the same. His first pitch was fast and straight. Beanie watched it all the way to the glove. The next was outside and after some arguing over whether it was a ball or a strike, we won the argument and he was one and one. The next ball came in right where we expected it, but Beanie's bat decided to be somewhere else at the time. Strike two. The next pitch was an obvious ball that no one argued over.

I called out to Beanie, "Now focus on the seams. Make a connection."

Beanie looked intent. He readied his bat. Dodger threw the ball and it was coming in a little lower and inside than most of his pitches. Beanie swung. I couldn't believe it, but the next thing I knew the ball was sailing over the first baseman in a blooper that fell short of Billy who was running in to retrieve it.

Mel had taken off the moment the bat connected with the ball. She rounded third as Billy threw the ball to the first baseman knowing he could never get it all the way in. Mel headed for home. The ball rocketed in from first, but it was too late. Mel had already crossed the plate.

I ran out to Mel and threw my arms around her in a bear hug.

Beanie raced in from first and jumped up on us. We bounced up and down together screaming, "We won! We won!" When we finally pulled apart to look over at the boys, most of them were already leaving the park.

Dodger walked up to us. "It's all yours."

Mel smiled. "Thanks. You won't understand, but that was for my dad."

"Whatever." He headed off the field with the rest of the boys in tow.

Mel watched until they were out of sight.

She looked over at me. "Dodger? What kind of name is that?" She looked at Beanie. "Can you imagine going through life with such a weird nickname?"

"No way. I sure do feel sorry for the guy," Beanie answered.

We all broke up over that one. When we had finally stopped laughing Mel's look turned more serious. "Okay, let's find that debris."

Chapter 21— Recovery

"So where is it?" I stood with Mel and Beanie near the edge of the ball field. We could see a few people at the far end of the park by the swings, but no one would be close enough to see what we were going to do. We looked over at the house.

"In the ground under the back deck," she answered.

"In the ground?" I said.

"Yeah, in the ground," Mel answered. "I'll explain when we get there." She looked at Beanie, "We'll need you to keep an eye out for anyone coming by. Frankie, you come with me."

I followed her up the slope. We stopped and took one last look around, then ducked past the shrubbery and into the yard like commandos in a war movie. We made our way along the back wall of the house. It stuck out farther than the rest. Mel whispered to me, "This was my mom and dad's bedroom." We got to the far edge and Mel peeked around the side. The deck was about two feet off the ground and sat in the recess of the main house.

"It's clear. Come on." Mel got down on her knees and crawled. I followed her. "There's a box buried in the ground under the deck. We need to find it."

We crawled beneath the deck and the smell of musky earth hit my nose. All I could see was dirt. "Why would a box be buried here?"

"A long time ago, I think I was about five, Dad made a toy box to store my outside play toys. But I cried because I was sure that kids from the park would see it and take them. Dad told me he would make sure that didn't happen. He buried the box under the deck where only the lid was exposed on the surface. He told me it was a great hiding place and no one would find my toys there."

I looked around under the deck. "I don't see a lid."

"I know it still has to be here." Mel thought about that for a second. "I think Dad would have covered it up with dirt after he put in the debris. That way no one else would know it was there." She started looking. "It's been like five years since I used it so I can't remember exactly where it is. It shouldn't be too far back though."

She probed the ground with her fingers, so I did the same.

"I used to keep my Barbie dolls and tea set there that my mom always wanted me to play with. But as I grew older, I got bored with them and spent more time watching the kids playing at the ballpark. That's when Dad figured it out and gave me the baseball glove on my eighth birthday. I kept our gloves and a baseball in the box for a while, but it was just as easy to take them inside, so I quit using it. I had completely forgotten about it until we found Dad's glove in the garage."

"Maybe it's not here anymore, or it caved in. Was it made out of—" My fingers hit something hard. "Mel, come here. I think I found it." I brushed away the moist dirt in one spot and felt a smooth surface underneath.

Mel scooted in next to me and worked her fingers in the soil. "This is it. Get the dirt off."

We worked at the dirt, pushing it aside. The box was bigger than I expected, about three feet long and almost two feet wide. When we had the lid uncovered we stared down at it. I could see the top still had the faint decoration of painted flowers.

Mel looked up at me, her eyes bright with anticipation. "Here goes." She pulled up on the front of the lid, but it didn't budge. We were on our stomachs and she couldn't get good leverage. "Help me get this open."

I grabbed the lid on my side and we lifted together. The hinges squeaked as it rose. We gave a last shove and the lid dropped to the back. We scooted forward and stared into the hole. It was dark inside, but I could just make out some sort of green bag.

Mel looked over at me and grabbed my arm. "That's my dad's backpack, the one he always used on his field expeditions. It has to be the debris."

We reached in together and pulled the pack out of the box. It was an army style backpack like the ones Beanie and I had seen many times at the army surplus store where we got our walkie-talkies. It was made of dull green canvas with all sorts of straps and loops for holding gear. The flap had a pocket on it and was attached to the main bag. The two straps for the shoulders also had loops on them and could be adjusted to fit the wearer.

"Let's get out of here," Mel said, scooting backwards and pulling the pack as she went.

We crawled along the ground until we were against the side of the house and then crouched down until we were at the far end. Beanie waved us over to indicate all was clear. Mel swung the straps over her shoulders and we raced out of the yard, past Beanie, and across the baseball field in a bee-line for the road.

"Hey, wait up," Beanie shouted.

We slowed to a walk as we neared the bus stop to let him catch up.

We were on Tacoma Street walking to where we would catch the final bus that would take us across the Sellwood Bridge and back home.

Mel was tired of Beanie's badgering. "Look, no matter how many times you beg, we are not going to open this back-pack until we get somewhere safe!" He had been on her about it all the way from the Bybee bus stop.

Beanie was leading the way. He just wouldn't let it drop. He turned around and said, "But what's wrong with taking a peek if no one sits near us?"

Mel looked at me and shrugged. "Is he going to be like this all the way back?"

"I think so."

Beanie turned to us again and started walking backwards, "I know so. I won't let up all the way home."

I could see Mel was giving in. "Okay, but just a quick peek, and only if there is no one in the back half of the bus. I don't want them to see, or hear, a thing."

I looked to see if Beanie was finally happy, but his expression changed that line of thought. "What is it, Beanie?"

He pointed behind us. "You know that Fairlane you described? The Baby Blue one with the out-of-state plates the mystery man was driving? I think that's it."

We turned around and there it was. It had just turned off 17th onto Tacoma and was headed toward us.

"You mean the KGB agent!" Mel corrected. She grabbed my arm and yanked me into the street. "Come on, Beanie," she yelled.

We cut across Tacoma to the other side, evading a truck that swerved to miss us. Another car honked as we raced in front of it. The Fairlane screeched to a stop in the middle of Tacoma and the door flew open. The man jumped out and yelled, "Stop. Stop! Come back here!" He started to chase us and then must have decided he couldn't leave his car just sitting there. He jumped back in.

There was a gas station on the corner. We ran under the pump island, through the parking lot and around the side. I looked back as we cut behind the building. The Fairlane had turned into the station.

"Keep going!" I shouted.

The pavement behind the building dead-ended at a grassy lot. There was a big barrier that kept cars from continuing, but not one that we couldn't get around. We ran along the side of the next building that butted up to the service station and then cut back to 17th Street through a furniture store parking lot. At the corner of the building I looked down 17th toward Tacoma. I couldn't see the car.

"Come on." We ran across the street to an A&W restaurant on the other side and in the door. We went to the far end and grabbed the corner booth. It was one of those wraparound booths with continuous seating on three sides. Beanie slid in on one side and Mel and I on the other where we could see out the window. It provided a good view of 17th Street and the intersection with Tacoma.

We were sweaty and winded. It took a minute to catch our breath.

"What are we going to do?" Beanie finally asked.

"Keep down and watch the streets," I answered. "I'm sure he didn't see us come in."

Mel nudged me. "Look."

The car came down 17th Street. It slowed and then turned into the furniture store parking lot. It pulled into a spot. The man got out and walked to the street. We ducked down to make sure he couldn't see us.

"Yeah, that's him all right," I said. "The same guy as at the town meeting and on Iron Mountain."

We watched as he glanced up and down 17th Street, then turn around and walk to the back of the furniture store.

Beanie looked worried. "Think he'll come in here?"

"I have no idea, but he can't do anything if he does," I answered. "There are too many people around." It was early afternoon. The place wasn't packed, but there were enough customers to make us feel safe.

"Here he comes," Mel said.

The man walked back to his car, got in, backed out of the parking spot and pulled onto the street next to the lot. The car headed away from 17th Street and disappeared down the road.

"He's looking for us," I said.

"And I don't think he's going to give up until he finds us," Mel added. "He saw the backpack. He's probably figured out we have the debris."

"How'd he find us?" Beanie asked.

We didn't have a chance to think about that until now.

"He must have followed us to my old house," Mel suggested.

"That would have been way too hard to do, what with the transfers and all. I bet he was staking it out," Beanie said. "These spies know their business. He probably figured the debris was hidden there somewhere."

"Well," I pointed out, "we can't just go stand on a corner now and wait for a bus. What are we going to do?"

We all thought for a minute.

"I'll try Mrs. Crowley," I said. "Maybe she will venture out when I tell her it's an emergency. Do either of you have a dime?"

Mel pulled out her coin purse, dug around a piece of paper in it to find a dime and handed it to me. She put the purse back in her pocket.

"I'll be right back. Cross your fingers." I walked over to the payphone, which was near the front of the restaurant. I dialed Mrs. Crowley's phone number and let it ring for a while, but there was no answer. I walked back to the table.

"She had to be there, but wouldn't answer. I bet it's because she's tired of getting calls from all the reporters. Now, what do we do?"

Beanie jumped right in, "Well, you can forget my mom. It would be twenty questions all the way home. We'd never make it through her interrogation."

"Same with my mom," I added.

Mel looked at us. "Well, you know my mom is out."

It looked like we were stuck.

Then Mel said, "Wait. What about Mike?"

I looked at her. "What?"

She reached back into her pocket, pulled out the coin purse, opened the zipper and took out the sheet of paper.

"We'll call Mike." She turned to Beanie to explain. "We told you about him. He's the new teacher that saved us the first time when my bike chain broke." She waved the piece of paper in the air. "This is his number." She looked over at me. "Remember, Frankie? He said to call anytime for any reason. I'm thinking this is a pretty good one."

I agreed. "It may be the only way we can get home without getting the third degree."

Beanie leaned forward over the table. "So, what are you going to say?" He flashed his eyes and pretended he was Mel. "Hi, Mike, oh, it's Melanie. We need a favor from you. Well, you see, there's this spy after us because he wants the debris from an alien flying saucer we just happen to have and, well, we're not sure about this, but he might try to kill us to get it. So, can you pick us up?" He dropped the Mel impression and morphed back into Beanie.

Mel just looked at him like he was a complete idiot. "Unless you have a better idea, like reconsidering calling your mom, he's our only hope." She waited. "Come on, Beanie, what *is* the big plan?"

Beanie dropped his eyes. "Not my mom. Not any of our moms. Sorry, you're right." Then he looked up at us with a little grin. "But you have to admit, he would think it a pretty crazy story if you actually told him the truth."

Mel got up from the booth. "I'll think of something to tell him. I just hope he's home." She walked to the payphone, dropped in a dime and dialed his number. She stood out against the reflection of light coming through the glass doors on the tiled floor. He must have been home because we could see she was talking and making gestures as she explained. After a while she hung up and came back to the booth, sliding in next to me. "He'll be here in about half an hour."

Beanie and I looked at each other with relief.

"So, what did you say?" I asked.

"I told him we went to my old house to get some things of my dad's. That the new owners had called to let us know they found some of his stuff in the attic. I also said my mom couldn't drive because she was still pretty upset about what happened at the meeting, so we had decided to make an adventure out of it by taking the bus, but were now stuck. We hadn't realized how much the buses cost and didn't have enough money for all three of us to get home."

"That's pretty good," Beanie confessed. "But didn't he ask why Frankie or my parents didn't come out."

"No, because I reminded him that he had offered to help me and my mom, and I really needed him to pick us up. I said we'd figure something out if he couldn't do it. But he told me he would be glad to."

I put my arm around her. "Mel, I'm amazed. You can whip up a really good lie pretty fast."

She leaned over, gave me a big kiss on the lips, and looked me in the eyes. "Scary, isn't it?"

Beanie stood up from the booth. "As far as I'm concerned, you're both scary." He dug into his pockets, pulled out some change and counted it. "Well, we've got half an hour."

I looked up at him. "What are you going to do?"

"Get a cheeseburger and a root beer float. I'm starved, and if there's any chance I'm going to die today, I don't want it to be on an empty stomach."

"Well, I'm not big on your logic," Mel said, "but none of us have eaten since breakfast, so that's not a bad idea." She reached into her pocket and brought out some bills. "Get the same for Frankie and me. I'll buy. While you're ordering the food, we'll keep an eye out for our KGB friend."

Chapter 22— Saved

We finished eating and were now sitting back to let the food settle. Cheeseburger baskets, wrappers, and empty float glasses were spread across the table as the result of our efforts.

We only saw the Russian agent's car one more time. It was heading east on Tacoma Street, but it never did come back down 17th.

"I'm sure he's still out there," Beanie said, grabbing one last abandoned fry from Mel's basket and wolfing it down. "He's probably staking out the area from somewhere, waiting for us to come out of hiding. I've seen lots of spy movies and that's what they do."

A Cherry Red Ford Mustang turned onto 17th Street from Tacoma.

"Wow, check out that Mustang," I said. "Isn't it cool? Ford just came out with it in '64. That's the '65. It has that neat two-plus-two fastback design they released last year. Look at the sleek lines on that car." It pulled into the A&W parking lot.

Mel said matter-of-factly, "That's Mike."

I looked at her, not quite sure I heard her right. "What?"

"You were too busy looking at the car to notice who was driving."

"You mean we're going home in that sweet ride? This is great."

Mike came through the door and looked around.

Mel waved to him and he walked over to the booth. "So here are the wayward travelers."

"Hi, Mike." Mel slid out of the booth and stood up. "You know Frankie, and this is our friend, Beanie."

Beanie gave a little wave. "Hey, Mike. Nice to meet you."

Beanie and I got out of the booth. Mel grabbed the backpack from where it had been stowed on Beanie's side.

Mike said, "Well, come on. Let's get you kids back home."

We headed for the door.

I had to ask. "What happened to your truck?"

"Oh, I borrowed it from someone for the move. I drive a Mustang."

"So I noticed."

All I could talk about on the way back was the sweet ride. Beanie and I had the pack with us in the back seat. Mel rode shotgun up front. I leaned forward between the bucket seats to drool over the console. I reeled off the whole history of the Mustang, how it originally used the Falcon's frame, and the various options of the '64 when it first came out.

Mike was impressed. "You sure know a lot about it."

"I'd love to have one. What did you pay?"

"Just over twenty-four-hundred with the upgrades."

Geez, that's a lot. I wish I could save up to get one. Maybe I can by the time I learn to drive. Is this the two-barrel V8?"

"No, I went for the four-barrel two-eighty-nine. It delivers two-hundred and twenty horses."

"Wow. And you went for the optional four-on-the-floor manual transmission. Way cool."

We were in Lake Oswego now, turning onto Iron Mountain. Mike shifted gears, with both the car and our conversation. "So, I have to ask you kids, what's really up?"

Mel looked over at him. "What do you mean?"

He gave her a quick glance and shifted again. "You weren't really stranded. If you were out of money, I wouldn't have seen all that spent food on the table."

Beanie and I looked at each other. *What do we say?*

Beanie tried his best. "Oh...I, uh...had some money I didn't know about."

Mike didn't answer at first, then he gave us the tone. "Want to try again?"

Mel looked back to us with a 'what do we do' expression on her face. Finally, she said, "There was someone after us."

"After you? Like in trying to get you?"

Mel kept going. "It's hard to explain. There's been some man following us. He drove by on Iron Mountain when you were helping us on the bridge. You were busy putting our bikes in the truck, so didn't see him. We think he tampered with my bike chain and was trying to catch us out on the road. Then he showed up over on Tacoma and 17th and chased us. We didn't know what to do. We couldn't go to the bus stop because he might find us. So we called you."

"And why would he be doing all this?" His tone was skeptical.

Wow. Once you get into this, how do you stop? "That's the part that's hard to explain," I said. "We think we have something he wants."

He nodded toward the back seat. "Is that what's in the backpack?"

Mel took over. "We can't, I mean, I wish we could tell you more, but we just can't."

"If you knew the whole story," Beanie added, "you'd just think we were making it up anyway."

We were coming toward the turn-off for Lakeview. The entrance to the Hunt Club came up on our right and Mike swerved into it.

"Where are you going?" Mel questioned.

"To get to the bottom of this." He drove to the far end of the empty parking lot, across a grassy area, and around the corner of the horse barn. He pulled to a stop behind it. "You see, your problem," he reached under the seat, brought out a knife and pointed it at Mel's throat, "is you've been worried about the wrong guy. I was the one who tampered with your chain."

Mel's eyes grew with the terror of the knife at her throat. "So, *you're* the Russian agent."

"I expected it would be much harder to gain your confidence in order to find out where the material was hidden. I certainly didn't expect you to deliver it to me."

The terror in Mel's eyes subsided into scorn. "Keep that in mind while you hold a knife to my throat."

"I don't want to hurt you, but what's in that backpack is vital to my country. Your Air Force has the spaceship. We need that material to advance our own capabilities. We can't allow your country to get ahead of us. That man you mentioned; I'm sure he was from your government. They don't want us to get this technology. Your death is of little consequence, if necessary, to make sure we do."

He looked back at Beanie and me. His eyes were cold and hard. "So, don't try to be heroes, boys. Sit still or you'll know what a lot of blood looks like, and it's not a pleasant sight when it's your own." He turned to Mel, bringing the knife up so the razor-sharp point hovered close to her eyes. "Get out of the car, close the door, and come around to my side. Try to run and your friends get to see what their insides look like."

Mel slowly opened the door and stepped out. She glanced down at me through the window as she closed the door, an apologetic look in her eyes, and mouthed the words 'I'm sorry'. She walked around the front of the car. Mike opened his door and got out. He spun Mel around, forcefully grabbed her by the back of her neck, and shoved her toward the rear of the car.

I wanted to look, but knew I had to stay still. "What's he doing, Beanie? Can you see him in the rearview mirror?" My heart pounded in my chest and my body felt weak. I took deep breaths to keep from passing out.

Beanie's voice trembled with fear. "Just a little, but I can't tell what he's doing."

We heard the trunk open and close. Mike walked Mel toward the front of the car on my side. He called to us. "Get out of the car, boys, and leave the pack."

I pushed the passenger seat forward and tried to get out. My legs didn't want to work at first. I had to pull myself out.

Beanie followed. Mel was cringing from the force of Mike's grip. His hand looked huge around her delicate neck. Tears from the pain formed in her eyes, but there was also a hint of defiance in them. Mike had the knife tucked into his belt and held some coiled rope in the other hand.

He nodded to me. "Put your hands behind your head and lock your fingers together." I did what he said. "And you." He threw the rope at Beanie. "Carry this." He took the knife back out of his belt.

"What are you going to do with us?" I asked.

"That depends on you. Try anything and the girl gets a new look."

The knife had a long, curved blade. The sun flashed off its cool steel. A chill went through my body at the thought of what that knife could do to Mel.

"Beanie, let's just do what he says and maybe we'll get out of this okay."

"I'm all with that," Beanie blurted back.

Mike motioned with the tip of the knife. "Into the barn and don't bother calling out. I've been watching this place for a while and it's hardly used, especially this side. No one would come, and if someone did, well, you would be responsible for their death."

We walked through the entrance. The smell of horse manure and mildewed straw hit me. It took a moment to adjust my eyes to the dark interior. Wooden stalls lined both sides of the main walkway that ran down the center of the building. Dim overhead lighting cast shadows across the rough concrete floor. A few harnesses, halters, and other equipment hung from pegs on the posts and walls. At the far end of the walkway I could see the entrance to the indoor arena. The whole place seemed empty, except for the whinnying of a few horses in the distance. A corridor ran along the wall to our left. It led to two more walkways that were parallel to the main one.

"Turn left and move slowly," Mike ordered, his voice cold and demanding.

We walked down the corridor along the wall, past the first walkway, and stopped where it dead-ended at the last one.

"Keep going," Mike said.

We headed down the walkway and past a few stalls.

"Turn into that stall on your left."

The gate was open and the stall empty except for a layer of dirty straw bedding on the floor.

"Go to the far wall, turn around and get on your knees."

A piercing scream sounded behind us. I quickly turned to see Mel wrench from Mike's grip with a sudden twist. She grabbed a two-by-four that had been leaning against a post and swung it at Mike's head. He ducked, putting his arm up to divert the blow. Her momentum threw her off balance. In one motion Mike made a quick spin move and launched his foot against the side of Mel's face knocking her across the rough concrete. I started toward him.

Mike pointed the knife at me. "Don't try it, hero. Step back!"

Mel lay still, sprawled across the floor. She moaned and then slowly pushed herself into a sitting position. Her knee was scraped and bleeding. She rubbed the side of her face, already turning red from the force of Mike's kick.

He grabbed her arm and dragged her over to the stall, where he stood over her. "You're just as strong-willed as your father."

Mel looked up at him, fury building in her eyes. "*You* killed my dad!"

"He should have turned over the material. He was stupid to think it was more important than his life. Now, get up."

Mel slowly rose to her feet.

Mike motioned to the stall with the knife. "Get in there."

Mel limped to the stall entrance and stopped.

"Go!" Mike rammed his foot into the small of her back, slamming her into the far wall. She crumbled to the straw bedding on the floor.

He flipped the knife point toward Beanie. "Now you. Get over by your friend."

Beanie went over by Mel and kneeled down to check on her.

I followed, but Mike suddenly grabbed me from behind, yanked back on my head to expose my neck, and pushed the knife tip against my throat. He threatened Mel. "Try anything like that again and you'll watch these boys die before I kill you."

I felt warm blood trickling down my neck.

Mel's eyes widened. "Stop! It was my fault. Don't hurt Frankie!"

Mike pushed me into the stall just as a loud whack reverberated through the air. I turned to see his head jerk forward. The knife flew into the stall and he slumped to the floor. The mystery man appeared, a flat-headed shovel in his hands.

I backed into the stall worried I would be next. I reached up to my neck. When I took my hand away blood covered my fingertips.

The man took a step forward. "It's okay. I'm here to help you."

Mel grabbed the knife from the floor and jumped up next to Beanie and me. She pointed the blade at him. "How do we know that?"

"You mean besides the fact I just knocked out the man who was probably going to kill you?"

"Yeah, besides that," Beanie demanded.

He looked at Mel. "Then how about this—I was with your dad at the crash site. I helped him get the material out."

Chapter 23— Roswell

"Okay? Can you put the knife down now? This guy isn't dead. We need to tie him up before he comes to." He laid the shovel on the ground and picked up the rope Mike had dropped. He looked at Mel, waiting for her.

"You were with my dad?" Mel was still trying to absorb what he had said.

He took a few more steps toward the stall. "My name is Tom Richardson. I'll tell you all about it later, but right now we need to tie this guy up and get out of here." He nodded at what Mel still held in her hand. "The knife?"

Mel looked down at the blade, which was still pointed at Tom. She slowly lowered it to her side.

Tom leaned down, grabbed Mike by the arms and pulled him into the stall. He rolled him onto his stomach. Blood oozed from the back of Mike's head. Tom took the rope and tied his hands behind his back. When he was done, he looked up and reached out to Mel. "I need to cut a section off this rope so I can tie his feet."

She looked down at the knife in her hand wondering what to do.

"It's okay, Mel," I said. I walked over to her and took the knife. "He's here to help us."

I handed it to Tom.

He took it, cut the rope, and then handed it back. "Hold it while I tie his feet together."

He moved to Mike's feet and pulled them together and tied them with the rope. When finished he said, "That should hold him. I'm parked out front. Let's get going."

I gave him the knife and said, "We need to get the pack from Mike's car."

Tom looked over to me as he got up. "I'm guessing that pack has the spaceship material, right?"

"Yes, it was hidden at Mel's old house. That's what we were doing there."

Tom nodded. "Then we had better get moving."

Mel finally snapped out of it. "Hold on." She knelt next to Mike, searched his pockets and pulled something out, showing us. "His keys, just in case, so he can't go anywhere if he gets loose."

We grabbed the backpack from Mike's Mustang and ran to Tom's car. Beanie and Mel jumped in the back and I got in front. Tom started the engine. "We need to go somewhere safe to talk. A place where we won't be seen. I'm sure Major Burnham has quite a task force looking for you, the pack, and probably me at this point."

I knew right where to go. "Take a left onto Iron Mountain and then across the railroad bridge. You know, where you saw us yesterday when Mike had the truck."

Tom answered, "I remember. Back then I was trying to figure out who this guy was and if he was involved in this thing in any way. I guess I got my answer."

We headed down Iron Mountain. I looked over at Tom. "How did you find us, back at the Hunt Club?"

"I saw you run into the A&W. The way you reacted when I tried to stop you on the street, I knew it was useless to go in and explain myself. So, I acted like I had lost you, and then parked nearby to watch what you did next."

I heard Beanie say from the back, "See, I told you guys so. Just like in the movies!"

Tom continued, "I followed you when you got a ride with Mike. Who is he anyway? I'm not thinking one of our own, the way he was holding that knife to your throat."

"He's a Russian spy," I explained.

Tom was surprised at this news. "Doesn't look like our crash debris is much of a secret anymore. When we're done here, I'll hit a payphone and make an anonymous call to the police. Let them know the major would be very interested in who's tied up in the horse barn."

We were approaching the bridge.

"Is this the spot?" he asked.

"Yeah, turn right here," I told him. When he got up on the bridge I said, "Okay, just across the other side of the bridge is a dirt road on the right. The road goes back far enough that no one will see us."

Beanie realized where I was talking about. "Yeah, it's a good place. Frankie and I used to go here all the time to play. We've never seen anyone else."

209

As soon as he took the dirt road, there was tall brush on either side of us and we were soon out of view. He bumped along the road for a few hundred feet. The railroad tracks ran parallel on the right. I could just barely see them through the trees and undergrowth. We came out into an opening at the base of a gully that rose on our left and in front of us. There was a large flat area where Tom turned the car around so we would be facing the way we came in.

"Is this the only way in here?" he asked.

"Yeah. I mean, someone could walk down from the hillside behind us, but a car can't make it because there isn't a road."

"Good." He put the car in park, turned off the engine, and shifted his body so he could see Mel and Beanie in the back.

He looked at Mel. "Your father and I have kept in touch ever since Roswell. Not often, but we always made sure we knew how to get ahold of each other and where each other was. You experience something like that crash site and it ties you together for the rest of your lives. Over the years we have managed to meet clandestinely to discuss what we saw there. It was kind of like therapy for us because it had created this bond. Well, the last time we met, your dad seemed distracted. I asked what was going on, but he wouldn't admit to anything. I don't think he wanted to alarm me. He asked that I keep an eye on you and your mom if anything ever happened to him. I think it was his way of letting on that he was being watched. It was almost like he knew what was going to happen. I gave him my word. When I found out he died in that car accident, I had to wonder. I've kept a pretty close eye on the two of you ever since."

Beanie leaned into the conversation. "It was faked. The Russians were trying to get the location of the debris out of him."

"They killed him and made it look like a car accident," I added.

"No wonder he hid the pack. He must have known they would get to him eventually."

Mel asked, "Were you the man who met my dad at the restaurant? The major was trying to get information out of my mom. He said a man gave my dad a package. Someone overheard them talking. That's how the major eventually found out."

Beanie added, "And because they've been infiltrated by more spies than a James Bond movie, the Russians found out."

"Yes," Tom answered, "that was me. I'm surprised they haven't figured out who I am, though that may not be the case any longer, after coming here."

"What made you come?" Mel asked.

"I live in Redmond, up by Seattle in Washington. The UFO sightings made the news up there and I saw the coverage on television. I knew you had moved to Lake Oswego only a few months ago and where your house was." We all raised our eyebrows at that. He saw our looks and said, "Like I told you, I promised your dad I'd keep an eye on you, so when you moved, I wanted to know where. When that first sighting was reported, and I found out it was here, so close to your new house, well, it just seemed like too much of a coincidence."

211

Mel, Beanie and I exchanged knowing glances, but didn't say anything. *Our UFO hoax had brought him here and it saved our lives!*

Tom continued, "I left that night to come out and see if they had anything to do with the material from the crash site. I found out about the town meeting, so decided to attend in case that turned up anything. That's when I saw you and your mother there."

"And we saw you," I added. "We could tell you were watching us. We didn't know who you were at first, but then we thought you might be the KGB agent we found out was after us. That's why we ran away from you and into the A&W."

"Well, that helps explain your reaction," he said.

"So why did you hide in the back at the town meeting when the major showed up?" I asked.

He looked at Mel. "Your father told me all about this Lieutenant Burnham who had interrogated him. I knew right away who the major was when he walked onto the stage. I also had my confirmation that somehow this did have to do with the material we took. I hid in the back of the crowd just in case. I've worked hard to keep under the radar. Ever since the town meeting, I've been trying to find a way to talk with you or your mom without exposing my identity. I'm sure the major has quite a surveillance set-up in place. Especially around your house."

Beanie broke in. "Okay...I can't stand it any longer. Tell us about the crashed spaceship. Were there aliens?"

Tom looked at Beanie for a moment, seeming to be going back to that place in time. "Yes, there were aliens."

"Wow!" Beanie's eyes widened. "What did they look like?"

Mel jumped in. "How about letting Tom start from the beginning? I want to know about my dad."

Tom settled into his seat. "It was a three-day weekend, what with July 4th being on a Friday. I decided to go camping in the desert to look for arrowheads. I knew a good spot about forty miles northwest of Roswell. That evening in camp, this is on July 4th, a big thunderstorm rolled through. Huge thunderclaps and lots of lightning. It was late in the evening. I was getting the camp ready to weather the storm when I saw something coming out of the clouds toward me. I thought it was a meteor. It had a brilliant blue-gray color and was really intense. It went right over my campsite. I then realized it had to be something else. What, I didn't know, but not a meteor. It crashed close to camp. I decided I would try to find it the next morning. I couldn't get to sleep that night. I kept trying to figure out what it was.

"The next morning I was up well before dawn. I had marked the direction of the impact the night before, so I got dressed, grabbed a flashlight and headed out. It was just getting light when I came upon the crash site. I topped a small rise and found myself standing on the edge of a gully looking down on what I first thought was an airplane. But the wings were different, hardly even there, really, and more crescent-shaped. It didn't look like any airplanes I had ever seen. The front was crushed in where it had hit the rocky side of the gully. Then I saw a man kneeling over something near the craft." He looked at Mel. "It was your father. He was kneeling over a small body. I thought it was a child."

"An alien!" Beanie deduced, shifting in his seat with anticipation.

Tom didn't acknowledge him. He was reliving the experience. "I worked my way down into the gully. There were two more bodies in the distance. I could see a large gash in the side of the ship. I figured they had crawled out of it and died. I walked toward your father. He looked up when he heard me coming and then back down at the alien. He didn't say anything. Then the alien's hand moved. *It was still alive.* It handed something to your father and he put it in his satchel."

"What was it?" Mel asked. We were all leaning on his story.

"I don't know. Still don't. When I got there, I knelt next to him. Your father didn't look up at me, but simply said, 'He's dying.'"

"What did it look like, the alien, I mean?" Beanie asked.

"Human...but different. Small, maybe a little over four feet tall. It had a metallic-looking bodysuit on. But the eyes were the most amazing thing. They were large and dark, with no pupils, but they weren't daunting. There was a kindness in them I can't really describe. When I looked into them it was like I could hear the alien's thoughts and feel its pain. All I can remember is the alien wasn't worried about dying, but was worried about us...humanity. He was so weak these were really just sensations I felt. To this day I'm not convinced they really happened...but I think your father was."

"Why?" Mel asked.

"Let me explain. Your father had arrived at the crash site well before I got there. It was a year later, when we met for

214

the first time since the incident, he told me how. He was with an archeology expedition from his school at Texas Tech. They were using the three-day weekend to survey an Indian site in the area. They all saw the ship come down the night before and some of them agreed to go look for it. Your father left earlier than the rest. He felt he knew right where the ship had gone down and didn't want to wait for the rest of the group to get ready. That's how he made it there before everyone else. So, he had spent quite a while with the alien. I am sure they were communicating when I arrived.

"It was a little while later that other members from his group showed up. We were all still examining the crash site and collecting pieces from it when someone shouted and pointed to the south. Off in the distance we could see a cloud of dust reflecting the morning sun. We figured it was the police or someone from the military base. Your father pulled me aside. He told me I had to take his satchel and get it out of there. He knew his group would be detained and they would take it away from him. But he was sure that I could get away. He gave me this really odd look and said, 'We can't let them take this!' I asked him why. He wouldn't tell me, but I think the alien had communicated with him, like the way it did when I looked into its eyes."

"Mental telepathy," I suggested.

"What's that?" Beanie asked.

Mel answered. "It's done with the mind. You communicate with thought, not words."

"Oh, so that's how my mom does it. Or maybe it's just the looks, but I swear I know what she's thinking every time she gives me one."

Mel gave Beanie a hard stare. "Can you tell what I am thinking?" She turned back to Tom so he could continue.

"Your dad pushed the satchel into my arms and told me there was a place in Roswell we could meet. It was a cafe. Katy's Cafe. I still remember the address...118 North Main...like everything else I remember from the crash. It's all fixed in my mind as if it just happened yesterday." He paused for a moment, thinking about that. "We agreed to meet one week later. We thought that would be enough time for things to die down. He wanted me to hang onto the satchel until then. He said it was very important. We could see the vehicles were getting closer. He pleaded for me to go. I climbed up the slope in a spot where no one could see me, went to my camp, threw my gear in the jeep, and took a back road I knew through a low ravine where my jeep's dust wouldn't be spotted."

"What was in the satchel?" I asked.

He looked at the backpack between Mel and Beanie. "I don't think it will be too long before you see for yourself. But there was one thing in it I found very interesting."

"I want to look now," Beanie said. He reached for the backpack.

"We don't have time," Mel said. "Tom needs to get to a phone and make that call."

"I don't want to see that stuff again, anyway," Tom said. "You have to understand, my whole life changed because of that crash." He continued with his story. "The satchel had all sorts of different material in it, but the most amazing thing was a small device of some sort. I'm sure this is what the alien handed to your father. It's about the size of a cigarette pack, but thinner. It was made from a very smooth metal, black in color. It didn't reflect light, but seemed rather to absorb it. I couldn't figure out how the device worked. There were no buttons or any obvious way to operate it."

"What was it?" Mel asked.

"I have no idea, but I'm sure your dad did. A week later I was waiting for him in a booth at the back of Katy's. I was facing the door so I could see him enter. When he came in, he crossed to the back of the cafe and sat down opposite me. The first thing he asked was if I still had the satchel. I took it off the seat next to me and handed it to him. He held it in both hands as if he wanted to make sure it never got out of his sight again. We sat and talked about the crash. Then he told me about his interrogation and the men in black suits who threatened him and your mom, and how they had torn his house apart looking for this satchel and what was in it. I couldn't believe what he was telling me. I could see him fingering the buckle on the flap. He really wanted to open it and check the contents, but knew he couldn't because of where we were. Then he asked if the device was still in the satchel. I told him yes and he showed a look of relief."

Beanie leaned forward and said, "I bet the alien told him what it was and how to make it work, you know, through his mind."

"I agree," Tom said, "but that's the last your dad and I ever spoke of it. We decided to meet again in a year. When we did, I tried to bring it up with him a couple of times, but every time he avoided the issue. And it's been that way every time we've met since. He would never answer any questions about the device. All I know is it was very important to him."

"Now it looks like we will never know," I said.

Tom gave Mel a sad look. "I'm sorry about your dad. He was a great man. Ever since Roswell I could tell he was driven by something he needed to do. It looks like he didn't have a chance to accomplish it...whatever *it* was."

"I wish I knew," Mel replied.

"I'd better get going to make that phone call. I can't give you a ride home. I don't want to take the chance of getting caught."

"We can walk the tracks back," I said. "No one will see us that way and then we can cut in at the end of Springbrook. We'll be safe."

"What are you going to do?" Mel asked.

Tom looked off in the distance. "Move, I guess. I can't take the chance of staying in Redmond in case they know who I am now. Don't worry about me. We'll see each other again in the future. I'll make sure of it. I promised your dad I would keep track of you and your mom and I'm not about to break that promise."

I opened the car door and got out. Mel and Beanie followed with the pack.

"Be careful, Tom," I told him, "and thanks for saving us."

"Yeah, thanks, Tom," Beanie said.

I closed the door. Mel walked around to Tom's side. Beanie and I followed.

He rolled the window down. "I just want you to know, your dad would be proud of you."

She leaned in and gave him a kiss on the cheek. "Thank you."

Tom smiled with the kiss. "You kids be careful. I don't know what you'll do with that debris, but the Air Force is still after it and they won't stop until they recover it."

"Yeah," Beanie added, "and Russia, and probably a few dozen other countries by now that we don't even know about yet."

"We'll be careful," Mel said. "Bye."

Tom started the car and slowly drove down the dirt road. We watched him until he disappeared where the road curved through the brush.

Mel looked at me and reached up to touch my neck. The blood had stopped flowing, but by her look, I must have had a pretty good cut there. "It's not real bad, but what are you going to tell your mom?"

"Oh, I guess I'll just tell her I cut myself shaving." We all laughed. I didn't have a hair on my face yet.

"Come on," Beanie said. "Let's get home so we can look at that debris."

Mel swung the pack over her shoulders and we worked our way down the bank and through the underbrush to the railroad tracks. We came clear of the brush, climbed a small slope and walked the railroad tracks toward home.

"I need to change when we get back," Mel said. "Look at me."

I gave her a good looking over. She had a red, slightly swollen spot on the side of her face, her hair was all tussled with straw in it, she had a scrape on her knee caked with dried blood, dirt covered her sweatshirt, and her shorts had

a brown stain on the butt from landing in a pile of horse manure. "Hmmm…I don't see anything different from how you
normally look."

Mel hit me in the shoulder. "Perv!"

I smiled. "Let's meet at my place after you change. We can
check out the debris down in my room."

"It's about time!" Beanie added.

We picked up our pace because we all wanted to see what
debris from an alien spaceship looked like.

Chapter 24 — Debris

Beanie and I waited impatiently in my room. The bedroom door was open so we could see out to the sliding glass door of the carport where Mel would come in. I had cleared my desk of all the accumulated junk and turned on the gooseneck lamp so we would have a good place to look at the debris. Mom and Suzie were upstairs in the sewing room busy working on Suzie's new clothes for school, so I knew they wouldn't be a problem. Dad was at work.

Beanie was currently going through my records to create a playlist for our viewing. 'Mood music' as he put it. He finally put on *Time Won't Let Me* by the Outsiders. I think mostly because it starts out with the lyrics: 'I can't wait forever, even though you want me to...' He was now pacing the room, very unusual for him because it was almost a form of exercise. "What is taking her so long?" he asked.

"I don't know," I answered. "But she *is* female and women always take a long time whenever a mirror is involved."

We heard the carport door slide open, and then close.

I looked out to see Mel walking to my room. She was all cleaned up and holding a wooden box.

"What's that and where's the backpack?" Beanie asked.

She came into the bedroom and I closed the door behind her.

"I didn't think it would be a good idea to carry Dad's backpack down the street, so I put everything in here." There was a difference in the tone of her voice, like she was troubled by something but trying to hide it.

I pointed to the desk and she set the wooden box down on it.

"Hey, are you okay?" I asked, reaching out and rubbing her arm.

She didn't look up to meet my eyes, tracing the outline of a flower on the box as an excuse not to. "Yeah. Why?"

"I don't know, I guess you just sound a little upset or something."

"You must be imagining things. I'm fine."

I shrugged. "If you say so," and looked at the wooden box. It was painted just like the box that was buried. "Your dad made this one too?"

She finally looked up at me. "Yeah, he wanted me to have one for my room. It's a hope box."

"Well, I *hope* we can look at the debris now," Beanie said, as he put on the record *Cool Jerk* by the Capitols.

"Not again, Beanie! How often do we need to hear that song?" Mel asked.

"Hey, it hit number seven on Billboard and is ranked as one of the top '66 songs. All the with-it stations have it in first rotation and are spinning it like crazy. It's popular, and besides, I like it. I'm not playing it any more than they are."

Mel frowned at him, opened the box and carefully tilted it over so the debris came out on the desk. She put the box on the floor and sat in the chair. Beanie and I moved in to kneel on either side of her.

All sorts of different material sat on the desk, but I couldn't see the device Tom had mentioned. "Where's the gadget Tom told us about?"

Mel looked up at me. "It wasn't in the pack. I've been try-ing to figure out why. At first I was thinking Dad might have been worried about putting it outside in the buried box. You know, because it might take a long time to be found and he didn't want it exposed to the elements."

"That makes sense," I agreed.

"Yes. But then I thought, he may also want it in a really safe place. Just in case. Remember when Tom told us my dad didn't want this to fall into the wrong hands? Maybe that's why it's not here."

"Oh, that makes even more sense," I agreed.

"Either way," Beanie said, "that's a real bummer. I *so* wanted to see that thing."

I looked down at the rest of the debris. "There's nothing we can do about it now. Let's check out what is here."

There were small bits and pieces of debris from the space-ship: some of the foil-like material in various shapes and sizes; a couple of struts that looked like little 'I' beams with squiggles of some sort on them; a few strands of the quartz-like material the major had mentioned; a couple oval pieces of clear, flexible plastic-looking stuff; and a bunch of little flat rectangle things that had very small metallic lines on them.

Mel picked up some of the foil material and held it out in the palm of her hand. "Beanie, I want to show you something." I could see Mel's eyes glowing.

"Okay," he said.

"See how smooth it is and not a wrinkle on it? Put out your hand." He did. She laid the foil on his palm. "Now crumple it up and drop it onto the desk." He wadded it up, making a tight fist and then dropped it on the desk. It sat for a second in a crumpled wad and then slowly unfolded, flowing back into its original form without a wrinkle showing.

Mel looked at me. "See, just like I had remembered."

"Wow, that's really neat!" Beanie said.

I picked up the biggest piece on the desk. It was paper-thin and very light. Mel and Beanie each grabbed a piece. We all inspected them, doing little tests. I tried to tear it, but that was impossible. I took a pair of scissors out of the desk and tried to cut it. I put as much force on the scissor handles as I could. The blades just slid back off the edge. I had Mel and Beanie hold the piece so I could put more pressure on the scissors, but I couldn't make any headway. There wasn't even a scratch on the foil.

"This stuff is really strong," I said.

Mel added, "This is way beyond any metal I've ever seen, if that's what it even is."

Beanie put down his foil and went over to the record player. In just a few seconds *California Dreaming* by The Mommas and the Pappas filled the room.

He slid back up to the desk. "I need to concentrate and I can't do it without a little background music." He picked up one of the quartz filament strands. At one end there was a thicker tube a little bigger than a piece of cooked spaghetti. About half way to the other end, the tube split into a dozen tiny strands. "Look at this tubing. See how flexible it is?" He twisted and turned the tubing into different shapes. He looked at the large end. "This isn't a tube at all. It's solid and it looks like glass. He moved it around under the lamp to see it better. When he pointed the large end to the light bulb a pattern of different colored dots appeared on the desk's surface.

I tapped Mel on the shoulder. "Did you see that?"

Mel looked up at Beanie. "Do that again. Point the big end at the light."

Beanie held it near the bulb. The dozen small ends all glowed, but each was a different color.

"See that," Mel observed, "how the light is broken out into different colors for each small strand?" She grabbed one and looked into the end. She squinted at the bright light coming from it.

I could see a small pinpoint of blue dance around her eye. "Mel, remember what Major Burnham said? He thinks it was used to transmit information. It could replace wires. Imagine what that would mean. I can see how this stuff is wanted by all those countries."

"Ya think?" Beanie kidded.

I picked up the strut from the desk. It was really light. "Look at these markings. They look like characters of some sort."

Mel leaned against me to get a better look. "They're like hieroglyphics."

"Like what?" Beanie asked.

225

"Hieroglyphics...symbols that represent words or meanings." She took the strut from my hand so she could look at the symbols better. "Dad studied them as part of his work on ancient civilizations." She examined the markings. Then she looked up at Beanie and me. "I think we are looking at alien writing." We all stared at the markings along the inside of the 'I' beam.

"What do you think it says?" I asked.

"Take me to your leader," Beanie said in a robot-like voice.

I reached across Mel and hit him on the shoulder.

Mel ignored us. "Do you guys realize we are looking at a written language from another world? Gives me goosebumps just thinking about it. There actually is intelligent life out there."

I picked up a strut and studied it again, turning it in my hands. The color of the writing had a purple tinge to it and changed slightly as the light hit it from different angles. "Why don't they just come forward?" I said. "You know, land on the White House lawn or something."

"Oh, I'm sure that would go over big," Beanie said. "We'd probably just blow them out of the air before they even got close."

Mel reflected on this. "Beanie's right. I bet they don't think we're ready yet. Mankind wouldn't be able to handle it." She paused for a moment. "Maybe someday we will."

Beanie picked up the small, rectangular wafer from the debris pile. "So, what's this?" He held it under the light so we could all get a good look. It was really thin and made from some sort of plastic-looking material. He turned it over in his hand. Both sides had very small metallic lines on their surfaces in intricate patterns. The lines originated at different points on the wafer, and then spread out parallel to each other until they ended at other points where more lines came in to meet them. One of the edges had a slot along it, like it could be plugged into something.

"What do you think it is?" I asked.

"No idea," she answered. "It looks like some sort of component from the ship, maybe used to help run it."

Mel picked up a piece of the clear looking plastic material and studied it. She moved it around looking at it from different angles. It was oval and flexible. She held it up to her eye like a lens from a pair of glasses and looked around the room. Suddenly her eyes grew large. "Guys, you have to check this out. Grab a piece of this." When we each had a piece of the material, she reached over and turned out the lamp. It was pitch black in the room with only a trace of light filtering in from the small window high on the wall in the back of my bedroom.

"Can you see anything?" she asked.

"Just barely," I answered.

Mel said, "Now hold it up to your eye like you saw me do."

I put it up to my eye and suddenly I could see the whole room. Not like daylight, but a whole lot better than without looking through the material. It was like seeing things at the very first light of dawn. I could make out shapes, but couldn't see detail. Everything had an orangish tint to it. "Wow, that's really cool." This coming from Beanie. He had moved across the room and was looking back at us. "I can see you guys when I look through this, but when I take it away, I can't see you at all."

"How do you think it works?" I asked.

"It must somehow collect whatever light is in the room and enhance it. But how it does that, who knows."

I turned the gooseneck lamp back on.

"Imagine what our military could do with this ability if they could figure out how to make it work," I said.

"No wonder they want to get this debris."

"And the Russians," Beanie added. "I'm sure that what this stuff does has leaked out to them just like everything else. No wonder they would be willing to kill for it."

We absorbed ourselves in the debris for a while longer, inspecting each piece and discussing what it could be. We agreed on one thing: it was way more advanced than anything we had ever seen or heard of before.

I looked at the clock. "Wow, we've been playing with this stuff for over an hour."

Mel stood up. "I'd better put it away. Mom almost didn't let me come over, so I have to get back." She looked at us with a set focus. "Now, I'm going to hide this debris and I don't want you guys to have a clue where. You know, just in case. I need to be the only one that knows where it is. I already have a good hiding spot figured out."

"You sure that's a good idea?" I asked.

She put everything back in the box. "Yes, I'm sure. I already thought it through and it makes sense. It won't take long to hide. Why don't you both meet me at my place in about fifteen minutes? I should be done by then. We can go to my room and figure out what to do with this stuff."

I gave Mel a look of concern. "I'm not sure I like this."

"Don't worry. It'll be fine." She kissed me. "We'd better meet in my driveway, otherwise Mom may not let me have you over."

I watched her leave. She closed the sliding glass door behind her and gave me a smile through it before disappearing from view.

Chapter 25 — Switch

Beanie and I rounded the corner of the hedge. Mel was already waiting for us at the bottom of her driveway. I expected her to be, otherwise Beanie and I might have known where the debris was hidden.

I gave her a look. "Fifteen minutes, huh?"

She smiled. "Well, it didn't take that long after all."

We walked up the driveway to the front door. Mel opened it and turned to us, "You guys wait in the living room while I check in with my mom."

I led the way inside. I suddenly felt a sharp blow to the back of my head and fell to the living room floor. Someone fell on top of me. It was Beanie. Then Mel ran over to us, not sure what just happened. The door slammed shut. Mel turned to the door and screamed.

I looked up to see Mike pointing a gun at us, a deadly-looking silencer fitted to the end of the barrel. Dried blood ran across the right side of his face in grotesque, dark red lines.

He gave Mel a repulsive grin and waved the gun at her. "Nice move on the keys, but still not smart enough to check the car for weapons."

Mel jumped to her feet. "Where's my mom!"

"In the kitchen, all nicely trussed up on a chair. She's been very well-mannered while waiting for you. Pretty much let me have the run of the place."

Mel raced into the kitchen and we followed. Her mom was bound to a chair by the breakfast table. Her hands were tied together behind its back and her ankles to the legs. A rag was firmly knotted around her mouth. Her eyes bulged at the sight of her daughter. She tried to talk through the rag.

Mel fell to her knees by the chair and wrapped her arms around her mother. "Mom, Mom! Are you all right? Has he hurt you?"

Mrs. Simpson shook her head. She looked over at Mike standing in the archway between the kitchen and living room. He slowly patted the gun against his thigh. Terror filled her eyes.

Mel ran to Mike and screamed, "Untie her!"

She hit him, but he pushed her away. "No, I don't think so. She's my insurance that you will do exactly what I say." He motioned to us with the gun. "Get back in the living room. I need to keep an eye on the street."

"What about my mom?"

"She'll be fine right where she is." He smiled. "Like I said…insurance."

Mike herded us with the barrel of the gun. We backed into the living room. He gestured for us to sit on the couch, and then walked to the far side of the room.

I sat down and felt the lump on the back of my head. There was a slight wetness coming from it. I looked at my fingers to see a little blood on them.

Mel sat down next to me and Beanie on her other side.

She looked down at my fingers and saw the blood. "Are you okay?"

"Yeah," I answered. "He beaned me pretty good when I walked in."

Mike stood in the corner by the row of windows and gave the street a quick sweep with his eyes. "So, who hit me and should I be expecting a visit from him again?"

"No," I answered, "He's gone."

Mike walked over to me. He slapped me across the side of my face with the back of his hand, grabbed my hair, jerked my head back and shoved the barrel of the gun into the cavity of my throat.

I winced from the pain. I wanted to do something, make some sort of move to overpower him, but knew it would be almost impossible to do and worried he would kill us if I failed. I felt so helpless.

He leaned down into my face and shouted, "I'm not fooling around here. Have you got that?" He looked over to Mel. "Is he telling the truth?" She didn't answer fast enough so he slapped me again.

He let go of me and turned to Mel, pointing the gun at her. "You want me to torture your mother instead? Is that what it will take?"

"It's true," she pleaded, tears in her eyes. "Please don't hurt my mom."

"Where is the backpack? I've searched the house and it's not here."

"Hidden," I answered. I wanted to draw his attention back to me and away from Mel.

Mike shifted over to me again and shoved me back against the couch. He pressed his hand into my chest and leaned into me until I couldn't breathe. He pointed the gun at my forehead. "Then get it."

The opening in the silencer looked huge just inches from my eyes. Cold sweat broke out on my face. All I could think of was what a bullet ripping through my head would do.

"He doesn't know where it is!" Mel blurted. "I'm the only one who does."

Mike directed his attention to Mel but kept the gun at my head. "Then you go get it."

Beanie jumped up from the couch defiantly. "We're not letting Russia get this stuff. She isn't going to turn it over to you!"

Mike stood and pointed the gun at Beanie. "We have a volunteer to be the first victim." He lowered the barrel to Beanie's leg and fired.

Mel screamed.

Beanie stared in shock at the hole in his pant leg, and then slumped to the floor by the couch. "Ahgggg...he shot me! He shot me!"

We jumped to Beanie's side. The bullet had hit him just above the knee. Red oozed from the hole in his pant leg. I reached into the hole and tore the fabric open. Blood pumped from the wound. I felt around the back and found another hole where the bullet had come out. I pressed my hands over the wounds trying to stop the bleeding. Blood seeped between my fingers.

Beanie cringed from the pain. He tried to sit up so he could see the wound. "Am I going to die?" He was turning white.

Mel pushed him back down. "Lie down, Beanie. Try to stay calm."

Beanie's eyes rolled back under their lids.

She looked angrily at Mike, "Why'd you shoot him? He doesn't know where the debris is!"

Mike moved back over to his position by the windows, doing a quick scan outside. "Because I'm tired that you think this is a game. I'm not into killing kids, but I will if I have to. I want that material and I don't have time for a discussion about it. Your friend has about twenty minutes before he bleeds to death. Does that help your decision? If not, your mother will be next. We can watch the two of them die together… slowly."

"No! I'll go get it." She looked at me. "Can you stop the bleeding?"

"I'm trying," I whispered, hoping Beanie couldn't hear, "but I think he's right. You'd better hurry."

Mel raced out the front door. Mike kept an eye out the window to watch for her return.

Beanie raised his head and then lowered it again. "Frankie, I'm cold."

"Just take it easy, Beanie. Mel will be right back with the debris. Then we'll get an ambulance. You're going to be all right." I couldn't stop the bleeding no matter how hard I pressed on the wounds. I doubted what I just told him was true.

It seemed like forever before Mel finally burst through the door, breathing heavily. *She held the backpack, not the wooden box!* She saw the puzzled look on my face but ignored it.

She backed up against the half wall of the dining area and leaned against it. She held the backpack out with her right hand. "We give you this and you're gone, right? You won't hurt anyone else?"

"That's right. Once you give me the pack, I have no reason to. Bring it here."

"I'm not coming anywhere near you." She tossed the pack across the room to the far wall.

I watched it land and then turned back to Mel. She had shifted her stance. Her stance? It was her pitching stance! I looked over at Mike. He pointed the gun at Mel while he walked over to the pack. He kneeled to get it, keeping the gun on her. I looked at Mel then back at Mike. I had to distract him somehow. "Hey batter, batter, batter, hey batter."

Mike gave a puzzled look in my direction. It was all Mel needed. He quickly turned back and raised the gun—just as the rock clobbered him between the eyes. The pitch was solid and knocked him backward.

"Nice throw, Mel!" I couldn't believe she took the chance, but it worked.

Mel raced over to Mike.

"Get his gun!"

She slid it to me and then jumped on top of him screaming and hitting him over and over again.

I couldn't leave Beanie. I yelled to her. "Stop, Mel! You've got to tie him up. Get something to tie him up."

The front door burst open and three men in police uniforms raced into the room, guns drawn. They pulled Mel off Mike. One of them shouted, "We have control, Sir."

Major Burnham walked into the room. "Get the medics in here."

One of the policemen called out on a radio.

Mel used the distraction to pick up the pack. She backed into the bedroom hallway and dropped it around the corner out of sight.

I didn't recognize any of these policemen. They weren't our local cops. Then I realized they were Burnham's men dressed like police officers.

Major Burnham looked over at Mike who was moaning and just now coming to his senses. "Secure that man and get him out of here."

They handcuffed Mike and dragged him onto his feet. He looked back at Mel as they took him out the door. A trickle of blood ran down the side of his nose from a spot in the middle of his forehead.

The major looked at Beanie's wounds and checked his eyes. He patted me on the back. "He'll make it."

I cringed at his touch.

The medics hurried into the room. I moved aside and they worked on Beanie's wounds and took his vital signs.

Mel grabbed the soldier still there and pulled him toward the kitchen. "Help me. My mom is tied up in here." They disappeared into the kitchen.

One of the medics prepared an IV drip while the other two raced out the door and reappeared with a gurney. They laid it down and lifted him onto it. I scooted in next to the gurney when they were done. Beanie's eyes were closed and it looked like he was unconscious.

Mel and the soldier helped Mrs. Simpson into the room, each with an arm around her. They took her to the couch. She was obviously in shock. Her eyes were glazed and had no focus. Mel brushed the hair from her mom's face, then came over and knelt down next to Beanie.

She leaned into me. "Is he going to be all right?"

"I sure hope so."

The paramedic looked up at us. "We've stabilized him and stopped the bleeding. At this point I think he has a pretty good chance, but we have to get him to the hospital. He's lost a lot of blood."

Mel leaned down and gave Beanie a kiss on the forehead. He opened his eyes a little and looked over at us.

"See you soon, cannonball," Mel said, giving Beanie a big smile.

I wiped my bloody hand on my shirt, grabbed Beanie's and squeezed it. "Hang in there, Beanie. We wouldn't be the Musketeers without you."

We stood aside while they lifted him up and carried him out the door.

Mel looked at the major. "How did you get an ambulance here so fast?"

The major signaled for the last soldier to leave. "That will be all." He watched him go and then looked at Mel. "We've been watching your place ever since you moved in. I decided to have it bugged, and it looks like that paid off in divi-dends."

Mel and I exchanged glances. *Tom had been right*.

The major continued, "When we got the anonymous call about a man tied up at the Hunt Club, we investigated. He was gone, but we found his car and based on what we discovered in it, knew he was the Soviet agent we've been looking for."

He walked over to us and leaned in so his face was close. "We had a good idea how he came to be that way, considering the close proximity to your house, so we figured he would come here." His stale breath washed against my face. He searched our eyes for hidden answers. Not finding anything of value, he moved over to the windows and looked out. "That proved to be the case, so we set up our surveillance operation."

"That doesn't explain the ambulance," Mel pointed out. "You knew Beanie was shot. You let him bleed while you sat outside."

He turned to face us. "We knew the agent was in here. We needed a position of advantage to take him down without endangering all of you."

"He shot Beanie!" Mel screamed. "You don't think that was *enough* danger to act on?" She put a hard focus on the major. "You were waiting until I got the backpack. That's what you were doing. You knew Mike would force me to get it."

The major twitched slightly before regaining his composure. "We needed to recover that pack. You know how important it is to our government."

I stepped into the argument. "Important enough to let our friend die?"

"I had an ambulance waiting nearby. As soon as the agent left with the pack, we could take him down and bring in the ambulance."

Mel walked over and grabbed the pack from behind the wall. "This what you want?" She threw it at the major, who had to act quickly to catch it so it wouldn't hit him. "Here, take it if it's so important to you."

I looked over at her in surprise. "Mel, what are you doing?"

"All it's ever done is bring harm to my family and friends. I want this over with."

The major gave her a self-righteous smile. "Now it will be." He set the pack on the table under the windows. He unlatched the buckles, opened the flap, and looked inside. His expression changed to one of uncertainty. "What's this?" He pulled out pieces of old rubber material, balsa wood sticks and aluminum-looking foil. It certainly wasn't the material we had seen in my basement.

Mel's expression didn't change. "It's the debris you wanted."

The major gave her a cold stare. "These are nothing but fragments from an old weather balloon."

Mel's look changed to disbelief, her acting paying off. "Really? We've never seen one before, or debris from a spaceship for that matter, so how would we know the difference?" She went over and sat down next to her mom and held her hand. Mrs. Simpson was still in shock. "Anyway, that's what was in the pack when we found it. I don't know what else you want. I guess if a weather balloon could fool your intelligence officer back in Roswell, then it could fool us."

"Where is the real material?"

"You think I switched it? What you have in your hands is what we found. It's not like I ran down to the department store and picked up an old weather balloon or something?" She looked at her mom and stroked her hand, then turned back to the major. "You know, maybe your informant was wrong, especially after so many years. His information was probably about as reliable as the Air Force's ability to keep secrets."

He shoved the pieces back in the pack and threw it on the couch next to Mel. "This isn't over, Miss Simpson. We're going to keep an eye on you." He walked to the door.

"Fine, but it'll be a big waste of time." Mel stood, marched over to the major and opened the door for him. "Do us a favor. Don't forget to tell your *intelligence* center what was in that pack. That way it will leak out and we won't be bothered by spies anymore. It's the least you should do, considering what you've already done to my family."

The major stiffened at the comment before walking out. Mel slammed the door behind him.

Epilogue

Mel, Beanie, and I stood at the top of the steps to the easement. He had been in the hospital for a week and we visited him several times, but there were always parents around, so this was the first time we would be able to really talk.

A cast covered Beanie's leg from above his ankle to his upper thigh, and he was still figuring out how to use his crutches. We worked our way down the steps, Mel on one side and me on the other.

"Luckily the bullet just grazed the bone and didn't break it," I said as we got to the bottom.

"I'm supposed to have the cast off in a couple of weeks, but it will be a while before I can go swimming again."

He made it to the picnic table on his own and sat down on the bench seat. I took the crutches from him and laid them on top of the picnic table. Mel sat down next to Beanie and I cozied up next to her.

Mel put her arm around my shoulder. With her other hand she fingered the medal hanging by a blue ribbon around my neck, inspecting it. "I can still see the look on Captain Thornton's face when he presented these medals to us at City Hall."

"Yeah, he seemed to be so happy about it," Beanie added.

Other than Major Burnham and Mrs. Simpson, we were the only ones who knew what really happened at Mel's house that day. To cover it up, the major concocted a story that we had interrupted a bigtime criminal on the run who had tied Mel's mother up as a hostage. We had managed to overpower him, save her mom, and capture the man, with Beanie getting shot in the process.

The major made sure the whole thing set us up as town heroes, and somehow a big cash reward was included. Apparently, he told the press that we had captured an FBI Most Wanted criminal with a big bounty on his head. It was all, of course, just a big bribe to keep us quiet on the whole Roswell cover-up. We weren't arguing.

After everything that Mel and her mom had gone through, Beanie and I agreed that most of the reward should go to them. I didn't take any money at all. Instead, I worked out a deal with the major. Somehow there happened to be a really hot Cherry Red, '65 Ford Mustang just sitting around with nowhere to go. Of course, it would be a few years before I could drive it by myself, but it looked really good parked in my driveway. Beanie did get a nice wad of cash, but he hadn't told us what he was going to do with it yet.

I'm sure the major did all this more out of need for a cover story rather than due to a guilty conscience. There was a big article in *The Oswego Review* about it and they set up a presentation at City Hall. Lots of people showed up for the ceremony. It was a big deal for our small town.

Captain Thornton hated the fact he didn't have a clue as to what really had happened that day, but I'm sure what got his goat the most was the fact he didn't get the glory for whatever did happen.

Our parents were sure proud though, and who knows how much Beanie's popularity at school would skyrocket. How could it not when he was a hero with a gunshot wound? There was a pretty good clue to how this would go, when at the presentation there was an abnormally large pack of girls all giving him their googly-eyed looks.

"Okay, you guys," Beanie said, "I've been really out of touch, so fill me in on the whole weather balloon deal." I had already heard the story, but Mel needed to share it with Beanie.

"We will," I said, "but only after you tell us what you are going to do with your money."

Beanie reached down to the transistor radio he had attached to his belt. He tuned it to his favorite station. Herman's Hermits, *Can't You Hear My Heartbeat* was playing. He looked over at us. "That's what I'm going to do. Become a DJ or a band manager, or something like that. I'm going to save my money until I find the right groove."

"The right groove," I repeated. "I guess it's just in your blood." I looked down at his leg. "Or, at least what's left of it."

We all laughed.

"Okay," Beanie said. "Now give me the details"

Mel started. "When I got home with the pack, I opened it. I really wanted to do this alone anyway because it was my dad's and there may have been something personal in it. Well, I was right. He left a letter." She pulled it out of her back pocket, unfolded it and read to Beanie:

Mel Belle..."

She looked up from the letter. "That's what he called me. Always said I could be the Belle of the Ball if I wanted." She started again...

Mel Belle,

I guess if you are reading this then I am no longer with you. I know my death will be hard on you and your mother. But I also know you have the strength to help her through it, and that gives me some comfort as I write this letter.

I buried the pack in your toy box because I knew you would be the only one able to figure out the clue to where it was hidden. You have always been a smart, resilient girl, so by now you must know why I died, perhaps even how, and that the reason is in this backpack.

I believe I am being watched. I don't know if it is our government or some other, but in either case, they should not get this material. It wouldn't be good for the United States if our enemies recovered it because the material is such a technological goldmine. On the other hand, our country already has the spaceship, so their only interest would be to quash the last bit of evidence that could expose their cover-up. And no, I don't think it should be released to the public either. Believe it or not, I agree with our government, that we as a civilization are not yet ready for this kind of revelation. One day the time will be right to share with the world what took place near Roswell in 1947. That is why it is important to keep the evidence, if at all possible. It is the only proof the crash really happened.

If they do think I have some of the spaceship material, these governments and their agents will never stop trying to get it. Not long after the crash, when the cover-up story came out, I went back into the desert to a place where I had seen an old Air Force weather balloon on a previous expedition. At the bottom of this backpack are some of the remnants from that balloon. If things become dangerous for you and your mom, and they think you have the material, give them the pieces from the weather balloon. Let them think this is what I had all along. They may believe it. Hopefully, it will at least throw them off enough so they leave you alone. But I don't want you and your mother in danger. If the weather balloon doesn't work, turn over the material. Nothing is more important than the safety of the two women I love.

Mel Belle, you are a very special girl. Work hard at school. You have amazing physical and intellectual talents. Develop them to their fullest. You will need them when you are grown. There are things yet to be done, and if you are reading this letter, then it seems you will be the only one able to continue what I could not finish.

I know this all sounds very cryptic, but one day, when you are older and wiser, you will understand. Mel Belle, I love you and your mother very much. I miss you both already.

Love,

Dad

Beanie had been hanging on every word. "What does he mean? It sounds like some sort of quest. Does it have something to do with the device that's missing?"

"Frankie and I have been discussing it. We think so. It must be hidden somewhere safe."

"And from what we can figure out from the letter," I added, "he feels she's too young right now to handle whatever it is and whatever needs to be done."

"Wow! I wonder what that is?" Beanie said.

"Well, I figure that somehow, when I get older, he has it worked out to get the device to me. And then I will be able to find out what he was doing and what he needs me to do."

"How old do you need to be?" Beanie asked.

Mel thought about this. "Well, I don't know. I guess it would be sometime after I get out of college. That's a long ways away, so there's not much I can do about it now."

"There's one other thing I've been wanting to know," Beanie said. "Why did you take the chance with Mike?" Your throw could have missed."

"He had already shot you and threatened to kill us," she answered. "I was pretty sure he would finish us off. I just didn't think there was any way he would leave us alive and take the chance that we could notify the police. And even if he had, he would have tied us up so we couldn't run to the neighbors." She looked over at Beanie. "If he did that, it would have meant a death penalty for you for sure!"

We all thought about that, and how close we came to it coming true.

I gave Mel a big kiss. "You saved our lives."

"Yeah, and now you are both indebted for life. Don't worry, I'll think of lots of ways you guys will be able to make it up to me." She gave us a big smile.

"What ever happened with the UFO landing out by Stafford Road?" Beanie wondered. "Was it real?"

Mel and I exchanged glances. "We don't know," I answered. "They couldn't disprove it as a hoax. A UFO actually could have landed there."

We all thought about that possibility.

Beanie hummed the theme from The Twilight Zone, and then said in his best Rod Serling voice, "You're traveling through another dimension, a dimension not only of sight and sound, but of mind…" He couldn't finish. We all broke up laughing.

I held my hand out to the middle, palm down. Beanie and Mel looked at me, and then placed theirs on top of mine.

"Three Musketeers," I said. "All for one…"

Beanie and Mel joined in, "...and one for all!"

"So, what do we do now?" Beanie asked. "We have two more weeks until school starts. After all this, it's going to get pretty boring around here."

"No clue," I said. "Maybe just hang, after everything we've been through." I put my arm around Mel and leaned back against the table. We all fell silent and stared out at the lake for a while.

I looked over at Mel. A little smile had formed on her face and her eyes were twitching back and forth.

She sat up and looked at Beanie, then to me. "Hmmm... you guys ever hear of the Loch Ness Monster?"

Turn the page for a sneak peek
at the first novel in the new

Melanie Simpson Mystery Series

You've seen things from Frankie's viewpoint...
...now it's time for Melanie to tell her story

THE TALE OF THE TAROT

I guess I figured that would be the end of it,
at least until I graduated from college…
but it wasn't.

Eight Months Later

Free Energy

I'm standing outside the classroom for freshman history, staring at the door. I want to go in, but I haven't been able to get my legs to move. I guess I'm a little hesitant. Things didn't go very well yesterday in there.

All semester, history has rarely been an adventure with Mr. Wolcott. He's a giant stuffed shirt. But yesterday was an exception. It got a little heated. Not as much for him as for me. I wanted to do better today, but didn't have high hopes. We would be talking about Marconi and I already knew where this would go if I didn't control myself. A couple of boys pushed by me to get inside and gave me the look for blocking their way. I took a big breath and walked in.

The desks were arranged in a semi-circle facing Mr. Wolcott and a couple of blackboards at the front of the room. Two aisles ran toward the front, separating the desks into three groups. I had to walk down one aisle and halfway up the other to get to my desk. A couple of girls locked eyes on me as I passed by. I think they had a pretty good idea of what might be coming. I ignored them and sat at my desk next to

Frankie's. He was scribbling in his notebook, working on some sort of anti-Vietnam war cartoon. It was his thing these days.

He looked up from his drawing. "Hey, Mel. How'd biology go?"

"Well, I'm pretty sure I have human anatomy down, so I didn't really need a refresher. What do these teachers think anyway, we're sixth-graders or something?"

"I know. I bet there are some students here who could teach them a thing or two."

I smiled. "No doubt."

Mr. Wolcott stood at the chalkboard, about to start class. Rumor was he would retire soon, which I totally believed since he looked like he had experienced most of the centuries he taught. His clothing supported the theory with his tweed jacket, sweater vest, and bowtie right out of last century.

If you want to picture his lecture style, think of a fly buzzing around your head you can never swat away, and it keeps droning on and on—sometimes louder, sometimes quieter, sometimes close, sometimes farther away. On and on and on.

Having this class with Frankie turned out to be pretty cool though, because he's helping me get through it. Last month we saw *Plague of the Zombies* at the Lake Theater in one of its Horror-Saturday Film Fests. Looking around the classroom, most of the students wore that same look. If there was a ground zero for zombies, freshman history would be it, and Mr. Wolcott the endemic source.

I usually like history, but this semester covered early twentieth-century inventions and inventors—and boy, can history get it screwed up. I had to wonder how our history books were so far off from the truth sometimes? Whenever

Mr. Wolcott told one of their lies, I could hardly sit still. He had been talking about Thomas Edison, who invented the light bulb, which was right, but also said he brought electricity to every home, which was way wrong. I got into it with Mr. Wolcott yesterday and it turned out to be an idiot move on my part. I mean, who ever wins a pitched battle with a teacher, right? But one good thing came out of it, because for the first time all semester, Mr. Wolcott showed even the narrowest hint of passion in his work. Thank God, he is human.

So, here's the thing: Nikola Tesla should have received credit for the electricity we use, not Edison. Now I'm sitting here this afternoon, and it's the same with Marconi and the wireless telegraph. I want to let it go, but can already tell I'm not going to.

Frankie must have noticed my tensing up. "Mel," he whispered, "you're looking like you did yesterday. What's the deal?"

I ignored him. I was too focused on Mr. Wolcott standing at the blackboard in front of the class, writing out Marconi's name in big, loopy characters, each letter grating on me. He turned to the class. "Guglielmo Marconi received the Nobel Prize in 1909 for inventing the wireless telegraph."

I couldn't stand it any longer and shot my hand up.

Frankie nudged me. "Mel, probably not a good idea."

I frantically waved my arm, but Mr. Wolcott ignored it.

"His invention eventually revolutionized radio and wireless communication—"

I jumped from my seat. "Sorry, Mr. Wolcott, that's not right. He didn't."

Mr. Wolcott shrugged, set his chalk on the blackboard tray, and turned to me. "What now, Miss Simpson?"

It showed in his voice and on his face. He wasn't happy with me, but I plodded on. "Nicola Tesla was the actual inventor of wireless radio communication."

I felt Frankie looking at me, no doubt trying to figure out what I was up to, but I stayed focused on Mr. Wolcott.

"Not Tesla again, Miss Simpson. We just did battle over this with Edison."

I held my ground. "Facts are facts, even if they are not in our textbooks. The DC electricity Edison developed deteriorated quickly and would barely even work in the big cities. Communities like Lake Oswego would still be using candles and kerosene if we had been stuck with Edison's system. But Tesla developed ways to use alternating current, AC, which could travel miles before needing a boost. And that's why we're not sitting here in the dark today."

"Which has *what* to do with radio technology?" Mr. Wolcott asked.

A few giggles came from the students. I looked around to see everyone waiting for what would happen next. "Well, Marconi studied under Tesla. He used Tesla's ideas, basically stealing them and calling them his own. Even back in 1900 Tesla could see that one day we would be able to speak to people on the other side of the world, and even be able to see them. And he thought we could do this using a device that could fit in our pockets." The giggles grew to loud snickers.

"We will not be getting into this Tesla hyperbole again, Miss Simpson, especially when what you say is quite ridiculous. We will follow the textbooks in this class, which I might add, were written by more accomplished historians than you, and perhaps less susceptible to wildish ideas." Now the snickers became subdued laughter.

Again, I ignored them. "Even the Supreme Court ruled Marconi infringed on Tesla's patents." I reached into my bag, took out my textbook, and tossed it onto my desk. It landed with a loud slap that reverberated off the walls. I wanted to make a statement, but not quite that big of one. It set me back a little, but I recovered and plodded on. "Maybe these old textbooks were written before that happened. We should get new ones."

Everyone broke out laughing. Not what I wanted, but I was way too into this to stop now. I stood my ground. "Tesla also should have gotten the Nobel Prize, not Marconi."

Mr. Wolcott stared at me for a moment, a frown forming in the area between his big, bushy eyebrows. Maybe I had gone too far, even if everything I said was true. I held my head high, still feeling defiant, but it wasn't quite the same defiance I felt a moment ago. Inside, I knew I shouldn't press it. I had enough going on.

"We are done with this rather tempestuous string-of-thought, Miss Simpson. Now sit down." He returned to the blackboard.

"No!" I couldn't help it. Maybe it was a case of self-destruction, but I couldn't let it go. I heard murmurs from the classroom.

He turned to glare at me. "What did you say?"

"No," I said again, but this time a little softer. I shifted my weight as if suddenly on unsteady ground. "Tesla deserves recognition for what he did for us. If we had paid attention to his genius, we would have free energy right now. We wouldn't need gas for cars, or planes, or have to pay a dime for any form of energy."

The students broke into outright laughter again.

It made me mad they couldn't see his vision. I looked around the classroom. "That's okay, go ahead and laugh. You're all a bunch of ditwads, anyway. They laughed at Tesla, too." I pointed to the lights above our heads. "But you all need to understand one thing—you sit here bathed in the very glow of his brilliance!"

"Stop. Now. Miss Simpson! I am done with your disruptions. Please leave this classroom immediately and report to the principal's office." He opened a drawer on his desk and dug out a hall pass. He scribbled something on it and held it out, motioning for me to come take it.

I stomped up to him and grabbed it out of his hand, turning to see everyone staring at me and laughing. I needed to settle myself. I closed my eyes for a moment. When I opened them again, most of the students were still snickering at me. I glared at them; my piercing stare emblazoned onto each of their faces, one-by-one, until they felt so uncomfortable they finally stopped. When the room became quiet, I walked over and grabbed my bag and books. I glanced down at Frankie to see a questioning look on his face. I leaned toward him. "I hate bureaucrats!" I wheeled around and walked between the rows of desks to the door and strutted out of the classroom doing everything I could to keep my dignity intact.

On Display

School had ended, and there I sat in the principal's office, still waiting to see him. Mrs. Darby, Principal Drake's secretary, would look up once in a while from whatever she pretended to be doing at her desk to give me a reassuring look. I guess she felt that was her role in this little play unfolding before the sea of students just outside.

A long row of half-high windows ran the length of the office, which overlooked the hallway near the main entrance to the school. My chair sat against one of the windows with my back to it. Everyone going by could see me. I might as well have been on display in a storefront window at Meier & Frank's in downtown Portland. I could hear students racing past the office in their hurry to escape prison. More than once, someone made me jump when they slapped the glass right behind me.

A small group of girls from my history class stopped when they saw me and chanted "We want free energy! We want free energy!" It was Madison Albright and her demonic friends. I'd tried to stay under Madison's radar all year. It hadn't taken long to figure out she could make someone's life miserable if she wanted to, and had a proverbial string of scalps to prove it. I guess I just blew that hope. I really didn't need this.

The door to Principal Drake's office opened. Mr. Wolcott and Principal Drake stepped out talking in low tones. I couldn't hear what they were saying. They both looked over to me. Principal Drake said, "I'll be with you in a moment, Miss Simpson." He shook Mr. Wolcott's hand and went back into his office.

Mr. Wolcott stood there for a moment and stared at me. If he was trying to make me uncomfortable, I wasn't buying into it. He finally walked over and leaned down close to my face. "You are a very bright girl, Miss Simpson. You know it and I know it. What—you think I don't realize these textbooks are antiquated? They may as well be clay tablets written in Sumerian for how out-of-date they are." His hot breath sprayed my face as he spoke. It smelled of centuries. "But they are what I am required to work with, and I must follow the State curriculum. So, it is a burden we both share, Miss Simpson. I only ask you one favor—don't *ever* show me up in class again. Do you understand?"

I was surprised by what he said. It wasn't even close to what I thought he would say.

I nodded. "Yes, I understand. I'm sorry I made a scene in class."

He seemed satisfied and stood. "I wish you luck on whatever path it is you appear to be wandering, Miss Simpson, rocky that it may be. But be careful. Footing can be unstable on rocky ground, and tenuous at best." He opened the door and walked out.

Principal Drake looked to be about finished with his "What are we going to do with you?" speech. I think it had been about ten minutes, but it felt like hours. I sat in a chair on the other side of his desk and played with a ring on my finger. His speech wasn't as bad as I heard they could be. Maybe it was because Principal Drake had an idea of what I faced at home, so felt sorry for me. I could only hope. I didn't want my mom to have to deal with this.

He sat forward in his chair. "Miss Simpson. I am not going to contact your mother about this." *Relief.* "But you must stop disrupting class. We work as a group here at Lake Oswego High." He intertwined his fingers and held them out to me in demonstration. "All together as a team. We don't condone those who want to hack out their own path. Do you understand me?"

I stiffened at his words. "I guess so." But I couldn't help myself. "So, what you are saying is independent thought is not encouraged here."

Principal Drake sat back and sighed. Everything around him cried out conformity. I doubted if he ever had an original thought in his life.

"Look, Miss Simpson, I don't understand what is going on with you, but you need to get that chip off your shoulder."

I looked up from studying my ring. I wanted to say, "That isn't a chip, it's the weight of the whole world," but I didn't. What I said was, "So be it." *So be it?* Where did that come from?

The principal got up from his chair in a way that had 'I give up' written all over it and motioned me toward his office door. We walked through the empty secretary's area. He opened the door to the hallway, gave me one last look, and held it open for me. I walked out without saying a word.

Frankie had been waiting for me, leaning against the wall across from the principal's Office. "Mel?"

I glanced at him, but wasn't in the mood to talk right now. And I certainly wasn't interested in explaining anything, even if I could. I headed toward the school exit.

Principal Drake's voice sounded out behind me when he saw Frankie standing there. "Can't you control her?"

"Me?" I heard Frankie blurt. "How is that *my* job?"

I pushed the door open and stormed out, hearing Principal Drake's condescending voice behind me. "Well, it sure has to be someone's, and everyone knows her mother is incapable of it."

Red Velvet Cake

Frankie knew from the moment Mel got into his car she needed her space. He could recognize such times, and this was one of them. They hadn't said much on the ride home. He pulled into his driveway, shut the engine off, and engaged the parking brake.

They sat in awkward silence for a moment.

Mel finally glanced over to Frankie. "Thanks for waiting for me, and for the ride."

"No sweat." He gave her a little smile.

Frankie found it tough going when Mel got into one of her moods. Even with that, he couldn't help being deep into her. It wasn't just those amazing blue eyes that penetrated into him every time she looked at him. Or an absolutely perfect face, as far as he was concerned, framed by blonde hair which seemed lit by the sun even on a cloudy day. It was more because her beauty came from inside. Her heart was built from kindness; always thinking of others. Just sitting next to her made him feel good about himself. Something that drove those ever-lingering self-doubts away for a while.

But she put a shell around her heart sometimes, like right now, and all he felt was awkward silence. He wanted to break that feeling and decided to do it with a piece of cake.

He looked over at her. "You ever been to an Elmer's Restaurant?"

"What?" Mel had been gazing off into space. His question brought her back.

"Elmer's. They have this red velvet cake. It has seven layers and a creamy icing on top."

Mel stared at him. "What are you talking about?"

He ignored the touch of attitude in her voice and kept going. "I ordered it one day. It looked so good. When I first started eating, I was sure I could finish the whole thing. But when I knocked off one layer, there would be another one, and then another. It was too much. I never did finish it."

"What is this, some sort of metaphor or something?"

He smiled. "Yeah, exactly," then thought for a second. "Or, maybe it's a simile. I don't know. I always get them confused."

Mel managed a smile. "And your point?"

"Layers, Mel. That's you. Lots of layers. And when I think I've gotten through one, another appears. And they seem to keep going and going."

"Huh. You just described every woman out there."

"I'm not sure if that's a good thing or not."

Frankie laughed and Mel did too.

Frankie had a hard time understanding a lot of things about Mel—those layers. Not that she hid her feelings from him. It was more like she either hadn't figured them out herself or didn't realize they even existed. All he knew was something seemed to be hiding deep within her. But there was one very special thing about her he appreciated more than anything else, and it was something few of us have—

she grew stronger when things got tougher. And last summer, with everything that went down, there were plenty of times where she proved it.

He wasn't sure what happened in the principal's office today, only what he saw in class, but he knew something was up. Frankie opened the door to get out. Mel did the same. He walked around to her side of the car. She stood by the door, bag over her shoulder and books in her hands, looking at him.

He leaned in and kissed her. A light one, but hopefully an icebreaker. "Can I ask you something?"

She looked into his eyes, as if trying to figure out where this was going. He thought maybe she had read a tone in his voice because she didn't answer right away. She finally said, "Sure," but held her books against her body, as if to buffer what might be coming.

Frankie put his hands in his pockets and kicked at some moss in a crack on the driveway. He turned to her. "We spent an hour last night studying together about the assignment for our history class, and you didn't say one thing about Tesla. Why didn't you tell me then what you said in class today? When you flipped out, I felt blindsided."

Her tension released a little. After a moment she set her books on the hood of the car and wrapped her arms around his waist, smiled, and leaned into him. He smelled the stimulating fragrance of her scent and, as always, it drove him crazy.

She gave him a kiss. "I'm sorry. I'm not sure why I didn't tell you. I guess I thought I would get through the class without saying anything. But it kept bugging me that our textbook was so wrong. And when Wolcott stood up there spouting a bunch of crock and writing Marconi's name on the chalkboard, well, I kind of lost it. It should have been Nikola Tesla's name." She let go of him and leaned against the car.

"How did you know all that stuff about this Tesla guy, anyway? I've never even heard of him."

"My dad. There was a bunch of stuff about Tesla in his notes. I guess that could be a big part of why I acted the way I did. I think I was defending my dad as much as I was defending Tesla. Remember back when we found the clue for the crash debris in his storage boxes?" Frankie nodded. "I went through them again to see if I could find anything important in there. A couple of boxes were full of his archeological studies and research. Some of the research focused on ancient man-made structures around the world. He was working with a group of archeologists and scientists who were studying whether they were built in relation to the earth's energy field. That's probably how he came across Tesla. He had a thick notebook full of information about Tesla and his studies." She pushed a strand of hair behind her ear, and seemed focused on the rock wall across the driveway. "So, I went to the library and found everything I could on him. There wasn't a lot. But between my dad's notes and the library, I learned about his inventions and patents, and how Marconi pretty much stole his ideas." She looked at Frankie. "You remember what I said about free energy in class?"

"Yeah. The kids thought it pretty funny."

"Well, Dad's writing pad was full of notes about it. I think it had something to do with the Orb."

"The Orb? What's that?"

"Oh. Remember when Tom told us about the device the alien gave my dad at the crash site? That's what my dad called it in his notes."

"That's right. It's been a ton of time since we've talked about the device. I kind of forgot about it. I mean, it wasn't in with the debris, and from what we figured out in your dad's letter, you won't see it for years."

"Well, from what I could get out of his notes, I think the Orb was directing him somehow. To what or where, who knows? But he was definitely looking into this whole thing about the earth's energy field."

Mel paused for a moment, focused on the rock wall again. Frankie wondered if she could be thinking of her dad. He reached out and held her hand.

She looked at him. "I mean, imagine a world where we can run things by drawing power from the energy around us. I know, very science fiction, but so was the idea of television a few decades ago. Now we get television reception with rabbit ears out of thin air, have color instead of black and white, three channels, and a remote-control box to change channels and volume all from the comfort of the couch. We're even building rocket ships that will land us on the moon. Things change."

Frankie gave Mel a startled look. "You have a remote control?"

She stared at him. "That's all you got out of what I just said?"

He laughed. "No, I'm just screwing with you. So why didn't Tesla do the free energy thing?"

"None of the big-buck guys would back him, especially when he told them the energy would be free. Nobody wanted anything to do with his ideas unless they could make some serious moolah. He went broke and lost everything."

"And so goes our capitalist society. That's too bad. Based on what you say, this Tesla guy might have changed the world."

"I know." She paused. "Anyway, about the blindsiding thing, I'm sorry. I didn't mean to do that to you." She let go of Frankie's hand and reached for her books.

Frankie stopped her, put his hand behind her head, and pulled her into him for a kiss. A longer one this time, where her soft lips lingered against his. She relaxed and returned it with equal passion. They separated. He was pleased to see her tension release. "Glad you're back. Sometimes you just go away somewhere."

Her eyes fluttered a little, like she was processing his words. She picked up her books and bag and looked at him for a moment, then said, "I need to get home. I've got to check in on Mom."

"Sure. No sweat." Frankie put his arm around her waist and walked her to the back of the car. "I'm glad you explained things. I get it now."

"Thanks." Mel stopped and turned to him. "I know sometimes I can be...well, *me*."

Frankie had to smile at just how true that was. "What if I come over later? We can hang out together and do our homework."

He hadn't been to her house for a while because she preferred to come over to his. Frankie figured it was because of her mom. But lately, Mel hadn't been able to come over at all. Last night was the first time in a week and only because he wanted her to help him with his homework. He wondered if her mother could be getting worse.

She seemed to think about his offer for a while, a pros and cons kind of thinking, then said, "Sure. I need some time for Mom first. How about seven, after dinner?"

"Sounds cool."

Frankie watched Mel walk down the driveway for a moment and then got his books out of the car. Ever since last summer, when Mel moved in next door, his life had completely changed. And in too many ways to even count. But if it meant never meeting her, he wouldn't have changed a thing, including having a gun held to his head…well, maybe that. Even then, he knew he was pretty lucky.

Revolver

Frankie walked into the carport and opened the sliding glass door to the basement. He crossed the rec-room to his bedroom, went inside and tossed his books on the desk. He looked around at the mess in his room, took off his jacket, shrugged, threw it on the bed, kicked off his shoes and headed upstairs.

His mom had the vacuum going full blast in the living room. She turned it off when she saw him enter from the stairwell. His little sister, Suzie, was nowhere to be seen, so must be over at a friend's house. Simple blessings.

"How did school go?" she asked.

Frankie smiled at the question. Every parent asks it, every single day, and they always get the same answer or some variant of it, every single day, yet they persist. As if we would slip up and give a detailed and insightful description of our school day. But this wasn't that day. "Same old, same old."

"You're late getting home."

Frankie had been heading for the fridge but stopped at the comment. He turned to see her standing there with her hand on her hip—a truth-seeking missile. "You didn't go anywhere, did you? You know our agreement. You only drive to school and back."

It took a ton of pleading and a big stack of chores, to get his mom and dad to sign a permit allowing him to drive the Mustang to school. He didn't want to screw that up.

"Yeah, I know. Mel got delayed after school, so I waited for her. Her mom doesn't drive much anymore." Frankie figured that should explain it. His mother knew Mel's mom had been sick and somewhat bedridden.

"Okay. Good. But remember, the privilege will be gone if you abuse it."

"Yes, ma'am."

"Well, don't go anywhere. The rec-room has somehow become an extension of your bedroom and is a complete mess. I need you to clean it up."

"Sure, no biggie."

"And get your homework done. Your dad and I weren't exactly thrilled to see your grades slip last report card." She turned the vacuum on again and attacked the carpet.

Frankie had gone a little slack with the studying last semester. "Okay," he shouted over the vacuum, knowing she couldn't hear, "I'll do everything I can to get Harvard to take notice." Like that would ever happen.

Frankie opened the fridge and stared at its contents—a daily ritual. And as always, it was full of food, but nothing to eat. It's not like a giant Dagwood sandwich sat on the top shelf, wagging its tail like a dog, waiting for him to get home. He was deep in the throes of food frustration when something caught his eye. Something barely noticeable tucked into the very back of the middle shelf. A glint of aluminum foil, in the unmistakable shape of a cold slice of pizza, somehow managed to escape consumption ever since dinner three days ago. Small wonders. He scooted everything aside and grabbed the pizza, along with a bottle of Dr. Pepper, and headed downstairs.

In his room, he went over to the record player and picked out one of the Beatles' newer albums, *Revolver*. He put it on the player, started it, and set the needle to the second cut on the vinyl, one of his favorites, "Eleanor Rigby." He remembered when he got it last Saturday at the Rexall Drug store.

He and Mel had just come from seeing the great Sci-Fi movie, *Invasion of the Body Snatchers,* at the Lake Theater with Beanie and his latest girlfriend, Katch. What was this, the third girlfriend in the last two months?

The girls were off somewhere else in the store. He looked around but couldn't see them. Maybe they were in the make-up section, though he doubted it. Frankie didn't know if Mel even wore make-up. If she did, he sure couldn't tell, and if not, she sure didn't need it.

He stared down at the Beatles section of LPs in the rack, trying to decide between *Rubber Soul* and *Revolver*. Both came out within the last year and he didn't have either of them.

He looked over to see Beanie checking out the 45s in the rack next to him. "Hey, Beanie."

He looked up from the 45 single in his hand. "What's shakin,' bacon?"

Beanie had recently fallen prey to such childish rhymes.

"Which album would you get, *Rubber Soul* or *Revolver*?"

Beanie was the go-to for such things. Frankie didn't doubt that someday he'd end up as a DJ on the local KGW radio station, his favorite. He knew more about the current music scene than Billboard magazine. They probably called *him* to get the latest scoop.

Beanie put away the single and walked over. He pulled out *Revolver* and handed it to Frankie. "Definitely this one."

Frankie looked at him. "I hate it when you hem and haw over a decision."

"*Rubber Soul* is really good and has a kind of folksy feel to it. Though it would have been better if the label hadn't screwed it up and dumped some songs from the original British release. But you have to go with *Revolver*. They changed up their style with this album and did some amazing things in the studio while recording it—techno-wizardry. Not just innovative, but putting a whole new level to their Beatles magic. Besides, it has 'Yellow Submarine', and if I'm going to have to hang out with you in that cave you call a bedroom, I want some good music playing."

Frankie knew Beanie hated the fact he had the downstairs pretty much to himself; and because the bedroom sat underground, being on the back side of a daylight basement, it did somewhat resemble a cave. Maybe it beckoned to the buried instincts of primal man.

"Well, you sure hang out there a lot considering how tortured you feel."

"Exactamundo, my friend. It's better than my place and the prying ears of my mom. Oh…" he reached out and took the album from Frankie, "one other thing about *Revolver*. You know how they came up with the cover name?"

Frankie looked at him. "Not a clue."

Beanie ran his finger in circular motions around the surface of the album cover. "Because that's what a record does when played. It revolves. They were into puns and must have really liked this one."

Frankie grabbed the record back from Beanie. "Sounds a little lame to me, but I'll get it anyway."

He sang the words to "Eleanor Rigby" as it played. It was at the top of his play list, right along with The Kink's "You Really Got Me," and The Doors "Light My Fire." He finished the pizza in about three bites, downed half of the soda, wiped his hands on his pants, and headed to the disaster in the rec-room. Looking around, he figured this shouldn't be too bad—clothes were strewn all over the place, but those could be tossed into his room, and it would only take about five minutes to shove the rest of the stuff into cabinets and drawers. Piece of cake.

Playing Mom

I walked down the hall to my mom's bedroom and knocked softly on the door. "Mom, it's me, Melanie."

I opened the door and peaked in. She was propped up on her bed with some pillows against the headboard watching *Gomer Pyle, U.S.M.C.*, the only light in the room coming from the television. She hardly touched the dinner I brought to her earlier. I could see a drinking glass in her hand. She held the glass tilted at an angle, about ready to spill. A half-empty bottle of vodka sat on the nightstand next to her bed.

I walked over, took the glass, and set it down next to the vodka. She looked over at me with a distant smile. I crawled onto the bed, put my head on her shoulder, and watched as Sargent Carter yelled at Gomer over some innocent thing he did.

"Why does he yell at him like that?" she asked me. "He doesn't deserve getting yelled at." She reached out and held my hand.

I squeezed it, happy to make contact. She was so out of it most days. This appeared to be a good day. "It wouldn't be much of a show without it. Right?"

She nodded and was gone again. That was it. The moment passed. She might as well have been on the other side of the world instead of lying right here next to me.

I battled over what to do. When Dad died so suddenly a couple of years ago, she started drinking. She hid it pretty well for a while, but after what happened last summer, she couldn't control it anymore. Now she was a full-fledged alcoholic. She got caught drinking at work, so lost her job, and ever since she hasn't been able to take care of day-to-day things.

I pay the bills, clean the house, run errands, make the meals, and do everything else around here—including forging her signature on anything needing to be signed. All she manages to do anymore is drive to the liquor store when her supply runs out.

I guess I could hate her right now, but I don't. She has gone through so much. I lay there holding onto her, thinking about it all.

It had been so horrible for her. First, she had to deal with my dad's sudden death. Then last summer she was gagged and bound to a chair, held for over an hour at gunpoint knowing I would be walking in at any moment. And before any of that, it was what the Air Force did to her and my dad back when the Roswell crash happened. They frightened my mother so much she lost a baby, which would have been my big brother or sister. It hurts every time I think about it, wondering what it would have been like to have someone to look up to. She was only in her early twenties when that happened. How could I blame her for being like this, after all she went through?

Thank goodness we got some reward money from capturing the Russian agent. Along with the insurance from Dad's death, it kept me from worrying about how to pay the bills. I miss the old mom. She used to be so much fun. Now

I can hardly get a coherent sentence out of her. Mostly just mumbling. It's getting me down. Maybe that's another reason for what happened today with Mr. Wolcott and Principal Drake. I'm getting worn out.

I looked at her. The light from the television danced in her eyes, but that's all. The shine once there, now gone. I squeezed her hand. "Mom, I need to get some things done. Frankie is coming over soon, okay? If you need anything, let me know." I kissed her on the forehead.

She gave me an out-of-focus look and smiled. "Love you, honey."

"Love you too, Mom." I got off the bed, gathered up the dinner plate and took it to the kitchen. I placed it in the sink and stood there thinking about my mom, having no idea she would absolutely freak me out in only a few hours.

————————————————

The Tale of the Tarot, Book One in the
Melanie Simpson Mystery Series,
is planned for release in May 2022,
and Book Two, *The Map of Orbis Terrarum*,
is scheduled for release in August 2022.
Look for them at your favorite online
publisher, bookstore, and library.

Shoot me an email at DJSchneider1947@gmail.com
and I will send you release notifications on these and
future Melanie Simpson novels, along with a bonus
short story not available anywhere else.

Acknowledgements

I would like to thank the many individuals who helped edit this work, especially the Magnificent Seven writing group—Coston Frederick, Frank Marvin, Kelly Jones, Byron Meredith, Maria Eschen, Liz Goins—along with The Cabin in Boise, Idaho, where we met in the perfect creative environment. I spent many hours honing my skills there with those talented writers, a dedicated group relentless in helping each other become better at our craft. Also, to Tony Doerr, an elegant writer and inspiration, who gave me a reassuring nudge on a short story that I am now developing into a novel, *River of Dreams*. And a special thanks to Suzi Wiser who helped me with the final edit of The Roswell Quest.

I also would like to thank Stanton T. Friedman, Kevin Randle, Donald Schmitt, Charles Berlitz, William Moore, and Col. Philip J. Corso (Ret.) for their research and revelation of the events that happened in July of 1947 in the New Mexico desert. Much of the information in this book is based on their research. Without their hard work, dedication, and commitment to exposing the Roswell cover-up, *The Roswell Quest* would never have been written. And finally, Janice Dunnahoo, Chief Archivist for the Historical Society of Southwest New Mexico in Roswell, who helped me get over a small hurdle that made a big difference.

About the Author

DJ developed his creative writing skills at the San Francisco Art Institute, and then at the Log Cabin Literary Center in Boise, Idaho with a writing group called the Magnificent Seven. DJ also spent many years in the advertising and marketing fields writing and producing creative content for radio, print, and television. When DJ isn't out traveling the stars following Melanie Simpson around and documenting her great adventures, he is buried deep in an Oregon burrow he calls The Writing Cave, honing his craft and building his novels. It is there under the light of a gooseneck lamp he can be found diligently working on Melanie's next story, and on an upmarket novel titled *River of Dreams*.

Call to Action!

Post a review and get an exclusive, unpublished short story!

If you really enjoyed *The Roswell Quest*, please go back to the site where you purchased it and write a review. You can also post a review at Goodreads.com by searching for the book's title. Then email me at DJSchneider1947@gmail.com to let me know where your review is posted and **I will send you an exclusive, unpublished short story.** Whether you do a review or not, send me an email and I will keep you up to date on when the next book in The Melanie Simpson Series is due out, along with early release information and sample chapters for you to read. Please help me get the word out about The Melanie Simpson Series!

Research Bibliography:

UFO Crash at Roswell. Kevin D. Randle and Donald R. Schmitt

The Truth About the UFO Crash at Roswell. Kevin D. Randle and Donald R. Schmitt

The Roswell Incident. Charles Berlitz and William L. Moore

The Day After Roswell. Col. Philip J. Corso, (Ret.)

Cover-up at Roswell. Donald R. Schmitt

Crash at Corona. Don Berliner and Stanton T. Freidman

Witness to Roswell. Thomas J. Carey and Donald R. Schmitt

Incident at Exeter. John G. Fuller

The Interrupted Journey. John G. Fuller

Made in the USA
Middletown, DE
25 April 2024